THE
SKIN
CODE

An absolutely gripping crime thriller
with an astonishing twist

STEPHEN WILLIAMS

Joffe Books, London
www.joffebooks.com

First published in Great Britain in 2022

Cover art by Nick Castle

ISBN: 978-1-80405-259-4

CHAPTER 1

Heather was scared. Her breath came fast and shallow as she focused on the rectangular slot of light in front of her: the exit from the alley. She could hear footsteps behind her; the bunch of youths who had been smoking and joking against the club wall when she'd passed. Even with her head down, she'd felt their hungry gaze cataloguing her body as she'd scuttled by.

She kept her eyes focused on the end of the narrow lane, walking purposefully towards the main road. She hoped that her body language would dissuade the gang from taking things any further. The alley stank of decomposing food and broken dreams. Heather tried to control her breathing as she put one foot in front of the other. She offered a silent prayer. *Please just let them leave me alone.*

'Hey, sister, what's your hurry?' The voice behind her, but not as far behind as she'd hoped, was rough with smoke and laced with bad intentions.

Heather didn't turn, just picked up the pace and aimed for the end of the alley, clutching her canvas shoulder bag tight to her side.

Why on earth had she turned into this alley? Just to save a couple of minutes? Being a few minutes late was better

1

than being robbed or killed. Or maybe worse. Fear-fish swam through her blurring vision, her throat constricted with fright and her lungs were on fire.

'What's your hurry, darlin'?' The accent was pure South-London-gang swagger, the words whispering in her ear like air pushed from an oncoming train. Heather felt the panic in her throat drop into her stomach as a rough hand pulled at her shoulder, spinning her around. The youths were dressed in hoodies and dark Puma tracksuits, all wearing run-away trainers and sly smiles.

Heather smiled weakly back, her insides crawling with fear.

'Please, all I want to do is catch the Tube home.'

She hated the pleading tone in her voice, as if she were in some way inferior to the thugs spreading out around her. She had hoped, when she'd moved to London, she'd left the pleading behind. Left everything she hated about herself behind.

The man who'd spun her — the leader, she guessed — grinned, his gaze dancing over her body. His teeth were stained from a lack of hygiene and an excess of drugs. He glanced at her shoulder bag. She watched as his reptilian tongue flicked across his lips, black in the LED glow of the lights beyond the alley.

'Maybe you'd run a bit faster if you weren't weighed down by that,' he said, hooking the strap and slipping it off her shoulder.

It was the *bag* he wanted. She felt absurdly grateful at the realisation. Just a robbery. Just another London street hustle.

'There's a laptop and my purse in there. You can have them both. Please, just leave the bag. It was a present from my sister.'

The man eyed her, appraising. Slowly, he reached forward and touched the peak of her hijab, pushing it back off her head, exposing her hair. Heather held her breath, sick with the intimacy of the movement.

'So beautiful,' he whispered, teasing a length of hair out and gently wrapping it around his finger. 'Such a shame to cover it.'

'Please,' she whispered again. The man slid the bag the rest of the way down her arm and held it up.

'From your sister?'

'Yes. It isn't worth anything, except to me.'

The man looked at her for a long second, then nodded.

For a moment she thought he was acknowledging her words, letting her keep the bag, maybe. Then she felt her arms being grabbed by the thugs beside her, pulling her back against the wall, away from what little light there was. They hooked their feet around the inside of her ankles, forcing her to stand with her legs apart. She could feel the hot air from the vents in the pavement snake up her legs and lick at her thighs. A scream lodged itself in the back of her throat. Fingers were digging into her arms.

Absurdly, she wished that she was wearing trousers rather than her long black skirt. Like her clothing was the problem.

'I reckon you'd enjoy a bit of rough, yeah?' The gang leader, stepping in closer, rubbed his hand gently on her jawline. His other hand pressed against her skirt, tracing the edge of her underwear, hip to thigh. The scream that was caught in her throat died, and she felt herself collapsing into the grip of the two men holding her. Heather's vision began to blur again and she felt herself disconnecting.

'*Please*,' she said a third time, but the youths just sniggered and closed in, her fear only exciting them more.

This is it, Heather thought. *This is where my life gets ruined for ever. This is the reason I never get to do all the things I have to do, because I'm broken and dead in a London alley.*

'I'm so sorry,' she whispered.

She braced herself for the attack, shutting off her thoughts. Squeezing her eyes closed. Retreating into herself.

There was the scrape of a boot on concrete.

'Well, it doesn't look like the lady is having fun, does it?'

A woman's voice, coming from a little further down the alley. Heather opened her eyes and peered into the dark.

'What the fuck?' The youth's hand slipped from Heather's thigh and he turned towards the voice.

'*What the fuck?*' the voice mimicked, amused and hard. Heather didn't understand. She wanted to tell the woman to run; to get out of the alley and scream for help.

Instead, the voice continued. 'That's not very original, is it? Next you're going to say something like, "Mind your own business, bitch, or you'll get some of the same."'

The woman stepped into the weak lighting. She was around five-five, with short, choppy, dirty-blonde hair. Black beret perched on the back of her head. Black Docs, combat trousers and a tight black top with some sort of shoulder holster. The would-be muggers stared at her incredulously. She gazed back at them, completely unintimidated.

'Wow, it's like you've never seen a woman before. You boys need to widen your social circle.'

Heather felt the grip on her arms loosen as the youths got ready to take the woman down. The main thug bared his teeth in anticipation. Now he saw that there was no threat, he began to enjoy himself. Heather could guess what he was thinking: *two for the price of one.*

'What the fuck you doing here, man?' said the youth holding Heather's right arm. She felt his grip slip another notch. 'None of this is your business.'

The woman turned her head to look at him, smiling widely.

'Well, first, I'm not a man, which I would've thought was obvious. And second, probably more pertinent to your situation, technically it is my business.'

'What is?'

The woman's forehead creased and her head tilted, as if she were considering the question.

'Common decency? The lady in the veil doesn't look like she's enjoying herself.'

4

'You want to try smart talk with us? I've got something right here that'll shut you up.' He smirked, stepping forward.

The woman grinned back at him. 'Oh, Luke, you have such a way with words. Your mother must be so proud!'

The youth froze, the grin melting off his face. The tension in the alley returned.

'How'd you know my name?'

'What, other than the fact that by saying that, you've just told me?' she said, wide-eyed. 'I'd know you anywhere, Luke! Drug dealer to the street boys and girls. Plus, roadman for hire for whoever's got the dollar to pay him — am I right?'

Luke stared at her, sizing up the situation.

'What's that on her chest, bruv?' The thug on Heather's other side said, his voice strained. He sounded wound up, ready to run. Ready to kick and knife and do whatever was needed to exit the alley. The woman was freaking him out with her constant smile.

'This?' she said, tapping an object attached to her shoulder harness. 'This is a life-logger.'

'What the fuck's a life-logger?' sneered Luke, trying to hide his rattle from his crew.

'Video audio surveillance device. It's a bit like the body cams the police wear, only better quality.'

At the mention of police, the alley paused.

'Which, in fact, is what I used to be, Luke. A police officer. But I hated the uniform and the terrible hours. Why I decided to do something more fun.' Her smile got wider, wilder. 'Like becoming a private detective and hanging with you boys. Now, why don't you smile for the camera?'

The youths looked at the woman, then at the device attached to her holster. Heather felt herself being released. She could hardly breathe for the tension in the alley.

'Wait a minute, sister,' began Luke, tossing the bag away from him. It made a crumpling noise as it hit the wall. Heather crouched down and grabbed it. 'I think you've got the wrong end of the stick here. All we were doing was trying to help this—'

'Not your sister,' said the woman, shaking her head, cutting him off. 'Not by birth or culture or religion.' She paused, considering. 'Although I would quite like to be a nun.' She turned to Heather. 'What do you think? I could totally rock a wimple, right?'

Luke cut in again. 'Lady, I don't know how you know my name but—'

The woman held up a hand, stopping him. 'Can I just point out that I don't have a nun obsession or anything. I just like wimples. I think it has something to do with *The Sound of Music*—' The woman clocked the bewildered expression on the thug's face and grimaced. 'You're right. Not important, sorry. Let's just move on. I know your name, and I've filmed and tagged you—' she tapped her holster again — 'assaulting this young woman.'

Luke stared at the camera, then at Heather, her hijab again covering her hair, then finally back at the woman.

'Don't know what you think you saw, lady, but it wasn't no assault. She was ready to party.'

The woman turned and addressed Heather.

'Did you give these men permission to touch you, miss? Because it seems like you're being held against your will.'

Heather shook her head.

'I'm telling you she was well up for it. Never told us to stop or nothing.' Luke grinned.

'It's all about consent, Luke. Did this woman consent to you restraining her? No. Did she consent to you taking her bag? No. Did she consent to you to intimidating her? All no.'

After a beat, Luke stepped forward, his grin widening.

'Maybe we'll just flip you both, fuck you with your life-logger until you're ripped up and begging me to stop.' He smiled his reptile smile. 'What do you think about that? Would that work as consent?'

The woman continued grinning at him. Heather couldn't understand why she was so sure of herself.

'I think,' the woman continued, musing, 'you've just uttered threats with menaces, so I reckon the police will have you and your boys in the back of their van in no time.'

Without warning, Luke stepped forward and drove his gloved fist into the side of the woman's face. The sound of his knuckles connecting with her cheek was like the snap of wet washing on a line. The woman staggered back a few feet, her beret slipping from her head. Luke's lips stretched in a feral slash of anticipation, and he stepped forward again and slapped her hard. As she fell to her knees he ripped her camera from its holster and threw it against the wall of the alley, narrowly missing Heather. Luke loomed over the woman, pulling his fist back for another blow.

'Wait!' the woman managed, her voice mushy.

'Why?' said Luke, clearly enjoying himself once more, now he was back in control. 'Do you want to consent? Because that won't be nearly as much fun.'

'No.' The woman got slowly to her feet, rubbing her cheek. 'I want to explain about the phone.'

'What phone, lady?' sneered Luke. 'Do you mean your logger?' He pointed at the device where it lay, smashed at the foot of the wall. 'It's fucked, and you're about ten seconds behind it.'

The woman grimaced in pain. 'That's not what I'm talking about. I'm talking about the phone.'

'The bitch is warped, Luke. I think we should—'

'See? "Bitch"! I knew one of you would get round to it!'

The woman reached down to grab her beret. Luke backhanded her across her face, making her stagger.

'Shut it! What phone?'

The woman spat blood onto the pavement.

'The phone in my pocket,' she said, touching her face with caution. 'You know, I think you might have cracked my tooth, Luke.'

'What about the phone?'

'Well, I don't claim to understand it because I'm about as technical as a brick, but the company I rent the body cam from set it all up for me.'

'Luke, I'm freaking here. The woman's boki.' Luke's side-kick skipped from one foot to the other, eyes skimming off the walls of the alley.

'You see, the camera's got GPS and a recording facility built in, which is all good and dandy . . .'

Luke stepped forward, fist clenched, ready to shut the woman down.

'. . . but it uses the phone for streaming.'

There was a silent beat in the alley.

'Streaming? What are you talking about?' Luke scratched compulsively at the back of his head, trying to alleviate the skunk itch in the centre of his brain.

The woman spat red again, wiping her mouth with her sleeve.

'The streaming, Luke. The live streaming of all the images it records. Images of you, in this case, sexually assaulting the woman over there and physically assaulting me.'

It took a couple of seconds for the implication of her statement to sink in.

'Fuck off. Who to?' spat Luke, backing away slightly.

'Well, that's the question, isn't it, Luke? Who to? The company I lease the logger off, obviously. They keep a digital copy of everything streamed in a vault somewhere. Not an actual vault, but a server room. Or a cloud. As I say, I don't really understand it. All I know is it's stored somewhere and I can send it to whomever I want. Shit, my mouth hurts!'

'Like who? Send it where?'

'Well, I don't know, Luke! Off the top of my head, the police might be a good bet for a start. And maybe a hospital to show them where you hit me. I think I might have a concussion, by the way.' The woman felt her head gingerly.

Her words brought a deeper stillness to the alley, broken only by the sound of sirens approaching at speed.

'Luke! We've gotta split!'

Luke shook his head, his eyes never leaving the woman in front of him.

'Live streaming?'

'Just like the TV shows, Luke. It's a brave new world.'

The sound of sirens echoed around the alley. It was impossible to tell which direction they were coming from. One of Luke's gang muttered under his breath, practically vibrating on the spot.

'Who are you? What's your name?' said Luke softly.

The woman smiled back at him, her lips distorting where he had punched her, the skin already beginning to swell and split.

'Why, do you want to send me flowers?'

The two youths next to Heather couldn't take it anymore. They turned on their trainers and fled the alley, leaving Luke alone with the two women. The siren sounded both nearer and further away, bouncing off the brick walls. As they stared at each other, a second joined it. Two police cars. Luke's eyes never left the woman.

'Just want to know who to look for, when it's time to come calling.'

If the approaching law worried him, he didn't show it. Heather stared from one to the other, the woman to the road-man, wondering who would be first to back down. Getting ready to run.

'Who are you?' repeated Luke.

'Tock-tick,' said the woman. 'In about two seconds this alley's going to be knee-deep in blue. Then you'll be in a world of trouble.'

'I'm dead anyhow if you live-streamed me to the feds.'

The woman shook her head, a puzzled look on her face.

'Live-streamed you? What, like on the telly? Is that even possible?'

Luke squinted at her, confusion and slow anger washing his features.

'But you said . . .'

The sirens seemed to take a sonic leap forward. Heather thought she even saw the first hint of blue and amber lights painting the walls. The woman stepped forward.

'I know what I said, Luke. You just don't know if it's true. Maybe I just said it because you were about to beat me and the lady over there senseless. Or maybe it is true, and I have a top-notch bit of up-to-date tech—' she glanced at the broken camera, dead at the foot of the wall — 'which you owe me for, by the way, that has in fact called the feds here.'

Luke looked up the alley, where emergency-vehicle lighting was washing the walls with streaks of colour. The sirens were so loud now they sounded like they were already in the alley.

He made up his mind and ran.

The woman watched him go, no smile on her face now. Only after Luke had skidded round the corner and disappeared from sight did she turn her attention to Heather.

'Are you OK?' Her voice was suddenly serious.

At the end of the alley, an ambulance screamed past. Heather's eyes widened as she watched it sweep from left to right across the mouth of the road, disappearing in the blink of an eye.

'I don't understand,' whispered Heather.

The woman reached down and picked up the camera, turning it over in her hands. She winced as a bit of it fell off, then looked up at Heather.

'Steady,' she said, taking Heather's arm. Heather realised she'd collapsed against the wall. She focused on the woman.

'You weren't filming? The police aren't coming?'

The woman shook her head.

''Fraid not.'

'I don't believe this. Who are you?'

Heather studied the woman in front of her. Close up, she could see that her rescuer was older than she'd thought. Maybe thirty. Her eyes were grey and full of concern.

'My name's Raine,' said the woman. 'Like the weather, only with an "e" at the end.'

'Right. And why were you . . . ?' Heather stared around helplessly. She felt sick and light-headed, overwhelmed by the terror that had just passed. She stumbled. Raine wrapped a strong arm around her.

'You've had a shock. You need some hot tea.'

Heather could see beads of blood on the woman's swelling face.

'Hot tea? How . . . ?'

Raine saw her looking and smiled, making the skin of her lip pull tighter. Like it was going to split.

'Don't worry. There's a cafe up the road. They know me there. A little blood isn't going to get us barred.'

CHAPTER 2

Detective Inspector Mary Hume gazed down at the body of the young man on the floor and felt like crying. He couldn't have been more than twenty, and the punishment inflicted on his naked torso was like a road map of torture.

'Cause of death?' she said quietly.

The scene-of-crime officer, Brendon Ho, glanced up at her. 'Specifically? Drowning. Through drug overdose, probably.'

The SOCO was kneeling by the corpse, a row of cotton bud swabs on a plastic tray at his side. He was taking samples from the dead man's mouth for analysis. Saliva. Blood. Regurgitated food. His nose clip made his voice monotonous. Hume tried to breathe through her mouth; the bouquet of death-odours coming from the body was solid as a wall.

'Choked on his own vomit,' said Hume, nodding at the victim. It was nothing she hadn't seen before. She glanced at the man's arms, legs and groin, looking for the telltale signs of a long-term user. Brendon carefully placed a swab in a vial and followed her gaze.

'No track marks, so the drug use wasn't habitual,' he said, voicing Hume's thoughts. 'That, plus the nakedness, looks more like a date-rape gone wrong to me.' He wrote an identifier on the vial and placed it in a zip bag. There were already several others inside: Hume was late to the party. She let her eyes travel the body, not concentrating on any one detail but rather making a mental map of the murder scene. Something she could revisit later. Her gaze ended back up at the mouth, at the flecks of matter stuck to the white veneer of the dead man's teeth.

Hume blinked. 'Nice dentistry,' she said. 'Expensive.'

'Everything here is.'

Hume gazed around the upmarket Soho flat. If it was his, the young man had money. The decor was sparse but stylish, with retro-erotica prints on the walls and an oak floor polished to perfection. The lacquer applied to it was so thick the blood leaking out of the body just sat in pools on the floor, rather than soaking in. Hume closed her eyes, playing out the scene in her mind. The invitation back. The spiked drink. Then the night of hoped-for passion turning to a murder dance.

Hume opened her eyes, layering her imagined scenario onto the room in front of her.

'Boyfriend?' She asked, finally. The erotica on the walls featured male bodies only.

'In the next room,' said Brendon, wincing. 'He came in off-shift three hours ago expecting to find a meal and a kiss and a Netflix-binge waiting for him before bed and a decent night's sleep. Instead, he found a reason never to sleep again.'

Hume winced back. She looked again at the damage to the body, skin goose-bumping under her shirt and jacket.

'Do we know what the numbers signify?' she asked softly.

'Haven't got a scooby. They were carved with something sharp, though. A scalpel, maybe. Or a razor blade.'

Hume gazed at the three numbers carved into the young man's hairless chest. The cuts forming the characters were straight, but she supposed they'd have to be. It would be difficult to carve curves into flesh and muscle so deep she suspected they scored the bone.

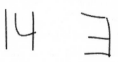

Hume looked at the neat slices of flesh, white ribbons of fat poking out. At the dead man's eyes, staring at nothing. Less than nothing. At his neatly manicured fingernails. At his perfect white teeth underneath the vomit. Then she slowly looked around at the meticulous flat. At the perfectly aligned paintings. At the immaculate furniture. Everything seemed exactly in its place. The whole flat coordinated to perfection.

'He didn't fight back,' she realised. 'No trauma to the hands. No blood other than from the wounds to the body. No damage to the fingernails indicating a struggle. No furniture out of place.'

The SOCO nodded. 'I noticed that, too. Which suggests he either knew the killer or perhaps was in the habit of bringing strangers back to his flat.' He glanced at the door that led to the next room, where the boyfriend was being comforted. 'Which will make for some fun questioning.'

Hume sighed, following his gaze.

'Good luck,' said Brendon, returning to his work.

Hume rubbed a hand through her grey crew cut. She took one last look at the dead man's rictus grin, then headed for the door.

* * *

In my day it was a rarity to keep drugs at home. They were exclusively bought on the night, ready to drop at parties or raves. No way would you have them just lying around your house. You'd either buy a pill at the venue, or maybe in the pub just before, so that when you arrived you had a nice buzz going.

A love-buzz, we used to call it. A secret inner nirvana caused by chemicals. An event. A special occasion kept for one or two weekends a month. But now it's just chips.

Now it's just every day.

I think the kids are so desensitised by their environment — their smartphones and their tablets and their world of immediacy, with no time and no need for reflection — that the concept of an experiential specialness is beyond them.

That's why they take the stuff at school. At home. On the fucking bus. Just for something to do.

I feel sorry for them. I really do.

Plus, they can't even keep it hidden.

The first time I found my son's stash I wasn't looking for it. I was just clearing up the crappy debris in his room.

Sixteen years old and incapable of bringing down a plate or throwing away an empty can of the never-ending energy drinks they all seem to consume.

Like living in a pigsty, as my mother would say — or at least she would if she wasn't dead.

One school day I walked into his room, opened the curtains and windows to air the place, and began clearing the shit off his desk.

Crisp packets. Old orange peel. Empty vape bottles. Mouldy half-eaten biscuits. And there it was: a small resealable plastic bag with a few grains of white crystal in it.

Of course, I immediately knew what it was. Or at least, the sort of thing I was looking at. I didn't know it was ketamine, but I knew it was drugs. I've been around enough to recognise it straight away.

Some parents, I suppose, would be upset. Angry, even.

Worried.

Maybe they would call the police. The doctor. The school.

Not me. That would be hypocritical.

I wasn't worried; I was delighted. I'd been thinking I was going to have to find a dealer to sort out my little problem, but here was this tiny plastic bag like a gift from God. Seeing my son's careless empty wrap, with its few licks of pleasure remaining, I could only think of two things.

There must be more.

He won't miss them.

Smiling, I began to search his room. I was so happy. I didn't need to buy drugs from some lowlife criminal. I could just steal them from my sixteen-year-old son.

CHAPTER 3

'It's so awful. Just so fucking, fucking awful!'

Hume watched the distraught man sitting in front of her, twisting his phone in his hands and staring into space.

'We're very sorry for your loss, Mr Brindley,' DC Echo said, his voice soft and sympathetic. Hume glanced at her partner. His expression was earnest and concerned. Hume wondered if he practised in the mirror. She turned her attention back to the man sitting miserably in front of them.

Cale Brindley. Cale who had come home to find his boyfriend naked on their living-room floor, with numbers carved into him like he was a human notepad. Who had gone out to work safe in a loving relationship, and come home to the end of his world.

'I mean, where am I going to live?'

Hume's gaze was steady, unblinking.

Unless he hadn't, of course. Unless he was, in fact, the murderer.

'The flat belongs to David, then?' said Hume, her tone neutral.

David Webb. David who lay dead in the next room, with some sort of code slashed into him as if he was a coordinate in a game of body-chess. Hume used the present tense when referring to the victim to keep alive any recent memory that might be of help.

'Yes, of course it's David's . . . Jesus! Do you think I could afford this place? I'm just a find-and-scan drone processing orders in a warehouse for twelve hours a day. David is the one working in the shit-hot property sector. They buy the shells and he designs the interiors.'

That explains the flat, thought Hume.

Cale looked up at her, snail trails of tears drying on his perfect skin. 'Designed, past tense. What the fuck am I going to do?'

'I know this must be awful for you, Mr Brindley,' said Echo. 'Do you have somewhere else you can stay? A friend, perhaps? Or a relative?'

Cale's eyes were wide with scorn. 'A relative? Are you kidding me? It took me two years of up-fucking to leave them behind. Why the hell would I go back to them now?'

Hume was impressed that Echo kept the look of compassion in his eyes. Only a slight tightening of his hand around the tablet gave away his shock.

'Were you aware of David engaging in any other relationships? Encounters with other men?' asked Hume. Cale stared at her like she was an idiot.

'Of course I was. David was into the screen-scene. It was no big deal. What's that got to do with anything?'

'Well, it's just that the flat doesn't seem to have been broken into, so we are working on the assumption that David knew his attacker; either well enough to let him in, or perhaps to bring him back here.'

Cale looked at her, then back at his phone, as if it had an answer to Hume's question. Finally, he said: 'Inspector, it may seem callous to you, but David and me understood each other. We had an open relationship based on sex and fun. I'm sad that he's dead and I'm freaked that he was murdered in our home, but to be honest, there's always that risk, isn't there? David often brought back his little treats. Bring back enough and you're bound to hit a bad one. David hit the

17

worst. And now it's happened, I'll grieve for him in my own way and on my own terms. I won't put on a show for you here and now when I've got my own skin to think about. You can judge me all you like . . .' Cale car-crashed a tearful smile at her and Hume felt a pang of guilt. 'But you can do it on your own time. I'd like to leave now, and try and find somewhere else to live that won't make me feel like a freak.'

Hume looked at the man; barely more than a boy. He had a slight accent, almost hidden, like he was from somewhere he didn't want to remember. Hume thought about what it must be like to grow up visibly gay in such a place. The courage it would take to come to London and carve out a life where you could be who you believed yourself to be. What sort of hard decisions you might have to make on the way.

'What's the screen-scene?' she asked. Cale blinked and waved his phone.

'Grindr. Hornet. Some slightly more . . . adventurous places. David couldn't get enough. Once the city started closing down the clubs in lockdown, there was a bit of an explosion.'

'So David often had men back?'

Cale smiled. Hume watched with amazement as the young man's armour was slowly reforming.

'Girls. Boys. David wasn't fussy.'

'Do you have any idea what the numbers might mean? On his chest?' This from Echo, fingers poised over his tablet.

Cale was back to playing with his phone. Hume wondered if he was looking for somewhere to live. Messaging friends. Or *what*? She made a mental note to have the device checked for messages or images. If Cale was more involved than he said, he wouldn't be the first murderer to film his crime.

'Cale?' Echo persisted. 'Mr Brindley? I take it you saw the numbers on his chest. Do they have any particular meaning for you?'

'One four three,' prompted Hume softly.

Finally, Cale looked back up. The detectives could both see the bitter glitter of tears in the back of his eyes. When he spoke Hume could hear the loss in his voice. The loss and the loneliness and the fear. He stared at each of them in turn.

'Fuck knows. Victim number? Maybe David was victim number one hundred and forty-three.'

Jesus, thought Hume, shuddering inside. *I really hope not.*

CHAPTER 4

Despite the late hour, the cafe was still busy. Raine and Heather sat opposite each other in a window booth, looking out at the London pavement. The cafe was tucked into Hanway Street, behind Tottenham Court, and the clientele seemed to be mainly police officers, either just on, or just off, duty. The atmosphere was tired and warm. Nobody seemed to notice the two women, everyone completely in their own little police bubble. Outside the window, on the opposite side of the narrow street, a group of musicians were lounging beside a doorway, smoking cigarettes; their instruments in cases beside them.

Heather took a cautious sip of her tea. It was black and sweet, with a nutty flavour almost like coffee. 'I feel so stupid. I know you should never walk down alleys like that by yourself, but I was late for the Tube and when I saw those boys I just panicked. If you hadn't come along . . .'

Heather kept her eyes on her tea. It was in a clear glass tumbler, with a flower floating in it.

'Not your fault. Anyone should be allowed to walk down any street in the centre of a city,' said Raine, sampling her own tea.

Heather glanced up. Raine had cleaned her face in the cafe toilets, but she still looked a mess. Heather could see that the hot liquid hurt the woman's torn lips.

'You can't live your life in fear and have to make judgements like that. Most people you meet would gladly have given you directions to the Tube station, maybe walked you there for safety. Despite what the media would have you believe, London isn't full of hoodied thugs wielding knives and selling drugs. People like Luke are just pouring petrol onto prejudice. How long have you lived here?'

Heather ignored the question, looking straight at the detective. 'You really believe that? That most people are good, and not just out for self-preservation? To get what they can?'

Raine shrugged. The soft light of the cafe, mixed with the distortion to her face caused by the swelling, made her impossible to read, and that made Heather uncomfortable. She liked to be able to read people. It was what kept her safe.

'No, I'm sure people are still out to survive, whatever that means to them, but in my experience, not every hoodie is a hoodlum. Life just isn't that simple.' Raine winced as she touched the side of her face. 'Fuck, this hurts!' She took a napkin from the plastic holder in the centre of the table and dipped it in the bowl of water that was supplied for finger-washing. She passed it to Heather. 'Would you mind wiping the blood off? I feel like the Elephant Woman here.'

Heather stared at the napkin, then at the beaten-up woman in front of her. Finally, she took the cloth and dabbed gently at the detective's battered face.

'Raine . . .' Heather said carefully, concentrating on her task and avoiding Raine's gaze.

'Ow!' Raine winced as Heather accidentally scraped across a bit of raw flesh.

'Sorry,' said Heather. She worked in silence then placed the napkin neatly on the table. Finally, she looked into Raine's eyes. They were grey with small flecks of purple. Heather was pretty sure she was wearing contact lenses. 'I just want to say thank you for saving me.'

Raine smiled. 'I didn't save you. I just got rid of the reason why you might have needed saving.'

'Oh.' Somehow Heather felt deflated, as she realised she was a side issue to why the detective had been there in the first place. 'Well, thank you anyway.'

Raine picked up her glass of tea, raising it in salute.

'You're welcome, Heather. And if you ever *do* need saving—' Raine smiled her lopsided smile — 'then feel free to give me a call.'

'So why were you there, if not to help me?' Heather turned her glass of tea on the table to occupy her hands.

'Doing my job. Luke and his road-boys have been putting the squeeze on some local businesses. I've been hired to observe them, maybe catch them in the act.'

Raine gave a shrug.

'So far they've been too slippery. But now . . .' Raine raised her glass again and tapped her holster. 'With the footage I have on my phone and the assault they made on me, I should be able to take them out of the picture.'

Heather frowned, looking concerned. 'I won't have to make a statement or anything, will I?'

'No. I mean, you can if you want. I would. What those boys were about to do . . . you should really get some counselling.'

'No,' said Heather quickly, shaking her head. 'I'm fine. I mean, I wouldn't be if you hadn't come along, but I'm fine. I just want to put it all behind me.'

Raine nodded. 'Sure, I understand. After I've walked you to the Tube I'll go and report the assault at the station. I won't mention your name. I'll say that you left after the gang had scarpered.'

She reached into her combats and pulled out a business card.

'At least let me give you this. Shock can be a funny thing. It can creep up on you. If you start feeling shaky you can give me a call, OK?'

Heather hesitated, then took the card and slipped it into her bag. 'Thank you.'

'No problem. And if you give me your number I'll ring you in a day or two. Just to check you're not having a panic attack or anything.'

Heather looked at her.

'Please,' said Raine, smiling. 'It would put my mind at ease.'

Heather hesitated longer this time, then seemed to make up her mind.

'Do you have a pen and paper?'

Raine grinned, causing her mouth to joker itself. The bruised half of her face had set rigid.

'Pen and paper?'

'Right, sorry. So, do you want to enter it on your phone or something?'

'Sure.'

Heather dictated her mobile number.

'Great,' said Raine, putting her phone away.

Heather pointed at the drink in front of her. 'What is this, anyway? I don't think I've ever tasted anything like it.'

'Bori Cha,' said Raine, picking up her own glass and looking at it. 'This cafe is run by a Korean couple. They're about a hundred years old and never seem to sleep. This place is open 24/7 every day until doomsday, as far as I can tell.' She gestured at the police officers dotted around them. 'That's why it's so popular with the gavva.'

'Gavva?'

'Police. It's what my mum used to call them. It's a Romany word.'

'Right.'

'The thing about this place is nobody comes here but the police, so they don't have to have their shield up. They can just relax and be themselves. Normally an officer has to wear a mask all day; be the job rather than the person. It can be a strain. Here, for a few minutes before and after a shift, they can take the mask off and . . .' Raine's eyes focused somewhere else for a beat '. . . decompress,' she finished, taking a sip then setting the glass down.

23

Heather gazed at her thoughtfully. Finally, she said: 'What's it made of? The tea.'

'Barley. It's meant to have healing properties.' Raine put her hands to her face, voguing. 'What do you think? Is it working yet?'

For the first time Heather smiled. 'How come we're here, then? If it's a police cafe?'

'Ah,' said Raine. 'That's easy. I told you I'm a private detective, right? Well, I used to be a police officer. A detective, to be exact.'

'Like now?'

'Only without the public hate and terrible pay,' Raine agreed.

'Is that why you left? The pressure of the job?'

A shadow muddied Raine's face for a moment, then it cleared. 'Not important. The thing is, I like to come here sometimes. To relax.'

'To decompress.'

Raine tilted her head in acknowledgement.

'Exactly. Everybody here knows me.'

'But they don't know me,' said Heather, feeling suddenly anxious again.

'Don't worry; you're completely safe.'

After a moment Heather nodded. She wondered if she should tell her? This woman she'd only just met. It would be such a relief to let everything out. But then what would happen? What if . . .

She shut her thoughts down, and picked up her Bori Cha.

'What about you?' said Raine.

'What about me?'

'Heather's a nice name. Are you Scottish?'

Heather looked at the detective to see if she was joking. Raine merely smiled at her, looking interested.

'No, I'm not Scottish,' she finally said. 'Heather is a very popular name in certain sections of the South Asia diaspora.'

She managed to keep a straight face for about two seconds before bursting out laughing. It felt good.

Raine did her half-grin, her bruised skin shining, and raised her glass again.

'Well, I asked for that. Finish your drink and I'll walk with you to the station. I need to report the assault and get home and take some tramadol to counteract Luke's street-facial.' Raine gently rubbed her jaw. 'You know, despite my profession I'm all about love and forgiveness, but when I catch up with that bastard I'm going to make him suffer.'

It was said with such matter-of-factness that Heather felt a shiver spasm through her. A shiver that went right to her core.

CHAPTER 5

'So, what are you saying to me?' Hume's face was a mixture of disgust and fascination.

She had spent the night searching through old cases of serial rape in the LGBT communities. Cale's theory about David being victim 143 had alarmed her. After reading several case histories late into the evening she had gone straight through concern into outright fear. The last thing she needed was an atom bomb in the shape of a sadistic serial killer.

'As I said, it's not possible to know for sure, but given the amount of ketamine ingested, coupled with the alcohol, it's likely that paralysis occurred before asphyxiation.'

Hume's DC, Echo, sat on the corner of the desk at Charing Cross Police Station. Although in his thirties, he could have passed for twenty. His carefully unstylish thick black hair cut above the collar placed him firmly in the geek camp. Reading his notes off the tablet in his hand, he could have passed for a big-tech work drone.

Which was pretty much what he did for Hume. DC Echo was recently assigned to her. A new type of detective constable for a new millennium. A DC who was also trained in tech analysis. Someone who could crunch the increasing amounts of data that could be recovered from a crime scene and feed it to her in bite-sized chunks. Hume glanced at the tiny tattoo inside his right ear, a homage to his Maori ancestry, and wondered how long his youthful looks would last. Dealing with the people caught up in London's underswell took its toll. Half the detectives she knew never made it to fifty in the job. It wasn't just the criminals that got to them, it was the grind of the city's machine, crushing the spirit of its citizens with its endless appetite for success. So many people got washed up on the shores of failure.

'So he was conscious as . . . well, when what was done to him was done to him?' Hume glanced at the crime-scene pictures displayed on the smartboard, showing in clinical detail exactly the damage done to David Webb, age twenty-four and no further. *Do not pass go. Do not collect anything at all, ever.* Hume felt a stab of pain deep inside.

'Stuck in a K-hole; a state of drug-induced paralysis. He'd be able to witness his own murder, but do absolutely nothing about it. Completely shut in with no ability to move.' Echo consulted the tablet in his hands. 'And given the amount of blood, coupled with how far it managed to travel from the body, the attacker took his time.'

'What makes you think it was a he?' said Hume mildly. 'The attacker?'

'The cuts to the chest were bone-deep. Slicing through muscle and sinew. Scoring the sternum and ribcage. Even with a scalpel or razor, the strength required would be considerable.'

Hume studied the photographs.

'Fair point. Tell me about the blood,' she murmured. 'About its travel.'

Echo wasn't fazed by the see-sawing of Hume's questioning. He was getting used to the way his boss worked. It was like watching a cake being baked. All the ingredients were added to the bowl, then the end result resembled something completely different. He stared down at his pad.

'David's flat was well maintained. Everything was new or kept in mint condition. The reclaimed oak flooring has been sanded then covered with a protective seal. Not oil-based, but some form of lacquer or polyurethane. The upshot of that is that the blood did not seep into the floor. That fact, apparently, means the tech guys are able to do some calculation between the severity and position of the injuries on his chest, the amount of blood and the distance it travelled, to work out the length of the attack. Lab puts the time of death in the early hours of yesterday morning.'

'And kids say maths is boring,' commented Hume.

'Dead boring,' agreed Echo.

Hume glanced at him sharply, then back at the photos. 'Nothing out of place, as far as can be seen?'

'That's what we guess, confirmed by the boyfriend, Cale. So we're working on the assumption that David knew his killer, however briefly. It seems that he was an avid user of various dating apps of the more transitory kind.'

Hume shook her head. 'You'd think, with all the horror stories out there, people would be more careful . . .'

Rapists using dating apps as their hook were headline news. Although few had gone on to commit murder.

Echo shrugged.

'You don't stop using taxis just because you hear of one rapist cabbie.'

'Good point. Anything on David's phone, or from the app account?'

'Nothing from the company. Data protection, blah blah blah. Not that it would help. Nobody gives their true details on these things anyway. As for his phone . . . it's locked, so we'll need to wait for the tech guys to unlock it. Maybe when they do, we'll find a message from him. The killer.'

'If it is a "him",' repeated Hume gently. Echo inclined his head.

'Although as I said, the depth of the cuts—'

'Merely suggests strength or skill of an individual. Not their sex.'

'OK.'

'Any skin DNA? Blood? Hair? Semen? Anything under the nails?'

'Not as yet. The lab is fast-tracking the samples taken at the scene but—'

'What about the vomit?'

Echo looked at her, his brow creased in confusion.

'What, what about the vomit? It was a result of the ketamine—'

'Not what caused it. What is it composed of?'

Echo stared at her uncertainly. Hume was gazing at the image of the dead man on the smartboard.

'I'm not sure—' he began.

'Was it all his? The vomit. Have the contents of his stomach been checked to cross-reference the material?'

Echo was aghast. 'Are you suggesting that some of the vomit might *not* be his?'

'Look at David's face.'

Echo turned to view the image on the screen.

'What am I looking for?'

'There was something that was bugging me at the scene, but I couldn't put my finger on it. David's got nice teeth.'

Echo swiped at his tablet and enlarged the image. The dead man's eyes stared past them at nothing. His skin looked pale and shiny in the camera's flash. Pale because he was lying on his back and all the blood had drained from his face. His mouth gaped open and Echo could see far more than he wanted to.

Hume looked at her partner, eyebrows raised.

'He died from choking, yes? Drowned in his own vomit.'

Echo nodded. Hume gazed at him a moment longer, then at David's image. She walked over to the smartboard and pointed at David's mouth.

'The vomit is all down his chin and on his chest. There is none on his cheeks or neck. Yet for him to choke on his own vomit, he would need to be on his back. Supine.'

It was a few moments before Echo got it.

'He was killed sitting up,' Echo breathed.

Hume nodded. 'I noticed his mouth at the scene, but didn't realise the significance. Most of the regurgitated matter is on the back teeth. The front teeth are relatively free of it.'

'Meaning?'

'Meaning the killer obstructed his mouth, either with a hand or some material, crushing David's lips against his teeth as he died; forcing the vomit to fill up the remaining space, drowning him.'

'Jesus.'

'That's why there wasn't much on the floor. It all went back down his throat.' Hume pointed at Echo. 'I want the contents of his mouth analysed. There may be contaminants from the killer. DNA or fibre that could give us a way into the case.'

Echo reached for his tablet. 'Full scan on the mouth and contents: check.'

Hume nodded and turned back to the smartboard. Finally, after staring at the pictures of the crime scene for another minute, she turned to her partner.

'OK, lay it on me. What the hell do the numbers mean? Please don't tell me we've got a triple-figure murderer out there.'

Echo swiped upwards on his pad until he found the information he wanted.

'One four three, slashed into the victim's chest. Carved with enough pressure to slice through muscle as well as skin. The graphology suggests the assailant was right-handed.'

Echo's reading was concise.

'And the meaning?' Hume glanced out at the officers working the computers beyond the glass wall, compiling and sifting through the data that the murder was generating.

'143 is the number of a bus travelling from Archway through Finchley to Brent Cross. We're checking TFL CCTV to see if David was on the bus, maybe meeting someone. We're also cross-referencing with social media to see if the route is a regular hook-up. Apparently, since the, er—'

Echo consulted the file again — 'screen-scene sprang up around the app trend, clubs are not the meeting places of choice. Bizarrely, transport is.'

'Makes sense.' Hume shrugged.

'Why?'

'If you're in a club or pub it's easy for someone to spike your drink. If you're meeting in a private car it's easy to be robbed.'

Echo nodded. There had been recent cases of gangs setting up Grindr accounts and arranging to meet prospective lovers, only to brutally attack them and steal their cars.

'Meeting on public transport is neutral,' Hume went on. 'There's no chance of your date finding out where you live, and if you don't feel safe or comfortable you can just step off at the next crowded stop.'

'Right,' said Echo. 'Smart.'

'What else?'

Echo blinked and looked down at his tablet.

'Psalm 143, verse 12 says: "In your unfailing love, silence my enemies; destroy all my foes, for I am your servant".'

Hume closed her eyes, feeling the pressure behind them forewarning a headache. 'Please, not a religious angle. I don't think I can cope.'

'Then you'll love this. 143 is also a magical angel number, apparently signifying changes in your love life. Also, it represents an angel that encourages you to learn the importance of tolerance and endurance.'

'Jesus.'

'You said it. And, according to the report of how long the assault went on before asphyxiation by vomit, David certainly learned the importance of endurance.'

Hume looked at her DC, then at the photograph of David's body.

'OK. Any other theories I should know about?'

'No, other than there's a certain ritualistic quality to it. Like a code. That's what put me in mind of the angel numbers.'

'And the toxicology report suggests he was conscious throughout it all?'

'In a ketamine-induced lockdown. Every minute of the three and a bit hours, yes.'

'And nobody heard anything because of the paralysis?'

'Seems that way.'

'Until the boyfriend came home and phoned it in.'

'Yes. He's given us access to his mobile. Everything checks out.'

'Jesus,' Hume said again. 'Poor David.'

The detective's room seemed to shrink a little, as Hume thought about what the young man's last few hours must have been like. The excitement of meeting someone. Bringing them back to the flat. She wondered if David had taken the drug willingly, thinking of increasing the pleasure without knowing the dangerous dose he had been given. Maybe he thought it was ecstasy or GHB. Or maybe he knew it was ketamine, but just not that much. Hume imagined the excitement, the arousal, then the disorientation and dislocation as the drug took hold, and the assailant showed their true intentions. The pressure behind her eyes increased.

'Then, of course, there's another possibility,' said Echo softly. Outside it began to rain, the noise of London-static on the window pane.

'Which is?'

'The boyfriend did it.'

'Cale?' said Hume in surprise. She thought back to the young man. To his comments about 'up-fucking' — having sex to climb the social ladder: for property or status. 'He didn't strike me as the murdering type.'

Echo smiled grimly.

'They never do, but nine times out of ten it's the partner.'

Hume felt the headache fully emerge and squat on her brain. She acknowledged the truth of her DC's statement.

He was right.

Nine times out of ten it was the partner.

CHAPTER 6

Raine sat at the table in her houseboat rewatching the evening's footage. Her earbud bleeped, telling her she had an incoming call. She tapped it, not taking her eyes off the laptop screen.

'Raine,' she answered, watching the footage from the alley play in front of her. The images were 4K-clear, despite the poor lighting. Much better than when she'd been with the force. The premium she paid her surveillance company for the hardware was worth it. She made a mental note to make sure she got Luke to pay for a replacement. One way or another.

'Hey, it's me.'

Despite the hour, the voice was clear, with no tiredness detectable. At the back of her mind, Raine felt a cog of tension click round a notch.

'Detective Hume, how lovely to hear from you. Now, what are you ringing me at dead o'clock in the morning for? I'm busy.'

On the screen, Luke's fist loomed large, just about to bust open her face. Raine blinked. Pressing a key on the laptop, she wound the footage back, reversing time.

'I don't doubt it, but I was hoping you might have spare capacity in your schedule in the next day or so? There's something we need help with.'

The Metropolitan Police occasionally outsourced work to the private sector. As a former officer, Raine was on their list as someone reliable. She had done legwork for Hume before the detective had moved over to the Major Investigation Team. Mispers — missing persons — and dealings with the various gangs. Now, Raine watched as the screen showed Luke harassing Heather. She hit rewind again.

'Sorry, I'm chocka with a job at the mo. It's going to keep me tied up for a day or two. Why, what's the gig?'

'No problem, a day or two won't make a difference; the victim isn't in a hurry.'

Raine could clearly hear the sadness in Hume's voice. She didn't have to explain what she meant. If the victim wasn't in a hurry they were dead. And if they were dead and Hume was phoning her then it was a jigsaw case. Pieces all over the board with no picture to guide her.

'What do you need?' Raine said.

'A couple of things. I need to find out where the gay community gets their sex drugs.'

Raine stopped studying the screen and turned to stare out of her window. Outside, the lights of the other boats moved gently in the water. In the distance, she could see the metal-and-glass gleam of the new office buildings outside King's Cross. So different now from when she had been growing up.

'What are we talking? Just murder, or rape as well?'

'I don't know. The victim is dead and can't tell us, but it doesn't read like a rape. No bruising in the usual places. We'll have to wait for the lab rats. He was up to the brim with ketamine.'

'Willingly?'

'There's no sign of a struggle at the scene. Either he participated without knowing the strength or purity of what he was given, or he was spiked.'

On Raine's laptop, Heather could be seen passing the gang. Her face in the streetlight was drawn and frightened. Luke's was Christmas-morning happy. Raine hit the button, taking it back again.

'Doesn't mean anything. Drugs are part of the deal sometimes.'

'I know, Raine, I'm not a complete imbecile. I've seen enough sex-deaths to know how it can happen. This was different though. Not like sex gone wrong and then the boyfriend tried to cover it up. This had an edge to it.'

Raine nodded. Sometimes when you first scoped a scene you got a feeling for the pieces. A sense of the greater whole. You could tell when something was off-kilter.

'What was the other thing? You said there was a couple.'

'That's the edge, literally. The killer left a message carved on the body.'

Raine blinked.

'A message? Now that sounds fun. What did it say?'

'Well, maybe "message" is stretching it. But he or she was definitely trying to tell us something.'

'She? I thought you said the victim was gay?'

'Jealous wife of a straying husband?'

On the screen, another image came up.

'Sorry, you're right. He or she. Carry on. What did it say?'

'Just three numbers: 143.'

Raine whistled.

'Wow. How were they written?'

'What do you mean?'

'I mean, were they written in ink, scratched on by a nail, razored in, or what?'

As she spoke, Raine studied the image on the screen. Heather, leaving her workplace. Before the alley. Before Luke. The road-boys had been the perfect excuse for Raine to make contact. When they'd started eyeing up Heather, Raine had seen her opportunity. Luke's image had pinged in the NeoFace software running on her phone — the facial recognition program used by the Met, among others, and linked to all persons of interest on their watchlist. Once she had the name, all she had to do was call an ambulance to the next alley and hope the timing was right. Luckily, it had all gelled. Heather had thought Raine had been there for the gang, rather than for her.

She split the screen on her laptop and called up Heather's file.

'Scalpel. Possible razorblade.'

Raine shrugged. 'Very thriller cliché. Well, as I say, I'm crammed for the next day or two, dealing with a missing person, but maybe after that . . . what do you think the numbers mean?'

Hume's sigh sounded like a bitter wind in Raine's ear.

'Echo's been checking bus routes and Bible quotes.'

'Echo's your new DC? Cool name.'

'He has a tattoo in his ear and plays Pokémon GO.' Hume's voice was dry and neutral. Raine wondered if she knew what Pokémon was.

'What a combination,' smiled Raine. 'I'm definitely going to his next party. Scan the print of the numbers through to me, OK? I'll have a butcher's in the morning and let you know if anything pings.'

Heather's file was not thick. She hadn't been missing for long. From a devout Muslim family in east Nottingham. Her parents said they had reported it to the police, but nothing had come of it. They also suggested that there might be some racial issue. That the authorities might not search so hard for someone from their community. Perhaps the parents had it right . . . It had been simple enough for Raine to find Heather. The woman had applied for a job and the company had followed up on her references. The parents had given Raine details of all her previous jobs and qualifications. All Raine had to do was check out who had looked them up in the recent past to find out who was employing her now.

'Thank you, Raine.'

'And make sure I don't have to do anything with the file to open it when you send it through. You know I'm useless with that stuff.'

Raine had a love-hate relationship with technology. When everything worked, she never thought about it. When it didn't, she felt ready to hit it with a hammer.

'Sure.'

Raine crashed the call, ending it, and started tapping in the evening's report.

CHAPTER 7

'Well, the second one's easy, at least.'

Raine sipped her coffee, absently stroking Melania, her cat. The animal purred and stretched her claws into her leg. Despite the painkillers Raine had taken as soon as she woke, she could only open her mouth gingerly, so quite a lot of the coffee dribbled down her chin. Outside, the day was London-gunmetal-grey, with a light rust of mist ghosting over the canal.

'What second one? And what's the matter with your voice? You sound like a ventriloquist's dummy.' Hume's own voice was fresh, ready for the day. Raine envied her. The pain in her face had kept her up half the night.

'Gottle of geer?' she tried.

She was rewarded with Hume's derisory snort.

'Seriously, what's the deal?'

'I ran into a fist. No big deal. What time do you get up to sound this good in the morning?'

'I'm not up yet; this is me in bed.'

'Bastard. Is Robert in there with you?'

Hume's smile reached all the way to Raine's earbud.

'Mind your own business. What second one?'

'Your second ask. About the numbers.'

Hume's voice became more alert. Businesslike.

'Did you get the file?'

'That's what's easy.'

'Really?' The excitement in Hume's voice was immediate. 'Please don't tell me it's a serial killer.'

'No idea.' Raine delicately dabbed her chin with a napkin. 'But I'm pretty certain it doesn't mean that your body is victim 143.'

'Tell me,' Hume said, all banter gone.

'It was the 4 that was the clincher. The 1 is always the one — unless you're weird — and the 3 could be because they were slicing through flesh: much easier to slice in straight lines.'

'What are you talking about, Raine?'

'The 4. The numbers carved into your victim. What do you know about numeric fonts?'

'Absolutely nothing. I didn't even know there *were* numeric fonts.'

'Sure there are, and the 4 is a big giveaway. Nowadays we just write it like a capital "L" with a line through the bottom of it, yes?'

'OK.' Hume sounded unsure.

'Some people used to do it like a right-angled triangle, only extending the lines down and to the right.'

'Yes, but this one is like the first. The lines—'

'No, it's not,' interrupted Raine. 'Your number 4 hasn't got the "L" carrying on past the line cut through it. It looks more like an upside-down "h".'

There was a pause. Raine heard the sound of tapping; Hume getting the image up on her tablet.

'OK, yes. But it could just be that the cut didn't carry far enough. It definitely looks like a 4.'

'It *is* a 4. Just in a very specific font. Do you remember when LED watches came out? Or clocks?'

'Well, not when they came out, cos I'm not a hundred years old, but I know what you mean.'

'Really? How's the face holding out?' said Raine, smiling. Or half smiling, due to Luke's fist-facial.

39

'Better than yours by the sound of it. What have LED watches got to do with anything?'

'Well, they had diodes in them; seven arranged in a zero shape with a line horizontally through the middle to make up each number. Depending which were lit up they would display a specific digit.'

'Raine—' Hume's tone was exasperated.

'Bear with me. The thing is, there were no curves; couldn't be. The numbers had to be made up of straight lines. Also, everything had to fit inside the zero, which means no lines sticking out. Hence the 4 looking like an upside-down "h".'

'This is all very interesting but—'

'The same number font got transferred to pagers when they came out in the '90s. And to early phones.'

'OK.'

'Well, I was a kid in the '90s.'

'Really? You're younger than you appear,' said Hume, returning the jibe.

'Fuck off,' said Raine amiably. '143 was shorthand. Like "lol" is now. Dates from before you could text. People became familiar with the meaning of certain combinations of numbers, just like most everyone today would understand what lol stands for. Each numeral indicates how many letters in each word in a message. 1 is one letter; 4 is four letters; 3 is three letters. 143. You see?'

'Just about.' The excitement in Hume's voice returned. 'So what does it stand for? 143?'

'You might want to take another run at the boyfriend. Or see if there's another boyfriend on the scene.'

'Why?'

'143 stands for "I love you".'

There was a pause. Through the ether, Raine could hear the sound of Hume's brain humming. Outside the window, floating on Regent's Canal, a disease-ridden swan glided past like a survivor of the avian apocalypse.

Raine sucked in another small dribble of coffee.

'Shit,' Hume said finally.

CHAPTER 8

Heather checked outside her window, pulling the curtain back a fraction. She always checked. There was never anyone there, or at least anyone she might be worried about, but she always checked. The smudge of street she could see was empty of people, with only the occasional passing car. But she waited. If someone was watching her place they would not be walking by; they would be a shadow in a doorway. Darkness against a wall. Biding their time. So she stayed vigilant, slowly scanning the street. Making sure.

The bags under her eyes showed her worry. She had spent a sleepless night; the near-miss in the alley had shocked her. Not in the way that her rescuer, Raine, thought it might, but in ways the detective could never guess in a million years. Ways to do with a past she would be incapable of understanding. How could she?

You really believe that? That most people are good?

That's what she'd asked Raine, and it had seemed that Raine did.

But Raine didn't know her life. Hadn't walked in her shoes.

In Heather's experience, most people were not good. Wouldn't even recognise what 'good' meant. In her experience

41

'good' meant something completely different. And any deviation from that definition involved . . .

Heather took a slow breath, checking the shadows for any deeper pockets of darkness, any hint of movement.

There was no way she was going to the police. If she reported the assault then there would be records. Records that could be traced. That was why she couldn't tell Raine. She simply wouldn't understand.

Heather gave one last glance outside, then turned and walked to the hall. Looking in the mirror, she adjusted her hijab to cover her hair and neck, leaving only her face exposed.

She stared into the glass, at the dark eyes that hid worlds of pain even from herself. She tried smiling, turning it on and off. It made her look like a mannequin.

She glanced at the small passport photograph stuck to the mirror and tried smiling again. This time it came more naturally, less showroom-dummy scary. This time she crinkled her eyes as well.

'Soon,' she whispered to the photograph, then opened the door and left her flat, stepping out into the grey.

CHAPTER 9

Raine spent the rest of the morning cleaning her boat, a wide-beam canal cruiser. She started on the outside, wiping down the surfaces and touching up the black paintwork where needed. She kept the decor simple, unlike the rentals with which she shared her section of the canal. The electricity and water hook-ups were buried, and the boat-mooring itself was protected by a high wall — all that remained of the original house that came with the berth her parents had bought.

When she was satisfied, she moved inside. The interior of the boat was one large open space, with a bed at one end and a sectioned-off bathroom at the other. In between were a desk, a sofa and a micro gym. Also, a small sink, a kettle and a tabletop fridge. There was no cooker; Raine had decided long ago that cooking was something best suited to other people. She either ordered in or ate out. She did, however, have a state-of-the-art Nespresso machine. Because life without good coffee just wasn't worth it. While rinsing out this morning's coffee cup she mulled over her encounter with Heather.

She was fairly certain 'Heather' wasn't the woman's birth name. Her parents' accents were clearly not native to the UK, and they had not given the impression that they would choose such a western moniker for their daughter, even though it was the name they had supplied. They'd told her that Heather had run away five months ago. That there had been some trouble — Raine guessed with a boy. Or maybe the mosque. Whatever. She had run away, like so many before her, to London.

When Raine had first got the commission, she had asked for background information. A list of Heather's friends. Any social-media accounts they might know of. Whether she had a bank account. How they knew it was London she'd run away to.

And that's when the alarm bells started ringing. Heather was educated, with a business degree. Heather had been gainfully employed before she ran away. Heather was in her twenties. She just didn't fit the profile of the usual runaway.

Raine had tactfully told the parents that as Heather was over eighteen, their daughter was an adult and, as much as they might want to get her back, they had no legal sway over her in this country.

The parents had assured Raine that they did not want to get Heather back; merely to know that she was all right. Perhaps open up a dialogue with her. That, although their daughter was indeed an adult, she was not wise in the ways of the world. Silently Raine thought that perhaps Heather was much wiser in the ways of the world than her parents were. Still, she took the job, found out where Heather worked, and followed her.

Now she had to decide what to tell the parents. Work out what the alarm bells meant.

She didn't get the sense that Heather needed help — at least, not in the way her parents were hinting. Whatever the young woman had run away from, it wasn't because she was emotionally disconnected from modern life.

Raine set her coffee machine going and opened up her laptop. She cropped an image of Heather outside her office and ran it through NeoFace and Clearview. Nothing pinged. She either wasn't on the system or the system couldn't read her face. Raine looked at the young woman's features, framed by the hijab. She couldn't see any of the telltale signs of plastic surgery.

Raine sighed in annoyance. She just didn't know enough about the situation to make a judgement. Then she picked up her mobile and scrolled through until she found Heather's ident. She primed the call and put the phone on speaker. Looking out of the little window at the urban leper-ducks, she listened until the phone rang out and the voicemail kicked in.

'Hi. Please leave a message and I'll get back to you.' The voice was definitely Heather's, despite the metallic tone.

'Well, well,' muttered Raine. She wasn't surprised the woman didn't answer, or mention her name in the message. If Heather had run away and didn't want to be found she'd be on her guard. She wouldn't answer the phone to a strange number. Raine was just intrigued she'd given her real number at all.

'Hi, this is Raine from last night. Just checking you're OK. I'll hang up and try again in case you're screening calls.'

She hung up and redialled.

'Hi. Please leave a message and—'

Raine hit the 'end' symbol, cancelling the call, and glanced at her watch.

'Fuck!' She was going to be late for her meeting with Hume. The cat looked at her, completely unfazed by the swearing.

Raine stuck her tongue out at him, poured her coffee into a travel cup, threw her phone into an army messenger bag and switched on her security system.

As she jumped from the boat to the path adjacent, she smiled. She let herself out of a side gate onto the canal path and began strolling. She wasn't really going to be late. She was never late. It was the rest of the world that was early.

* * *

Heather felt jittery, and she didn't know why. When she had got the Tube into work she had been constantly looking

45

over her shoulder. Every face seemed to hold menace. It was driving her crazy.

Maybe it was nothing; just ghosts in her mind. Maybe it was the aftershock of last night, the attack by the gang, that was spooking her.

What had she been thinking, walking into that alley? That one poor choice could have ruined everything, destroyed the fragile reality she had built around herself. She had been so stupid!

She took a sip of coffee and tried to focus on her work. She had only been employed there for a few months and needed to show that she was reliable. The dynamic structure of the company, a marketing start-up, was too fluid for her to lose concentration. As she looked at the rows of figures on the spreadsheet, neat and known and logical, she found her thoughts turning to Raine.

The woman had been so sure of herself. So completely comfortable in her own skin. It was like the world wrapped itself around her. So utterly different from Heather's reality, where she clung to the skin of the world by her fingernails.

And last night she'd almost lost her grip.

Heather sighed, adjusted her hijab, and turned her gaze outward, back to her laptop. Inside her bag, hanging on the back of her chair, her phone began to ring.

CHAPTER 10

'How do you even find these places?' asked Hume, staring in horror at the fried bread on her plate. The middle had been removed and replaced with an egg, also fried. Possibly in butter.

'That's a Vendetta egg, that is!' said Raine through a mouthful of heart attack. 'Like in the film. There are probably only two cafes in London who make that.'

'And I bet both of them have a direct line to a hospital.' Hume tentatively poked the egg with her fork. It began seeping yellow yolk like it was infected. She felt her stomach roll, actually visualising the fat congealing inside her. She normally had a vegetable smoothie and decaf coffee for lunch in a desperate attempt to stave off the middle-aged spread most of her colleagues seemed to be experiencing. If she ate all of what Raine had ordered for her she seriously doubted she'd make it to the end of the day, let alone retirement.

'You're funny.' Raine took a slurp of her full-fat Coke, hardly spilling any of it, then stuffed a piece of sausage into her mouth.

'Seriously, though. How do you know about this place? I mean, it hasn't even got a sign on the door.'

They were sitting in the back garden of what Hume had first thought was an office, overlooking the canal. In one corner of the garden was a chicken enclosure, with a dozen birds happily scratching away. The detective suspected that was where the eggs came from.

'I grew up around here,' shrugged Raine. 'I've lived here all my life. Way before it all started being gentrified.'

'Round here?' said Hume, amazed. In all the years they had known each other Raine had never revealed any personal details. Which, all things considered, was amazing. 'I knew roughly where you lived, of course, but here? All the apartments are for the super-rich. No way could you afford this on a detective's salary — private or public.'

Raine smiled and pointed at the soupy brown water a few feet from them. Hume peered at the canal. A couple of holiday narrowboats were tied up on the opposite side, with tourists eating their own brunches while looking at the shiny glass-and-steel buildings that seemed to be erecting themselves all around King's Cross. Hume stared at them enviously. One of them seemed to be enjoying a bowl of salad.

'A canal boat? Really?'

'Back in the '80s, when my parents moved here, this was one of the most run-down areas in London. A lot of prostitution and drugs. People used to arrive at King's Cross and just get sucked in. Half the houses were squats, and the rest were drug dens or brothels.'

'Lovely. Your parents must have been—'

'My parents were fantastic,' cut in Raine, her voice hardening slightly. 'They were part of the dance scene that took over warehouses for raves. They bought a wreck of a house with mooring rights for practically nothing and lived on a houseboat. Loads of arty types were living on the water back then. There was a real community. It was like Soho was supposed to be in the '60s. One entire barge was a kind of school for the boat-kids.'

'But didn't the authorities get involved?' asked Hume. She had grown up in Basingstoke, and the nearest she had ever got to the traveller communities of the '80s was watching

48

the television, seeing dirty teenagers with dreadlocks protesting about trees being cut down.

'Are you joking? The authorities didn't give a toss. Not until the end, when nice middle-class kids started coming to the house parties and taking ecstasy. When it started affecting the mainstream, that's when they took notice. And then, when the property boom happened, the whole place got demolished and rebuilt for millionaires. None of the old community could afford to live here.' Raine gestured around the garden, with its smattering of tables and riverside views. 'But if you know where to look, there are still a few places left. Properties that were bought outright with no ground rent.'

'But the business rates here must be phenomenal! How on earth can the likes of this place afford it?'

'Ah,' said Raine, stabbing a piece of bacon from her plate. 'Technically this isn't a cafe.'

'What is it then?'

Raine looked at her wide-eyed.

'A farm. Agricultural ventures don't have to pay business rates.'

'A farm,' Hume repeated, her voice flat.

Raine nodded and jutted her chin at the chickens. Hume glanced at the birds. As she watched, one of them pecked a worm out of the ground and swallowed it.

'You're kidding me.' Hume shook her head.

'Each time we sponsor a chicken we get a free meal.'

Raine wiped the last of her sausage from her chin. The tramadol she had taken had done its job, and she hardly felt any pain at all.

'But anyhow, discussion of the oddities of London history isn't why we're here. Like I said on the phone, I think you need to look at the boyfriend. But first I want you to look at this.'

Raine took out her phone and showed Hume the photo of Heather she had cropped from her surveillance video.

49

'What's this?' said Hume.

'This is why I'm not doing the other thing, the drug angle, for you.'

Raine briefly filled her in on what had happened the previous night.

'Ouch,' said Hume when she had finished. 'Did you get it checked out?' She examined the younger woman's cheek. The bruising was a tight oil-slick of colours.

'No, it's not broken. The point is that there's something off. The girl I met and the person her parents described just don't seem to gel.'

'The parents?' Hume glanced at the phone again, surprised. 'She doesn't seem young enough to—'

'I know, but that's just one of the weird things. She also isn't the type. She appears to have her life completely together. No sign of substance abuse. Holding down a decent job.'

'Family argument? Maybe a boyfriend here in the city? Or girlfriend?'

Raine raised her eyebrows, her eyes steady.

'Running away to London for love? I didn't know you were such a romantic, Detective Inspector!'

Hume felt a deep bell of pain inside her and quickly changed the subject.

'Where are you going with this, Raine? Only . . .' she raised her own eyebrows.

Raine smiled at her.

'There's something not quite right. She gave me a mobile number she's not answering and avoided giving me her home address. Plus, she seemed unduly wary.'

'Well, she had just been assaulted.'

'Unduly wary of me,' said Raine.

'Contrary to your image of yourself, Raine, you are actually quite scary. You have a way of smiling at completely the wrong time that makes sane people want to run away.'

'Rubbish. They're just dazzled by my natural charm. The point is that there's a disconnect. I put her picture through all the usual channels available to me but came up with zero.'

'So?'

'I thought you might run it through the ones that are not available to me?' said Raine, eyes wide. 'As I've helped you with the body number thing. Plus, if I get this cleared up quickly, I can look into the drug angle for you.'

Hume sighed. Raine reached into her messenger satchel and pulled out a clear zip bag containing the napkin Heather had used to dab Raine's face clean.

'I got her fingerprint as well. If you could run that for me too?'

Hume eyed the blood-splattered tissue through the plastic. There was a clear red fingerprint in the corner. She nodded, taking it and placing it in her own bag.

'Ping the image over to me. If I get time, I'll have a look. Now, tell me about the numbers. Why would the killer write "I love you" in . . . what was it you said?'

'Pager code,' said Raine, changing gear. 'I haven't got a scooby. Maybe it's become popular again, or maybe it's an app thing. To protect you from being understood by the mainstream muggles.'

'Is that why you know it? Because your parents were part of the illegal dance scene?'

'You see?' said Raine, smiling her joker smile. The tramadol may have taken the pain away, but it had done nothing for the mobility of her mouth. 'How mad were the '90s? Even saying "illegal dance scene" sounds insane.'

'Whatever,' Hume said, batting away the chit-chat now. She needed to get down to business. 'Why would the killer write "I love you"? Toxicology says that the victim would have been conscious the whole time. Possibly feeling everything too. Cale, the boyfriend, said he knew that David slept around. Even partied around in their flat.'

'David's the victim?'

Hume nodded, then continued: 'Surely it's far more likely to have been a predator? Someone who has something against the gay community in general perhaps, or David in particular.'

'Maybe David was going to throw the boyfriend out? Replace him with a newer, hotter model?'

'Maybe,' mused Hume, thinking about the high-end flat. 'Have you ever heard of "up-fucking"?'

A man in his early sixties, wearing fussy clothing, paused, his coffee cup halfway to his lips, and gave them a hard stare. Raine waved at him.

'Nah,' said Raine cheerily, 'but it sounds fun. And what do you mean, he was conscious the whole time?'

'The amount of ketamine in his body meant that he was paralysed, but fully conscious.'

'On purpose?' Raine was shocked at that.

'The lab guys think so.'

'That's sick.'

Raine stared at the canal. The tourists on the narrow-boat had finished their lunch and were steering their vessel towards the station.

'So, he was meant to read it. Understand what it signi-fied, maybe,' Raine said quietly, watching the retreating boat.

'Understand what? That the killer loved him?'

Raine shook her head. 'That's not what it says. Not once you factor in that he was conscious.'

Hume looked at her, confused. 'But you said—'

'One four three. Yes, I know. But that's not what it says,' she repeated. 'Not from his point of view. From his POV, it's upside down and backwards. The other way round.

'Shit,' said Hume. 'You think that was on purpose too? We were working on the assumption it was for our benefit.'

The gentleman with the coffee deliberately turned away, his posture a straight-board of disapproval. The two women ignored him.

Raine gazed at the older detective, suddenly aware of the lines on her face. Cut deep in the thick, grime-filled air of the city.

'For sure. Especially now you've told me he was conscious through the assault. You really need to look at the boyfriend again. It doesn't say "I love you". It's the opposite.'

'I don't love you,' said Hume, softly. 'Is that what you think it might mean?'

'Or "You don't love me".'

On the table, her phone beeped into life, a picture of Echo filling the screen.

* * *

Raine stood looking at her boat, her head tilted slightly. The vessel was tied to the bank by two mooring ropes. The ropes were ever so slightly slack, allowing the boat some small movement. Even though the canal water seemed still, there were tiny variants in height, and small waves when other vessels passed. If the boat was tied up too tight then pressure could be put on the hull. Each of the ropes was attached to a sturdy metal bollard.

Raine tilted her head the other way, causing a stab of white heat in her bruised cheek. She ignored the pain.

When she was young, her parents had endless problems with mice and rats. It wasn't surprising, living on the water. Her father had broken the necks and bases off wine bottles, and fed the mooring ropes through the remaining glass tunnels. If a rat tried to climb up them, the glass tubes would spin, sending the rodents into the fetid water. Keeping the boat meticulously clean was another deterrent. If food was left out or crumbs not swept up then you had no hope; once the rodents were on-board it was nigh on impossible to get them off.

Unless you had a cat.

These were lessons that Raine had learned well. Which is why she cleaned the boat every day, scraping and painting and varnishing; wiping and disinfecting and polishing.

Which is why she never kept food on the boat, clearing away any takeaway meals as soon as she had finished.

Which is why she had Melania. Between the good housekeeping and the deadly instinct of her feline, she hadn't had a rat on-board for years.

Until now.

The rodent was pure London brawl, almost two feet long from the end of its whiskers to the tip of its tail, covered in scabs, with pink flesh showing where its fur was missing. It was on top of her barge, nose twitching and paws worrying at the central hatch that gave access to the interior of the boat. Even from where she was standing, Raine could see that the latch had been compromised, prised from the wood of the boat. That somebody had broken in while she had been at her meeting with Hume.

Raine stared at the boat a moment, then scanned her surroundings, checking for anything out of place. All she could see were swans and ducks. Her eyes unfocused for a second, then she slowly removed a can of Farbgel, a high-impact personal deterrent spray, from her messenger bag.

'Oh, I don't think so,' she whispered, stepping quietly across the path and onto her boat, her eyes never leaving the rat.

CHAPTER 11

The interior of the church seemed wrong in the garish lights that had been set up by the police incident unit. The stone looked fake and the disrepair was all too obvious. Hume wondered if it would ever be used as a church again or whether the stigma of a murdered and mutilated vicar might hold too strong a memory for the parishioners . . .

She let her eyes wander the space, taking in the wood and the velvet and the stone, but could find nothing that sent up alert-flares in her head. Everything appeared as it should be. Except for the body, of course.

She turned her attention to the corpse on the floor, and the SOCO collecting samples from it. It was the same man as last time. She sifted through her memories until a name popped up.

'Morning, Brendon. Similarities?' she asked. Of course there were similarities. She wouldn't have been called if there weren't.

The SOCO looked up from his work. Beside him were vials and swabs, tablet and ruler — some of the tools of his trade. He raised a spatula in greeting.

'Morning, Detective Inspector. Pretty much the same, apart from the setting. The numbers are different but the graphology matches, as far as I can tell. Straight cuts with a scalpel or razor. The body is kneeling this time. The killer positioned him that way, leaving the head resting against the front pew. It must have been soon after death as the blood hadn't fully coagulated. You can see where it has pooled.'

Hume nodded. The victim's skin was noticeably darker around the buttocks and knees, suggesting that these were the areas to which gravity had taken his blood while it was still thin enough to flow.

'He was found by the cleaner who came in to tidy up and light the candles before the early service. When the local police saw the carving on his chest they called us.'

The scene freeze-framed as a camera flash went off, photographing areas of the body for later analysis.

'How did they see the numbers if the vicar or whatever he is was kneeling? Surely they would have been hidden.'

'The officer didn't see the whole sequence, but she could see the first two numbers. Your murder flagged, and she passed it on. After the prelims, when DC Echo arrived, we moved the body.'

Hume nodded again.

'Where are his clothes? I can't see them here. Did the killer take them with him?'

'No. In the vestry. There's a walk-through leading to it behind the organ. Good chance that's where the vicar was killed, too.'

'Right.'

'I've managed to deduce that from my years of diligent training, both in the field and at one of the top forensic institutes in the country.'

Hume looked at him.

He shrugged. 'Plus all the blood.'

Hume smiled. 'Splatter patterns?'

Echo answered from behind her. 'Just puddles. It seems like the vicar was incapable of putting up a struggle. He just sat there and took it. Sound familiar?'

Like David Webb, Hume thought. She turned to look at her DC. She wasn't surprised that his youthful features looked even more youthful. Behind his glasses, his eyes shone. Two murders was moving up to celebrity status. One more would hit serial-killer level. Hume glanced at her partner's trim body and wondered if he'd ever had a Vendetta egg. Probably not.

'Have you ever had a Vendetta egg?' she said.

Echo stared blankly at her.

'What, from the film?' said Brendon, looking interested. 'Are they a real thing?'

'What are you even talking about?' said Echo.

Hume took a deep breath and turned her attention to the corpse. The skin had puckered around the cuts, pale and waxy. The vicar's knees were a deep shade of purple.

'Nothing. Don't worry about it. How far away is this church from Soho?'

'David Webb's flat, you mean? About twenty minutes' walk, or three stops on the Tube from Russell Square.'

Hume nodded. 'Have you examined the mouth?'

'Filled with vomit,' confirmed the SOCO. 'Making the cause of death as per the last: drowning.'

'Lovely. So the same killer.' Hume squatted down and started a visual examination of the body.

'But the Rev here was not gay,' said Echo. 'Or at least not publicly so. He has— had a wife and kids. No record of soliciting or any of the usual if he was living a double life,' he added, pointing at the bio their tech team had quickly gathered together and pinged through to his smart pad.

Hume stared intently at the reverend's face, and thought about all the stolen years. The years he wouldn't preach forgiveness. The years he wouldn't offer hope or baptise babies or marry couples in love. She sighed and turned her attention to the numbers.

'But still, he's clearly ours. Any ideas?' she asked the room.

'Three lines of numbers, centrally placed down the chest. 11 34 on one line; single numeral 2 on the next; and finally 06. I've tried running them through bus routes, train numbers, taxi licences. Nothing. No sequence rings any bells. The numbers don't seem to correlate to any pager code either.'

After Raine had spoken to Hume that morning she had relayed the possibility that it could be some form of text code. Hume wasn't convinced; neither David nor the vicar seemed old enough to remember pagers.

'OK, well, keep working on it. They must have some significance. Has the wife been informed?'

'There's a support officer with her now. The children are at school and will be picked up once . . .' Echo left the sentence hanging.

Hume nodded. The wife would need to be ruled out of the murder before the children could be allowed to come home. If there was a question mark over her then the children, depending on their age, would need to be taken to a neutral environment. Another relative or safehouse.

'Good. Once we've finished here we'll head over and interview her. Two murders mean we need to get a lid on this before we lose control. There must be some connection between the murders besides just carved numbers on random victims.'

Hume looked at the cuts on the victim's body. Like those on David Webb's chest, they were bone-deep. She thought about the strength that must be applied to cause such damage. And the control required to make them so neat.

'Do we know what was used to make the cuts yet?' she asked.

'Still working on it. There's no serration, so a straight blade. Not a Stanley or craft knife because the blade is too narrow; it would most likely snap with the pressure required.'

Hume frowned, then focused on the face of the late Reverend Peters. The eyes were already covered in a thin film of dust. Hume felt tired and wired at the same time. She wanted to go home and put on her running gear. She wanted to pound the park until her mind cleared and the jigsaw began to put itself together. She wanted a seed salad to take away the taste of the appalling meal she had eaten for brunch. She wanted to feel clean.

Instead, she kept her focus on the dead vicar. The thought that there might be a serial killer stalking London was awful enough, but that there seemed to be no common denominator between the victims was absolutely terrifying.

Of course, there was nearly always a common denominator, even if it was only understood by the killer. And possibly the victims.

'Get a swab from his mouth — like you did with David. If there's anything in there that doesn't belong to him I want to know about it.'

The SOCO nodded, reaching for his kit. Hume turned back to the cuts.

She looked thoughtfully at the corpse; at the numbers carved into his torso.

Upside down. That was what Raine had said. From the viewpoint of the victim.

She moved to a position behind the dead vicar. Then she squatted down and looked past the head, down the body to where the numbers were carved.

'Jesus,' she said, completely forgetting where she was.

Brendon stopped what he was doing and looked up.

'What?' said Echo. 'What is it?'

'The numbers. They're not numbers at all. They're letters.'

'What are you talking about? Of course they're numbers,' said her DC, brow creased.

Hume shook her head. 'No, they're not. It's like when you're a kid, and you make words on a calculator by turning the numbers upside down.'

'My kids do that,' Brendon chipped in eagerly.

'Sure, we all did,' said Echo, walking around to join Hume. 'So what does it say?'

Hume swallowed, feeling a shiver rack through her. Echo squatted down next to her. She heard him draw a quick intake of breath.

ꟼO2 hЕ11

'Go to hell. It says, "Go to hell".'

CHAPTER 12

Raine's eyes were fixed on Melania. She lay on her side on the small sofa, her blood sticky on the fabric. Her eyes were glass marbles, with no life to give them depth. Her head was the wrong shape, Raine assumed because it had been hit repeatedly with a blunt instrument.

A hammer, maybe, or a crowbar.

Raine went with crowbar. When she had got on the boat and sprayed the rat with the red dye, causing it to fall into the water, she had discovered the hatch lock broken, the lock prised off the wood.

The interior of the boat was a wreck. All the cupboards had been emptied out and her laptop stolen.

Raine froze, completely still. The only part of the space she couldn't see was the bathroom at the rear of the boat. She looked at the wooden door, closed, and rewound her mind to when she had left to meet with Hume. Had she left it open, to allow the cat free rein? Rats and water voles were clever; if there was even the smallest of holes they would find their way in.

Raine nodded to herself.

Which is why she had left it open. Why she always left it open.

She gently stroked her dead cat, then walked towards the bathroom, taking small, careful steps to avoid the creaks of the wooden floor, her personal deterrent spray held straight-armed in front of her. She took slow breaths through her open mouth. As she approached the door she ducked down, moving to the left. If there was someone in there with a gun they would most likely shoot at head height, straight in the middle of the opening. Silently she took her phone out of her pocket and tossed it to the other side of the door. It clattered to the floor. Raine didn't look at it, keeping her focus on the wooden handle, waiting for movement. She strained her ears trying to detect any sound that might emanate from the small hidden space that could indicate that the intruder was still here.

Nothing.

Raine glanced back at her cat, then focused again on the door. She took a deep breath then kicked it in, spraying as she did so. 'Don't fucking move!' she screamed, propelling herself into the bathroom. She slammed against the sink, immediately spinning to her right, her arm out and spraying, covering the entire space in red dye.

The little bathroom was empty. Raine did a slow circle, slowing her breathing, then stepped back into the main living area. The hatch was still broken and the laptop was still stolen and the cat was still dead. Other than that, there was nothing. No robber waiting to lunge at her. No rapist waiting to rip off her clothes. No one for her to hurt.

She placed the Farbgel on the little side table under the window and moved over to her cat. Softly, slowly, she stroked his ruined head.

From the floor, where she had tossed it, her phone rang.

'Shit!' She scuttled over and picked it up. The ident read 'HUME'.

'You nearly gave me a fucking heart attack!' she shouted into the mouthpiece.

'Sorry, but I thought—'

'This had better be important, Hume. Somebody's bashed in my cat's head and I've just caused a horror-film decorating catastrophe in my bathroom and I promise you whoever's behind this is going to get fucked up really soon.'

There was a pause.

'Raine,' said Hume softly.

The tone of Hume's voice pulled Raine up short. She caught hold of herself and sat down.

'What is it?'

'That girl you pinged to me? The misper? Heather?'

Raine felt a tightening in her chest. A fly was walking through the mess of her cat's head. She could practically feel its legs sticking and unsticking to the congealing blood and brain matter.

'What about her?'

'She's dead, Raine. She was shot in the face fifteen minutes ago, outside her office.'

CHAPTER 13

'You know, I think those are the cleanest nails I've ever seen on a police officer.' Hume was gazing at her constable's hand as he pressed his finger on the doorbell. 'How do you keep them so neat?'

Echo shrugged. 'There's a nail bar in my block of flats.'

'You go to a nail bar?'

'It's included in the rent.'

Hume's eyebrows rose, then she glanced down at her own nails, ragged with broken cuticles, dirt packed tight underneath that had seemed to secrete itself out of nowhere. Just standing next to Echo made her feel grubby. She made a mental note to spill something on him when she got the chance.

'Your rent includes personal grooming?'

Before Echo could answer, the door opened and a young woman peered out at them. Hume flashed her ID and the door opened wider, allowing them entrance. The woman introduced herself as the family liaison officer.

'What's the status?' Hume asked as the officer closed the door behind them. The house was completely silent.

'The wife, Carole Peters, is in the sitting room. She's in shock, but coping well.' The officer gave a one-shouldered shrug. 'Maybe a little too well. She's offered everybody tea and biscuits.'

Hume understood the woman's unease. The liaison officer was clearly not used to bereaved spouses being so in control.

'Do you think she might know something?' said Echo. 'That's why she's taking it so well?'

'I think she's a vicar's wife,' said Hume. 'And therefore used to dealing with grief, death, and God knows what else. We can't read anything into her reactions.' She looked at the liaison officer's name-tag, nodding. 'She's as much of a professional counsellor as you, Browning. Now where's the sitting room?'

Browning led them through to where Carole Peters was seated, drinking tea from a china cup. The woman rose and smiled when they walked in, but the smile was automatic, developed from years of shell-building. She was dressed in a simple skirt and blouse that blended with the room, as if she were part of it, another object to make the setting seem safe. Unthreatening. Hume wondered what it must be like to be the wife of a vicar with an inner-city parish. The people she would have to meet. Have to welcome into her home. She wondered how far one would have to bury oneself to project the level of calm and reassurance needed.

'Mrs Peters, hello.' Hume stepped forward, extending her hand. 'I'm so very sorry for your loss.'

Carole Peters looked up. The brittle smile on her face looked like it had been stapled there by a child: slightly lop-sided and broken at the corners. Her eyes weren't smiling, Hume noted. Deep down, in the darkness at their centres, her eyes were screaming. There was no way this woman had known her husband was in danger. Not consciously, anyway. When she took hold of the detective's hand, Hume could feel the tension in her; little tremors and jolts just under the skin.

'Where are my children? I assume they've been informed?'

No mention of her husband: of the dead. Just her children: the living.

'They have. One of my officers picked them up from school.'

'Then why aren't they here?'

The smile was still there, but only just. The brittleness was creeping towards fracture.

'Until all the facts are established, then the children's safety must be taken into consideration. We believe the attack on your husband was not random, suggesting that he was known to the perpetrator in some capacity. Until we have more intelligence we cannot be certain your home is secure. I'm sorry.'

'Not random? So, you're saying my children aren't safe?' Carole's voice had risen slightly, her smile completely gone. 'They must be going out of their minds. I need to see them.'

'As soon as we have finished here, Officer Browning here will take you to them,' Hume attempted to reassure her. 'Then I'm afraid you will need to stay with a friend or relative for a little while, until we have established that whoever killed your husband is not also interested in you.'

Hume did not also repeat Echo's earlier observation: that nine times out of ten the murderer is known to the victim. Looking at the vicar's wife, Hume did not think she was capable of murder, but until the timeline of her movements could be established she would remain a person of interest.

'Could you tell me what time your husband left for the church this morning?'

Carole looked deep into Hume's eyes, as if searching for a lifeline. Something that would help her make sense of her terrible new reality. Hume watched the woman take a shaky breath and sit back down on the sofa. Composing herself.

'Jeremy left at the usual time: 5 a.m. The church is a good forty minutes' run away and he likes to be there in plenty of time to . . . well, some of his congregation . . .' She floundered to a halt.

'He runs to work. Like, for exercise?' Echo asked. If the Reverend Peters had a set routine then that would've made things easier for his killer. Easier to discover his weaknesses, his vulnerabilities.

Carole smiled. It was like watching a butterfly die.

'Jeremy likes to look after himself. His work is quite demanding. Many of his congregation are somewhat . . . colourful.'

Hume watched as Carole's face spasmed.

'Liked. Liked to look after himself. Oh my God, what am I going to do?'

Her fragile grip on normality finally broke and she began to weep. Hume felt her heart empty a little more. She and Echo waited silently until the woman pulled herself together enough to continue. She gave them another weak smile.

'I'm so sorry. What must you all think of me? My husband was murdered and here I am wondering where my children and I are going to live.'

'I'm not following. Won't you stay on in this house?' asked Hume.

Carole shook her head.

'It belongs to the Church. I'm sure they'll let us stay here for a while but . . .' She shrugged her shoulders. 'The new vicar will need it, and prices in London . . .'

She shrugged again, and in the movement Hume saw the woman's precarious future. The future of someone who had moved with her husband's job, never making any real friends. Never making any solid connections, because being the partner of a vicar was a job in itself, a mask that required you to act a role in a certain way. And in so doing she had probably lost every connection with her past. And now that her husband was dead she was cut loose from that role, and had no rudder to guide her. She and her children would have to find somewhere else to live. Somewhere cheaper. Somewhere further out of the city. Which might mean the children would have to move schools, along with the trauma of losing their father.

Hume reached out and took Carole's hand, squeezing it once then letting go.

'It's quite all right, Mrs Peters.' After a beat Hume continued. 'Can you think of anybody who might have visited your home recently? Or perhaps your husband mentioned somebody following him on his run? A particularly difficult parishioner he had been dealing with? Anything that could be relevant?'

Carole shook her head.

'Jeremy loved his work. His parish contained a sizable proportion of prostitutes and drug addicts. Jeremy used to say that they were exactly the sort of people Jesus would have gravitated towards. People who needed him.'

Hume nodded in sympathy.

'Would you by any chance know your husband's pass-codes?' Echo queried gently.

Carole looked at him, confused.

'For his mobile and laptop,' clarified Echo. 'There's a possibility that whoever murdered him attempted to contact him prior to the assault.'

Carole's eyes widened.

'You said earlier that my husband's attack wasn't random. Are you suggesting it was someone we might know?'

Hume thought of the numbers carved into the Reverend Peters' body, almost certainly the work of the same person who murdered David Webb. She shook her head.

'It's too soon to say for certain, but perhaps the killer may be connected to your husband's calling. You say that his parish was partly made up of sex workers. Would that include any from the gay community?'

'Detective, within this part of London when it comes to sex work there *is* no gay community. Or straight community. There is only the work, which is usually merely a means to an end.' Carole smiled thinly. 'That end being contained in the vial of a needle or a clingfilm wrap of whatever. The men and women who do the work will perform their services for anyone. Sexuality means nothing to them. They have already sold their bodies so many times that they no longer belong to them. They belong to the monsters who control them and the drugs that sustain them.'

'I understand,' was all Hume said.

'I will get you the passcodes,' said Carole, standing abruptly. 'And then I'd like Officer Browning to take me to my children.'

Hume and Echo got to their feet.

'Of course,' Hume nodded. 'Once again I'm so sorry for your loss.'

When Hume and Echo were back in the car, Hume let out a long sigh.

'Well, that's her life completely ruined.'

'Interesting connections to Cale's situation, though,' commented Echo.

'In what way?'

The car pulled out into the quiet road, heading back to the station. Hume couldn't remember the driver's name.

'Well, both Cale and Carole are going to have to find new places to live. Both seem to have left a past they are not keen to go back to and both partners potentially have a connection to drugs and transactional sex.'

Hume turned and looked at him, an eyebrow raised. 'Transactional sex?'

'The date-app scene appears to skirt prostitution, as does Cale's rental arrangement. And the vicar's parish seems to have a crossover.'

Hume wasn't convinced by this. 'A little thin.'

'Maybe there'll be something more concrete in the vicar's phone.'

Hume stared out of the window, watching London's buildings slide by in various shades of grey.

'Echo?'

'Yes, gov?'

'What sort of apartment do you live in that includes a nail bar in the rent?'

Echo looked up from his phone and smiled at her.

'A very clean one.'

CHAPTER 14

Echo breathed in slowly, looking at his mother on the screen. It was incredible: he only had to glimpse the house where he grew up, electronically reproduced in perfect detail across eleven and a half thousand miles, to feel like a child again.

'I've told you before, it's not a hall of residence, Mum. It's cutting-edge urban living with a community-first approach.'

Echo winced inside. Here he was, a grown man, justifying his lifestyle to his mother.

'It's making you all live like chickens in a coop, is what it is. Are you eating OK? Have you met any nice women yet?'

Echo wondered if it would be possible to set up a virtual copy of himself to talk to his mother. It needn't be a complicated model, seeing as she asked the same questions every week. Why was he still living in shared accommodation? Had he met any nice girls yet? They didn't have to be from Aotearoa New Zealand. Had he been to Ranana's yet?

Ngati Ranana was, according to his mother, the London Maori club where he would find the required nice girl who didn't have to be from back home. Having come halfway round the world to experience new cultures and different thinking, there was absolutely no sodding way Echo was going to Ranana's.

He smiled at his mother, who, being twelve hours ahead, was busy making a traditional Maori breakfast of croissants, coffee and fresh orange juice. Echo kept his bottle of beer out of the scope of the webcam.

'Work's too full-on to go meeting women, Mum.'

'Of course it is. And then one day you'll wake up lonely and dead. What good will the work have done you then, eh?'

Echo didn't point out the impossibility of waking up dead.

'I've been promoted actually,' he said mildly.

His mother paused in her breakfast preparations and beamed at him.

'Promotion! Excellent!'

'I've been assigned to a detective inspector. We're working on a murder case.'

'Murder! That's good, isn't it? Important? What's he like?'

Echo shuddered inwardly. His mother was about as subtle as an earthquake when it came to what she wanted for her son. Echo understood it. His immediate cultural history was one of disenfranchisement, poverty and social abuse. Anything that gave power, status and independence was a top priority in her eyes.

'Murder is never good, Mum. And he's a she. My boss is a woman.'

'Well, no, of course not. Not for the poor victim. But for you! For you, it is an opportunity to shine! Is it high-profile? Can I look it up on the web? Is she single, this boss of yours?'

'Mum! She's about your age.'

His mother suddenly raised her hand, as if she were a child in school.

'Will there be a picture of you? Doing your detective thing? Have you got a smart suit? Because this could be the perfect opportunity for you to find a nice g—'

Echo held up his hand and tapped his watch. He needed to shut down the conversation before he fully reverted to an adolescent.

'I've got to go, Mum. I've got a meeting in half an hour and I need—'

'Meeting?' His mother's eyes narrowed. 'It's the middle of the evening over there. What meeting?'

'Well, you know London never sleeps, Mum. I'll Zoom you next week, OK?'

'And tell me all about your murder, yes?'

'Bye, Mum. Love you.'

Echo ended the call and flipped the shutter over the laptop camera. He looked out of the window of his tiny apartment across Shoreditch. In the distance, he could see the Canary Wharf skyline, like some future Manhattan in miniature. He had been in London for two years and was only now beginning to understand it. The perpetual change that seemed to occur, like a vast machine that constantly needed feeding. The swell of people that moved in its currents. The unbelievable loneliness that came from the way people seemed to live.

Which was why Echo had chosen to live in this block of flats: one of a new breed of communal living spaces that were cropping up all over London. He supposed his mother wasn't far off with her comparison to student living. The flats themselves were tiny, with no cooking facilities or even space to entertain. But then that was the point. The block itself contained a selection of restaurants and cafes, along with bars, gyms, a swimming pool and a rooftop garden. The flats were just for sleeping, with a small desk for work. Everything else was done in the shared spaces.

Instant community. Nobody left to spend their evenings alone in some shitty flat, slowly becoming isolated until they didn't know anything else.

Echo raised his bottle to the skyline and took a swig.

Plus, on his wage, there was no way he could afford to live anywhere else habitable this close to the centre. Even with the promotion and the living subsidy, it was still almost impossible to actually buy anywhere. Not that he wanted to live elsewhere. The vibe of the block suited him. And, after working with Hume on the murder case, it was nice not to be going back to an empty flat in some anonymous road. The images of those numbers carved into the two bodies still flashed across his vision in quiet moments. What kind of killer left redundant text codes behind as clues? It was just plain freaky.

There was a knock on the door. Almost immediately, before he could answer, a young woman with spider-bite piercings in her lower lip stuck her head in and smiled at him.

'Hey, Echo. Fancy grabbing something to eat and being crushed at Mario?'

As well as the swimming pool and gym, there was also a communal games room, complete with Nintendo consoles and pool tables. Echo smiled back and stood up.

'Hey, Bitz. Just what I need. Winner buys the food, yeah?'

The girl smirked and gun-cocked her finger. 'That's why I didn't bring any money with me.'

Grinning happily, Echo grabbed his jacket and headed for the door.

CHAPTER 15

Heather's death made the news.

> *Young woman murdered on a London street.*
> *No obvious connection to extremist groups.*
> *Suspect a possible case of mistaken identity; perhaps*
> *gang-related. Maybe drug-related.*
> *Parents are devastated and ask for privacy at this terrible*
> *time.*

Her story was worth two days' airplay, before being washed away in the swell of never-ending chaos and conflict that occupied the London headlines.

Raine watched the coverage from her new laptop. The swelling on her cheek had reduced, but the pain had increased with the greater mobility. The boat seemed quiet without Melania. Not quiet in the sense that there was any less noise — there was always noise on a boat. The creaking of the structure. The water *snucking* against the hull. Other boats on the canal, or people strolling beside it. The swans and the ducks and the rain hitting the water.

Quiet in the sense that there was no cat. Melania had been Raine's companion for a long time. Longer than she cared to think about. The warmth of her body as she sat on her lap when she worked, or lay on her bed as she slept, had become part of the fabric of her life. The thought of never having the cat with her again made Raine ache inside.

After the phone call from Hume, she had wrapped up Melania's body in a rug. Raine couldn't face putting her in a bin bag. The next few hours had been taken up with arranging for a pet cremation service to come and pick up the body, and reporting the break-in to the police. Once the officer had been, and Melania's remains removed, she began cleaning up her boat.

Apart from the laptop, nothing had been stolen. Raine kept all her work online, using a cloud data service to store her digital files. Any hard-copy materials to do with her business she kept in a rented lock-up in Shoreditch. The intruder had prised their way in through the roof hatch, ignoring the sturdy padlock and just ripping the entire bolt away from the wood. Then it had been a simple matter of disabling Raine's alarm. Her system wasn't linked to the police or any security company. Given the shrill sound of the alarm, plus the fact that there was nothing worth stealing on her boat, she had considered herself reasonably safe.

Stupid of her. What was the point of having a big fuck-off padlock if the hinge it was attached to was bolted into the wood?

She'd called out a locksmith to secure the boat. It took a bit of explaining to let them know where she actually was but, eventually, she arranged a time. After that, she began cleaning up the interior. The burglar had been thorough, ripping through her drawers and cupboards, emptying out the contents and leaving them in piles on the floor. After Raine had put everything back she got a bottle of water from the fridge. Taking a sip, she looked around her home.

Whatever had been used to bash Melania's head in had been brought and taken by the intruder. The police had given her a crime number for her insurance but held no hope of retrieving her laptop.

'It's likely been sold for a vial or a wrap by now,' the young constable had said, shrugging his shoulders. He had glanced curiously at her bruises but had not made any comment. She could see it in his eyes, though. What he was thinking.

Domestic.

Maybe that explained why he hadn't tried very hard; just given her the paperwork to sign and left.

Or maybe she was being unkind. Maybe he was right and there was no point in following it up. There were over 50,000 burglaries per year in London. In a large majority of them, the police didn't even show up, just gave the crime number over the phone. It was only the killing of her pet that had brought them out this time. And now her pet was gone — picked up by a teenager in a black van, the ashes to be returned to her in ten days' time.

Ten days. Enough time to avenge Melania's death and to find out why she had been robbed; because she was quite certain it wasn't so her hardware could be sold for drugs. Stepping onto a boat when it is two feet away from the towpath may look easy, but not for your average wired-up junk bunny. Plus, whoever had broken in had to have been carrying a hefty crowbar about their person on the off-chance, and have enough *nous* about them to find and turn off the alarm as soon as they had jumped in, all while dealing with a genuine London killer-cat clawing at their eyes.

Raine had checked: there was no blood on Melania's claws. Whoever had broken in had been prepared.

Double plus, a pill-head would have taken her tramadol. Tramadol was a prescription-only drug. Addicts would recognise it immediately. The tiny green-and-yellow capsules would easily sell on the street. Much more valuable than the laptop. All anyone would need to do was put them through a grinder to get rid of the time-release control — a sure-fire way to an almost instant high. Yet, all Raine's blister packs of tramadol were scattered on the floor along with the rest of her medicine cupboard, untouched and untaken.

So here she was, two days later, sitting with her new laptop, the smell of fresh paint coming from her bathroom, viewing news footage of the murdered young woman she had been tasked to find. Maybe arrange for a return to her family if that was what she wanted.

Well, she'd found her. But she hadn't returned her.

Raine sighed, reviewing the report she had been assembling for the parents. All the information that had been on her old laptop had automatically downloaded to her new laptop from her cloud account, so none of her information was lost. But what was she going to do with it now? The parents had paid her bill and sent an email thanking her for her work, and telling her they would not require her services anymore.

Why would they? Their daughter was dead. Lying cold in a police morgue somewhere. Easy to find now.

Raine's eyes lost focus for a moment. She glanced up at the bitter grey of the canal, then took out her phone and scrolled through her contacts.

'Mary Hume,' said the crisp voice on the first ring. Raine smiled. It hurt.

'Very good. Offering the first name makes you sound human. More approachable. They'll never know your true nature until it's too late.'

'Raine.' Hume's voice changed from polite to concerned. 'How are you? I tried to—'

'I know. I got your messages. Thank you.'

Hume had left a half-dozen messages on Raine's voicemail.

'I just wanted to check you were OK,' Hume said softly. 'When you didn't get in touch I—'

'I'm fine. Everything's back together and I've got a security company coming to fit a proper alarm in a few days.'

'I'm so sorry about your cat, Raine.'

Raine closed her eyes briefly, wrapping the words in silence, deadening them.

'So am I.' She opened her eyes and looked at the corner where Melania's blanket was. When she had scrubbed through the boat she had left that corner as it was, keeping a little of yesterday in the dust and cat hairs. A yesterday where her companion was still alive and purring.

'And your misper, Heather. What an awful thing to happen. Have you had any follow-up?'

'Nothing. Case closed. The parents don't want me to try to find out what happened. As far as they're concerned, their daughter ran away from the family and the family got punished by God. They think it's their fault. That the street shooting was divine intervention for their failure as parents.'

'I'm so sorry,' Hume said again.

Raine kept her eyes on the skin of the canal.

'Anyhow, with my client dead, there's no need for you to follow-up on her fingerprints. But there is one thing you could do for me.'

'What's that?'

'The thug who broke my surveillance equipment: would it be possible to track him down? Those things aren't cheap.'

There was a pause down the line. Raine stayed focused on the canal.

'I'm not sure, Raine.'

'He assaulted a woman, Mary. I just want to give him a friendly warning and make him pay for the stuff he broke.'

Like Heather, she added mentally.

'You know I'll be able to find him anyway, Mary. I have his name. It's only a matter of time before I track down which particular postcode he hangs with. All I'm asking is if you can save me a little legwork.'

Finally, Hume said, 'Ping me through the details; I'll see what I can do.'

'Great, thank you. And now I have some time, do you want me to check out that other thing?'

'Other thing? What are we talking about?'

'The drugs from your murder. 143. "I don't love you",' Raine prompted.

'Oh, right. Well, I'm not sure how relevant the gay angle is anymore.'

'What do you mean?'

'You haven't been following the news?'

'No. I've been putting my boat back together. What's the latest then?'

Hume quickly told Raine the bones of what had happened to Reverend Peters, being careful not to give any sensitive information away.

'So the connection is the numbers?' said Raine when she had finished.

'There are one or two other details that led us to believe the murders are connected,' said Hume cautiously.

'Ketamine again?'

A pause.

'Yes.'

'And have you had an analysis done on the ketamine?'

'Nothing to analyse. It's not the drug that killed them; it was just used to incapacitate them. They died of asphyxiation in David's case, and—' there was a pause on the line — 'a myocardial infarction brought on by the attack in the reverend's.'

'A what?'

'A heart attack. His heart gave out before he drowned in his own vomit.'

'Lovely.'

Raine thought for a moment.

'Why not let me look into the drugs anyhow? The murderer had to get them from somewhere.'

'I'm not sure of the point, Raine. If the murders were confined to the LGBT community then it might have been relevant; the scene is quite closed and it might have been possible to find the supply chain. But now . . .'

Hume let it hang. There was no sound coming down the line, but she could practically hear the cogs turning in Raine's mind.

'Yeah, fair point,' Raine said finally, wiping a hand through her hair. 'But I need to do something to keep me busy.'

'Look, if you really have got some time maybe you could do some surveillance on the boyfriend. I'll need to put it down as something else on the sheet but—'

'Cale? Is there a problem with him?'

'Cale, yes — good memory. And no problem. But there was something that felt a little off. It's probably my own prejudice; the whole up-fucking thing . . . But for peace of mind. There's no way I could justify putting a surveillance team on it but . . .'

Hume's voice sounded tired.

'I understand. That would be great. Send me over the details and I'll get right—'

'Just for a day, though, to put my mind at ease. I know you have access to some places that a police officer wouldn't.'

'You'd be surprised,' Raine said, a tight smile on her face.

'I really wouldn't,' said Hume.

* * *

I knew this was coming, but I wasn't sure how I'd feel. I have the list, so it's not like I don't have time to prepare.

The house is filthy again. I don't know who my son thinks clears up all the shit he leaves scattered around.

But it's just me and him since his mother died. Not that anyone knows how his mother died. They think it was cancer.

That's why we moved here. A brand-new start.

And to be fair, I haven't really taught him the life-skills required for taking care of his environment. How to use the washing machine. How to cook and clean.

I'm too much of a control freak. It's part of my personality.

Anyhow, I can't really complain about his mess. After all, he's the one supplying me with the drugs.

Like I say, I wasn't sure about this one. David and the young reverend were easy. They practically did all the work for me. David with his unusual appetites. The reverend with his ambition to save the unsaveable.

But Alice . . . Alice is something else. She's a woman, for a start. I'm not being sexist or anything, but there's a difference. It just feels . . . more intimate. Plus, people could get the wrong idea; think it's about sex. Abuse or something.

Although of course, with Alice, abuse defines her. She's dripping in it.

She's clearly had a difficult life, according to her records. Violence at home. Misuse of substances. In and out of mental institutions.

Really, she's dead already. Looking at the life she's had, being born was a death sentence for her. Everything that's happened since then has been an attempt to take her back to a pre-life state. Before the pain. Before the hurt.

Because, just like David and the Reverend Peters, she was born wrong.

Well, that's something I can help her with.

I just need to work out how.

CHAPTER 16

Hume watched her husband, Robert, trying to do yoga at the foot of their bed.

She had already done her own morning regime — a daily programme, starting at five, of exercise and meditation. Running. Spinning. A series of light weights in rotation. A low-GI breakfast. Plus coffee, because the work she'd done holding back the creaks of the body deserved some treats.

'Are you sure you're doing it right?' she enquired after her husband let out a particularly spirited string of swear words.

Watching him cuss his way through a twenty-minute relaxation exercise was, she considered, a fantastic way for her to gear up for the day. She had even got back onto the bed so she could take it all in.

'Of course I'm bloody well doing it right. It's the skeleton with the robot smile and the dead eyes who's doing it wrong,' he said, attempting to balance on one foot. 'I'm pretty sure she's cheating.'

Hume looked at the woman on the screen. She appeared to be made out of plastic.

'How? How is she cheating?'

'I think she's had some of her screws removed so she can bend easier. And she's not really wearing any clothes. That's got to help.'

'She's wearing shorts and a sports top.'

'Only just. Yesterday she suggested I go down on a dog! What's that all about?'

Hume smiled.

'I think you'll find it's called "downward dog".'

'I think you'll find it's called let's take the piss out of the old bloke.' Robert punched the remote. The screen went blank.

'Well, I think you're already looking fitter,' Hume said. 'Two or three more years and you can probably move on to tai chi.'

'Two or three more years and I can definitely move on to the cemetery,' he said, tossing the remote onto a chair.

'I can't work out the connection between the two murders,' said Hume, staring at the ceiling. 'And I need to find it quickly before something else happens.'

'Like what?'

'I don't know. It's just that . . . it feels unfinished at the moment. As if there's more to come.'

Her husband turned away from her, pulling his top up as he did so. Hume found it endearing that he still brought modesty into their marriage. She wasn't sure if it was for her benefit or his. His, she suspected.

'Maybe the connection is sex?' he suggested. 'You say it's often about sex.'

'I don't think so,' said Hume, shaking her head. 'Or at least, not in an obvious way. One victim was gay and the other was a happily married heterosexual vicar.'

'Well, that sounds about as ripe for a sex murder as you can get,' Robert wrapped a towel around himself and slipped out of his shorts.

'You know I *have* seen you naked before,' she commented.

'Not with my new robot-woman-yoga-body, you haven't,' he said, throwing the towel onto the chair by the remote. 'I'm saving it up until I'm happy with the end product!'

Hume smiled inside.

'There *are* sex connections. Both scenes have transactional sex crossover—' Hume grimaced at Echo's term — 'but I don't think that's it. The numbers don't seem to fit a sex crime. And the whole scene-setting seems . . .'

'What?'

'Both the murders feel more . . .' she blinked, trying to work out how the killings made her feel. 'There was a coldness about them. A staging that suggested something being played out beyond the murder itself. 'Like some sort of game I don't know the rules for.'

'Family then. You always say that nine times out of ten it's the wife, or husband.'

Hume shook her head again.

'The Reverend Peters was happily married and his wife is devastated. David's boyfriend seems clean. He wasn't scamming him or selling him drugs. He wasn't mixed up in any nefarious activities, as far as we can see. All he's guilty of is exchanging sex for bed and board, which frankly could be applied to anyone. I'm getting Raine to follow him just in case, but I don't think there's a motive there.'

At the mention of Raine's name Robert paused.

'How is Raine?' he asked after a moment.

'Good, as far as I can tell. Have you ever had a Vendetta egg?'

He stared at her, eyebrows raised.

'What, like in the film? I thought that was made up.'

'How come everyone knows about this film apart from me?' said Hume. 'And before you ask, it doesn't appear to be money either. Cale is independent. He has a job and has given us access to his bank accounts. As far as we can tell he's legitimate.'

'Well, if it is a serial killer with no connection to the victims, won't they just have a motive that only means something to them? A code or something that you'd have to break?'

Hume shuddered.

'Please don't use the "s" and "k" words. Two bodies with a code carved into them are bad enough. Any more and the news outlets will go into meltdown. As it is, they're already frothing.'

'Fair enough,' said Robert amiably, sitting down next to her on the bed. 'Now how about some sex?'

Hume smiled and patted him on the leg.

'Absolutely,' she said. 'Straight after work we'll go and find a dog for you.'

She gave him a peck on the cheek, stood up, and started walking towards the door.

'Anyhow, I should get the lab report back today. Maybe that will shed some light.'

'H'm,' said her husband, a touch grumpily.

'Don't wait up,' she said as she reached the door. 'I can't see me being home early while all this is going on.'

'What's new?' said Robert, raising his eyes to the ceiling.

She smiled. Thirty years of marriage allowed for very little in the way of surprises.

'Mary?'

She paused. Turned to look at him.

'Send my love to Raine, if you see her again.'

She stayed looking at him a beat, then nodded and left the bedroom, closing the door softly behind her.

Outside the flat, as she walked down the corridor to the lift, her phone bleeped. She took it out of her jacket and glanced at the ident: Echo.

'Give me a break. I'm on my way,' she said, pressed a button to summon the lift.

'The lab just got back. You were right.'

Echo's voice sounded strange. Excited, but with a hint of something else. It took Hume a moment to identify it. Confusion.

'What about?'

'There was something in David's mouth that didn't belong there.'

Hume winced.

'You're not going to tell me it was vomit, are you? Because it's too early for—'

'It was a tooth,' cut in Echo.

Hume blinked. 'A tooth? It's a mouth, Echo. That's where the teeth are generally found.'

'Not his tooth. The killer removed one of David's teeth and replaced it with a different one. One from another person.'

In front of Hume the lift doors opened. Hume ignored them, stepping back. She watched as they closed again.

'That's . . . odd. Somebody else's tooth? How did it stay in?'

'The killer stuck it in with superglue, according to the report.' Hume could hear her partner's shudder in the speaker. 'The only reason they spotted it was because of your request. He must have cleaned away the vomit to place it. Once they started investigating they found the anomaly. Apparently it was the wrong size and a slightly different colour.'

'Jesus.'

'And belonging to a female.'

Hume listened to the dead noise on the phone as neither of them spoke.

'You know what this means, don't you, Echo?'

'What?'

'It means David wasn't the first. It means that we have a multiple murderer on our hands.'

'Pretty much.'

Echo's voice sounded flat, like the top notes had been stolen.

'Right. Chase up the vicar's status. Ask the lab to search for . . . foreign matter in his mouth.'

'Already done. I'm waiting on a call.'

'Good.' Hume glanced at her watch. 'I'll be with you in twenty.'

She ended the call and pressed the button to call back the lift. As she stepped in she felt a shiver spasm in the small of her back.

Teeth.

The day had only just begun and already it was spiralling into a nightmare.

* * *

Alice had to find something to take her out of her head, literally. She needed to not be inside her own thoughts because they were killing her. She didn't care what it was. Alcohol. Pills. Needle. A fist. She didn't care. She just couldn't stand another second listening to what her head was telling her. She needed to feel numb.

She had tried tapping the nurses. It was always worth a go. Sometimes one of them would give you something out of pity, but not this time. Or you could get the cleaners to score something if you were prepared to trade favours. Alice didn't care. Her body had long ago become an enemy rather than an ally. If she made it do something unpleasant, then it was all it deserved as far as she was concerned. But the cleaners hadn't delivered either. Which left her only one option: leaving.

Not always possible, and definitely not on occasions when she had been sectioned. But this particular visit to the mental-health unit of the hospital had been voluntary, strongly recommended by her GP. Alice had looked at him and agreed at once. It was clear from the concern on his face that, had she refused, she would have been taken forcibly.

On one level Alice was happy. Life inside the unit was simple and regimented. She ate when she was told and took what they prescribed. No one expected her to act in any particular way. No one pushed her or shoved her when she suddenly stopped moving. No one minded if she spent hours just feeling the texture of the wallpaper in the unit's corridors.

Nobody even minded if she screamed and screamed until her voice was nothing but a hoarse whisper. Which eventually became the problem: nobody cared. Not really. Nobody had ever cared.

Slowly, the voices would come back, slinking out of the corners of her mind like long-lost ghosts and whispering deep within her. *Nobody cares. Nobody knows you. Don't tell them anything.*

Then the voices would get louder, more insistent. When they began they were always friendly, on her side. By the end, they were always angry, not on her side but *inside*, leaving her with no place to hide. No place to run. Except into numbness.

'Ok, Alice?'

Alice smiled at the security guard, hoping her face did not give away the rage inside her. 'Good, thanks, Joe. Just going out for a vape. Could you?'

Although patients were allowed to keep cigarettes in the ward, electronic nicotine delivery units were forbidden. Too easy to deliberately set the wrong voltage. Too easy to smash and use the sharp edges that remained.

'Sure.' Joe turned to the open-fronted lockers behind him and reached into Alice's. Handing her the vape device through the slot beneath the safety glass, he punched the button on his desk, releasing the outer door. Voluntary patients often stepped out to smoke or vape. Sometimes to walk the grounds of the hospital. He had no right to stop them.

Alice waved and stepped through the doorway, the thick reinforced glass closing behind her with an electromagnetic snap. Once outside, she pulled on the tip of the pod, activating the draw. Nicotine vapour flowed down into her lungs. There were no other patients smoking here, which was a blessing. Alice knew she was close to exploding, and if she did they would section her for sure. She pulled out her mobile, swiping the taxi app. She didn't have any money but that didn't matter. Money was old-world. She had her phone, with all the apps she needed to survive. Uber for transport. Tinder for ready money. Gpay for transactions. Snapchat for scoring drugs.

One way or another she was going to get numb.

CHAPTER 17

'You know I can't authorise an outside agency to oversee any part of this operation, Mary. You already have two uniforms working with you full-time for interviews and follow-ups, not to mention the office staff collating data for DC Echo.'

Hume slowly counted to five in her head, while nodding at the man in front of her. Since the linking of the second murder, she had been summoned to report on her progress, or lack thereof, with David's case.

'I understand, and I realise that it's not common practice, sir, but this is Raine we're talking about. She's not really—'

'I know who she is, Mary. I am fully aware of her credentials when she served with us, but the fact is she is now an independent, and it is not the Met's policy to—'

'We outsource half our backroom enquiries, and almost all our IT,' said Hume, frustration creeping into her tone. 'We even recruit from the private sector for gathering witness statements and CCTV analysis. How is this different?'

'Because none of those roles could end up in a potentially dangerous situation for the recruit!' snapped the chief inspector. 'For goodness' sake, Mary, imagine the outcry if a civilian got hurt while carrying out duties for us? Imagine the litigation!'

'All I'm asking is for her to do a little surveillance. No contact and no engagement. She won't mind if we write it up as—' Hume shrugged — 'witness analysis.' As the chief inspector raised his eyebrows she quickly continued, 'Or we can put her down as a CHIS.'

Her boss raised his eyebrows. 'A CHIS? Using the Covert Human Intelligence Source route to get around a staffing problem is a bit—'

'Normal these days, sir,' said Hume. Before the chief inspector could tell her that using the money set inside for informants was misappropriation, she pushed on.

'It's just for one day. I just want to check that David Webb's boyfriend is on the level. Confirm he is where he says he is. Make sure he's clean. Putting Raine on him for one day will save us hundreds of hours. Surveillance of one suspect alone requires a six-person team. We're already massively under-staffed because of the terrorist grading, and—'

'Yes, Mary, I am well aware of the overtime situation,' said the chief inspector wiping a hand over his eyes.

'Just one day, sir, and no contact.'

Hume watched as her boss mulled it over. Finally, he said: 'Just one day, and only distance surveillance.'

'Thank you, sir. And if you could get the lab to prioritise the results from the mouth of the vicar. We've—'

'I've read the report from your DC.'

The man smiled. Hume tried to remember the last time she had seen him do that.

'He's quite on it, isn't he? It really is a brave new world. In my day you'd have to wait for a daily briefing to get infor-mation. Now it seems it's uploaded for group chat.'

'Real-time information-hubbing, he calls it,' Hume said. It didn't make her smile; it made her feel old.

'So I understand. I've sent a hurry-up to the lab. The whole tooth angle . . . is just . . . well, it feels different.'

Hume agreed. There was something so invasive about inserting a tooth into a dead man's mouth that it was difficult to comprehend.

'You should have something back ASAP,' the chief inspector concluded.

'Great. Echo is following up on the numbers carved into the victims and we have uniforms canvassing both areas for any witnesses to colour in the events.'

'Anything?' There was a tinge of hope to his voice.

'Not as yet, sir.'

'Right. Keep me posted.'

Hume took this as a dismissal and made for the door.

She'd considered telling him Raine's theory about the numbers, but it was best not to push her luck. Getting him to agree to the surveillance had seemed like a win; revealing that Raine was already more involved in the case than he thought might be counterproductive.

'Mary.'

Hume turned and regarded her boss. He was nearing retirement age but looked much, much older. Seeing the amount of brutality and violence that running a murder squad exposed you to would do that.

'Yes, sir?'

'Try to hurry this one up. It smells bad to me.'

'Yes, sir.'

She shut the door and texted Raine, telling her to go ahead, then headed off to find Echo.

CHAPTER 18

'Different ages. Different sexual preferences, as far as we know. Different social circles. Different life trajectories, with no immediate crossover other than the killer's MO and the tenuous sex angle. Different areas of London — so dissimilar they may as well have been living in different cities.'

Echo scrolled through his pad, flicking and swiping, sending information up onto the smartboard. He was dressed in distinctly unfashionable chinos and a plain black T-shirt under an open-necked linen shirt. Hume thought he looked like a child playing at being grown-up and smiled inwardly. Then she realised that was probably what she was supposed to think, and that she was getting old.

'So, what are the connections?' she muttered, focusing on the board. Echo had created three columns, placing a victim on either side, leaving the middle blank. Under each name he was listing what was known about them. Age. Physical features. Education. Jobs. Regular routes or repeating patterns in their lives. If they were dealing with a random killer, one who didn't know the victims personally, then the connection would be found in these columns. Even if the murders were done on the whims of a madman, there might still be commonalities. Something in the syntax of their lives that had singled them out for murder.

And if the killings weren't random; if there was actually some real-world logic or motivation behind it all . . . well, there would definitely be a hook. It was just a matter of recognising it.

'Both male,' said Echo, swiping the common facts into the middle column. 'Both white. Both incapacitated by application of alcohol mixed with ketamine and possible other drug or drugs, full toxicology report pending.'

Hume scrubbed a hand through her hair. It felt thick with London grime. She made a mental note to get Robert to clip it soon. She rarely let it grow past a number two.

'Exactly how did the stuff get into Reverend Peters at 8 o'clock in the morning, by the way?'

'It was mixed with the communion wine.'

'At 8 a.m.?'

'It seems he gave a bespoke communion offering to those who couldn't make a service for some reason,' said Echo. 'The homeless. Sex workers. People in the grey economy.'

Hume nodded; given where the church was situated, it made sense. She had an image of the vicar cycling through the early morning. Arriving in time to tend to those no one else cared about. And then being killed for it.

'And somebody spiked the wine?'

'Looks that way.'

Hume frowned. 'But if the wine was laced with drugs wouldn't that affect everyone? All the other people who took communion?'

'There wouldn't have been anybody else. The actual service wasn't until later in the day. The early morning slots were for individual communion, with any wine remaining in the cup drunk by the vicar between each one. Our killer would only need to slip it into the wine when Reverend Peters handed him the cup and . . .' Echo shrugged his shoulders.

'Fake drinking from it,' finished Hume. 'Neat. What else?'

'Text code carved into their chests, which suggests our suspect is in their forties or upwards, as that sort of code was only popular in the '80s and '90s.'

'Anything new through from the lab?'

'Actually, yes.'

Hume raised her eyebrows. The boss had clearly made good on his word.

'Good news?'

'It depends on what you mean by good.'

Hume eyed her DC. He looked back at her, clearly excited. And uneasy, she realised.

'Come on, Echo, don't keep me in suspense. Has the tooth fairy been visiting our vicar?'

'The lab found traces of foreign material in the mouth. Not just DNA, but different substances.'

Hume felt her own twinge of excitement. Mixed with revulsion.

'Another extraction?'

'Yeah, and replacement. Once the lab knew what to search for there was no missing it. Although this time the tooth was a better fit.'

'A male tooth, then?'

'Yes. From someone of similar build. Once the lab people had removed the tooth, they extracted DNA from the—' Echo paused, his face pinching slightly — 'tissue trauma; apparently the tooth was removed with some kind of pliers or metal grips. There are abrasions on the tooth's surface that suggest—'

'I get the picture, Echo,' said Hume, shuddering inwardly.

'Evidence from the attached gum tissue suggests that the tooth was removed while the victim was still alive,' Echo finished quietly.

Hume felt slightly nauseous.

'OK. Get the lab to run the DNA. See if there's a hit in the system. If the victim was still alive there might be a report—'

'We already have. And we got a hit immediately.'

Hume looked at her DC.

'And you waited this long to tell me?'

'I was building up to it. The tooth is David Webb's. It was removed from his mouth, probably when he was still alive, and replaced with that of a female, identity unknown. Then the reverend's tooth was removed and replaced with David's.'

Outside the office, the day seemed to click a degree closer to absolute zero.

'Oh my,' said Hume quietly.

'Beautifully put,' said Echo. 'This is super freaky. What's going on here, boss?'

Before she could answer, Echo's phone rang.

* * *

I watch Alice as she leaves the hospital and orders a cab. She's using an app rather than calling a service. I'm watching her do it. Not just through the windscreen of my car, but on my tablet.

People are funny. They download all these apps without checking the permissions: just ticking the 'I accept' box. And yet they still think their business stays private. Hilarious. Take the taxi app she's using, for example. Once she's signed up, the company sends all her user information, as well as lots of other information on her phone, to at least nine different servers.

The metadata.

Bank details. Address. Phone contacts. GPS. PayPal. All using a public encryption key that is completely open.

If she's using it over a public system — like the hospital Wi-Fi, for example — then it's really not that hard to perform an MITM attack. A man-in-the-middle attack. Where a person inserts themselves between the sender and the receiver, digitally speaking. So, as far as Alice is concerned, she is messaging the company, ordering herself a pick-up. When in fact I've intercepted it and she's messaging me.

It's child's play. You could do it. My son could do it.

Look at her, pulling on her JUUL vape like it's her mother's breast.

Helping me. Showing me how wrong she is. Not just now, after the years of abuse, but always. Always wrong.

I smile at her as she climbs into the back of my car, already giving me the eye in the mirror, checking to see if I'm interested in her. She probably needs drugs, or money. I let my smile widen, and start the car.

Poor Alice. Wrong from the moment she entered this world. Wrong from the start. Born wrong.

CHAPTER 19

'A woman, this time?' said Hume, as the car sped along the Westway.

'More like a girl than a woman. Alice Watkins was only twenty years old.' Echo was rapidly scrolling through his phone, as data from the crime scene they were hurtling towards was being relayed to him.

'And we're certain she's one of ours?'

'Code sliced into the chest,' read Echo. 'Body stripped. Suspected drug overdose. SOCOs called us as soon as they got there.'

'What about her teeth?' said Hume. She found the new angle involving the removal and replacement of the tooth very disconcerting. More so even than the codes carved into the bodies. It was just so bizarre. 'Are they all hers?'

'No info as yet,' said Echo. 'But I have asked on-scene the question.'

Hume stared out of the window of the unmarked car as it wove in and out of the traffic. The day, drab and cold before the news, had taken on a dark, ominous look. *That makes three*, she thought. Three murders, connected by brutality and torture, with some kind of sick game as a garnish. We need to stop him. Now.

She gritted her teeth. 'Tell me about her. The victim.'

'Alice Watkins. Aged twenty. Recently walked out of Barnham Mental Services Unit where she was on a thirty-day self-referral programme.'

'That information was volunteered to us?' Hume was surprised. The police had no right to a person's medical records without a court order, and there was no way one could have been granted in such a short time.

'She still had her hospital identity tag around her wrist. An officer on-scene contacted them.' Echo paused for a second. 'The unit where she was registered weren't even aware she'd absconded.'

'Brilliant. Who found her?'

'Unknown. It was an anonymous 999 call.'

'Right. And where was the body found?'

'Disused building near the Hammersmith Ark.'

The Ark was a well-known landmark, a spectacular ten-storey office failure developed in the '90s. It had spent much of its life unoccupied, which in turn had affected the buildings around it. Hard to attract commerce when there was a massive architectural albatross blocking out the sunlight.

'Access?'

Echo continued scrolling. 'No word on that. A full forensic team is on-site. I'm dialled into their data hub so I should get something soon.'

Hume stared at him. 'Their *data hub*?'

Echo shrugged.

'Everything is connected these days, boss. Live-streaming the crime scene, 3D digital scanning of autopsies. Whatever. There are so many data points to a crime that a metadata overview is necessary.'

The detectives were thrown sideways as their driver swerved to avoid a cyclist.

'I don't even know what metadata is,' said Hume, as she gingerly straightened up. Echo's expression became suddenly very excited, but Hume held her hand up. 'And I don't want to know. That's why I have you. How long until we arrive?'

'Twelve minutes,' said the driver, glancing at them in the rear-view mirror as the car screeched around a corner.

'Make it fourteen. That way we might actually get there without dying or killing anyone.'

The driver looked disappointed, but obligingly slowed the car down from certain-death to mere likely-accident. Hume let out a sigh of relief.

'Information coming in says there was a witness,' said Echo, peering at his phone.

'A witness? What, to the murder?' Hume was immediately energised.

'Not to the actual killing, but to a person running away from the scene. The information is a bit sketchy, but the witness is still on-site, so I guess we'll find out soon enough.'

Hume smiled and looked out of the window as London blurred past them. 'Maybe we've got lucky. Get a sketch artist to meet us there.'

When Echo didn't reply she turned and looked at him. He was staring at the information streaming into his phone.

'Is it even safe to receive information on an open network?' muttered Hume. 'I thought it was easy to hack into that sort of thing? The media and such.'

'Graphene operating system and Titan chip,' Echo replied, his eyes never leaving his screen. 'Hardened kernel. Practically impossible to hack.'

'Oh good,' said Hume. She had absolutely no idea what he was talking about. 'What's so interesting?'

Echo finally looked up at her. His expression was puzzled.

'Initial inspection of the body has been completed. Obviously, it is preliminary, and there are instructions that she shouldn't be moved until we have viewed the scene.'

Outside, London sped by, its wealth status changing street by street.

'And? Is there an alien tooth?'

There was something new in Echo's expression. Something beyond puzzlement. It took Hume a few moments to recognise it. Fear.

'What, Echo? What did they find?'

Echo licked his lips.

'Alice was found naked on the floor. She was clearly dead, although, other than the cuts on her chest, no indication of what killed her was apparent.'

'Was there vomit? Did she suffocate like David?'

Echo continued scrolling. 'Looks like it.'

There was a tension in the car as Hume had to prompt him again. 'And the teeth, Echo? Had she had one of her teeth replaced?'

This time Echo read from his phone. 'First examination suggests the lower-right incisor has been replaced with a larger one.'

'How can it have been replaced with a larger one? There wouldn't be room.'

Echo's gaze remained fully on his phone. 'Right, yes. Which probably explains why the tooth appears to have been hammered into position.'

CHAPTER 20

As she surveyed the building Hume felt a fresh wave of sadness wash over her. She heard the car door slam as Echo got out to deal with the officers already marking out the crime scene, leaving her to take it all in. The building was beyond run-down; it was on its knees. Covered in gang tags, the windows cataracted and cloudy with decay. Even the scrub of grass, bleached by years of chemical residue from the abandoned factory, looked like it had died where it grew. The door leading into the structure was half off its hinges, hanging at a jaunty angle that screamed 'run away' rather than 'come in'. Hume wondered how desperate you would have to be to voluntarily enter such a place. How desperate, or how completely numb.

Hume entered the building, careful not to catch her suit on the ragged metal of the door. Inside, the building was even worse, not helped by the dead woman lit up like an art exhibit. She lay framed in the LED lighting set up by the technicians. It made Hume want to turn around and leave. Maybe have a shower. Possibly exchange her skin for a new, clean one.

It wasn't just because the victim was a woman this time — although, God knew, the sight of the naked girl on the floor was enough to set you crying forever. Alice had been positioned like she'd been thrown away. Her naked body lay sprawled on the filthy floor of the abandoned building, surrounded by the debris of junkies and the excrement of rodents. There was a damp, musty smell in the air that Hume suspected was wet fox. She hated to think what might have happened to the body had it been left to lie here for any length of time.

'You said there was a witness?' she asked softly, being careful not to disturb any potential evidence. The FOS team had started gridding out the building and there were little metal walkways down to allow access. There was so much detritus on the floor it was going to take Forensics hours to catalogue the site.

'Sex worker,' said Echo. 'Apparently, this is a safe place to bring a client.'

'Sex worker again,' muttered Hume. She looked around at the crumbling walls and the broken windows, and felt even more desolate.

'I thought you told me the 999 was anonymous.'

'The sex worker wasn't the one who called it in; it was her client, or at least that's the supposition we're working on. Deborah — that's the prostitute's name — said she fainted as soon as she saw the body.'

'So instead of helping, the punter legged it. Very gallant. Well, at least he bothered to call us.'

Hume paused, then eyed her partner.

'Fainted? That's quite something considering her line of work . . .'

Echo nodded his head in acknowledgement.

'588, I'm afraid. For "fainted" read "passed out".'

Hume understood. 588 was an old army term, now adopted by the Met, to describe street prostitutes, women and men who would turn quick tricks to score drugs then go straight back out to tout for business, because it was easier that way. Less to feel. Less to remember. The downside was that it was easier to get robbed, or raped. Taking quick drugs on the street could easily result in unexpected bouts of unconsciousness.

'Got it. So absolutely no use at all, then.'

'Shouldn't think so. She said she saw someone running away, but couldn't give a description.'

At once Hume perked up. She eyed Echo keenly. 'Male? Female? Did she get a good look?'

Echo shook his head.

'Not even that. All she could tell us is that the person was, and I quote, a devil.'

'OK,' said Hume evenly.

Echo shrugged.

'That's what she said. A devil with wings.' He pointed at a door towards the back of the derelict floorspace. 'She said she watched it fly across the room and exit through there.'

Hume looked from Echo to the door, and then at the woman lying dead on the floor, with cuts on her body and blood in her mouth.

'Fucking drugs,' she muttered. 'Make sure the SOCOs check the door anyway . . . Do you have any idea what the cuts mean? Is it another text code?'

On the woman's chest was the familiar slashing, the blood wet and obscenely vibrant in the arc lighting.

'No idea. These seem random. More brutal. We'll have to wait for the lab results but my sense is that they are frenzied, as if the murderer was in a hurry.'

'Or maybe deteriorating. Losing energy or focus—'

A flash from a camera bulb suddenly highlighted and froze the cuts on Alice's chest, making them somehow separate from her body.

Hume slowly circled Alice, viewing the cuts from all angles, but all they said to her was slashed flesh and brutality. She peered at the girl's mouth, trying not to think of pliers and hammers. Finally, she straightened up.

'OK. Get the report to me ASAP. And DNA the tooth. I'd better go and interview Deborah about her devil.'

She had already begun walking away, but stopped and looked down once more at Alice. 'Why was the tooth bigger?'

'Not sure what you mean, boss.'

'Well, the murders are clearly not spur of the moment. They're planned. How come the tooth doesn't fit?'

'You think it's the vicar's, don't you? A man's tooth rammed into a woman's mouth.' The revulsion in Echo's voice was undisguised.

'I think our killer is making a chain, for some reason. Overlapping the bodies by shuffling the teeth forward.'

'This is really dark, boss,' said Echo quietly.

'Which would make the owner of the tooth in David's mouth victim number one — unless of course there have been earlier, undiscovered killings.'

Hume's gaze moved back to Alice's body. To the blood and the cuts and the too-prominent ribs. To the old scars that signified a lifetime of self-harm. A lifetime of harm inflicted by others. And those were only the scars she could see on the girl's skin . . . She looked at Alice's eyes, staring sightlessly and already beginning to film. She felt heavy. Heavy from the inside out.

'Get to work on trying to decipher the cuts. I agree they look random, but we may be missing something.'

'Will do.'

Hume let her gaze wander to the dead woman's mouth. She grimaced.

'And find me a dentist.'

* * *

I'm not a monster. I just thought I'd point that out.

In the end, it was surprisingly easy. After I picked Alice up she asked me if I knew any way she could make some quick money.

I suppose it must work a lot of the time, or she wouldn't risk it. Or maybe she just didn't care.

I could tell she was offering me sex from the pathetic smile stitched to her face. Not pathetic like I felt sorry for her. Pathetic like she thought I would take her up just like that. Without her even having to make an effort. Maybe it was because of her desperation that she couldn't read me. Or maybe it was my face. People always have trouble seeing beneath the surface.

Which is, of course, the point.

As we drove, I thought about the visit. The meeting that had sparked all this up again.

There I was, living my quiet life with my son, then ring-ring *goes the door. I had absolutely no idea that opening it would explode my life. Break down the perfect barrier I'd placed between now and then.*

Well. Almost perfect.

After the visit I was petrified. I'm better now, of course. Now I've started on my new path.

Because I'm beginning to understand.

There's a theory in science. It's about gravity. For gravity to work the way we think it does, there needs to be more energy in the universe than is actually created by it. Dark energy, it's called.

Apparently, one of the most popular theories to explain this proposes that there must be many versions of this universe, surviving for a single moment as different decisions are made, then exploding their energy into ours. Over and over again. Millions of millions of times per second.

Isn't that beautiful?

Immediately after the visit I thought my universe was ending; everything I'd so painstakingly built ripped apart by the person sitting so prettily on my sofa. But now I realise it wasn't that; wasn't that at all. It was just the universe bringing together all the possibilities.

Because it's me. I am the dark energy. I am the explosion.

Alice knows that now. Even as she struggled, I could see it in her eyes. Even as I hammered in the tooth, seeing the pain written on her face.

I could tell she knew what she was.

Bad to the bone. I could see it in her eyes, even as she fought me. She knew she was born bad.

* * *

The woman wrapped in the emergency blanket and sitting in the SOCOs' tent was probably only in her forties, but looked like she had lived every second of her years twice over. Beneath the battle make-up of her profession, hard choices mapped her body with lines that cut all the way through. Scars of a life lived in the shadows of a world that didn't even notice her existence, let alone care. Hume saw that the woman was shaking, her left leg doing a jittery dance.

'Could someone get Miss Frane a cup of cocoa, please?' she said, seating herself opposite the woman. When the witness raised her eyes, Hume saw that she was frightened. Her gaze kept shifting to the flap of the tent.

'Did you find it?' she whispered. 'The devil who killed that young woman?'

'That's why we're here,' said Hume, smiling warmly, trying to cut through the woman's shock. 'To get a description from you, Miss Frane. Deborah. Once we know what he looks like we'll be able to—'

'It wasn't a man. I told the officer that. The one who talked to me before.'

'Detective Echo,' nodded Hume, keeping eye contact. The woman was beyond frightened, Hume realised. She was terrified. 'He told me that you caught a glimpse of the killer before he ran away.'

'I'm telling you: it wasn't a man.' The woman's eyes were haunted, reliving the experience she had just suffered. The PC returned, wrapping Deborah's hand around the steaming cup of cocoa. The woman barely registered it.

'I understand that you were here with a client. Is that correct?'

The woman nodded slightly, her gaze still yo-yoing between Hume and the entrance to the tent.

'And that you saw an assault on the young woman, and your client ran away to get help?'

Deborah snorted. 'He wasn't running away to get no help. He was running away, period. Fucker hadn't even paid me.'

'Right. But he left when you interrupted the assault?'

'Wasn't no assault, either. Was a . . . feeding.'

Hume felt the chill of the word. Feeding. She thought of the blood and the tooth and the tears in the victim's chest. She saw the terror stamped on Deborah's face. She thought how hard and strong a woman would have to be to do what she did. Allow strangers to take her dangerous places. Risk her life daily to support a habit. To find the strength to just get up every day to wade through God knew what, with the only reward being to repeat the whole sorry process the following day. Whatever this woman had seen had managed to frighten someone long inured to horrors, and that frightened Hume as well.

'What did you witness, Deborah?' she asked softly.

Deborah's leg finally stopped its jitter and the woman turned to face Hume fully.

'What did I witness, love? I witnessed a fucking monster. When we came in, I was already going out. You know what I mean?'

Hume nodded. 'You'd already taken something.'

'I just wanted business to be over, yeah? So I could get paid and be gone. So I always save something to soften the blow. It's my method.'

'Good method. What did you see?'

'Punter had started to do his thing when we heard it. I thought it was a fox. Those fuckers get everywhere, and their barks sounds like baby screams, you know?' Deborah took a sip of her drink. If anything, the shivering had increased. 'But then we heard it louder and I saw movement on the floor.'

'He had her down on the floor?'

'I told you. Wasn't a he. Was an *it*.'

'Why do you say that, Deborah?'

'Because when it saw me, it stood up and I saw its face.'

Hume felt a tingle of excitement.

'And what did it look like, Deborah? Old? Young? Can you describe its features to me?'

Deborah smiled, and Hume thought it was about the most hopeless thing she had ever seen.

107

'It was evil. Face looked like it had been melted onto its skull. Like a melted jigsaw face, and its eyes . . . looked at me like I was nothing.'

'You could see the eyes? Even in the half-light?'

'Less than nothing,' continued Deborah as if Hume had not spoken. 'My punter fucked off then, but I couldn't stop looking. Whatever it was, it had blood all over it. Slippy with it. And I thought it was going to come for me. I thought it was going to come and eat me like it had that poor girl.' Deborah's leg started to jitter again. 'But instead, it just spread its wings and flew away across the floor. And then I must've passed out.'

Hume gave a small nod. 'Thank you, Deborah. Detective Echo will come and take a formal statement soon.'

'You'll never get it, you know. Not without the help of a priest.'

He's already killed a priest, Hume thought, but said nothing. She merely gave the woman's arm a light squeeze, in a futile attempt to reassure her.

CHAPTER 21

Dressed in black combats, black shirt and jacket, Raine watched Cale from the doorway of an anonymous building. Raine hadn't managed to secure a new recording device yet. The company she leased it from were demanding a hefty deposit and she didn't feel she could claim it off Heather's parents. Instead, she was making do with her phone.

Not that she needed a recording device right now. Cale wasn't doing anything suspicious, or at least not suspicious in her eyes. She had followed him around all day; from gym to bar to this late-night cafe in the centre of Soho, where he now sat drinking with an older man wearing an expensive-looking woollen coat, unbuttoned to reveal an expensive-looking suit underneath.

Raine hated Soho. It used to be so much fun when she was younger. The peep houses and mysterious open doors and stairs lit by fairy lights leading upwards. The vintage record shops next to decaying buildings with blacked-out windows with *XXX* flashing in neon above them. Clubs full of exotic-looking boys and girls, and everything in between.

Now it was just hipsters and grifters. Food bars where no average person could ever afford to eat and offices full of a seemingly unending supply of cutting-edge architects.

She stood in the shadows, toxic London rain wet and dirty against her face. Opposite her, at the cafe, Cale laughed at something the man said. Even though it was raining, the air was hot and they were sitting in the covered seating area outside. Cale had some sort of curry in front of him and a small glass of colourless liquid; Raine guessed vodka. The man had a bottle of mineral water. He appeared to be in late middle age, but it was hard to say. Partly because of the distance but also because the man was so lean. The skin on his face seemed tight, smooth and slightly oily. His frame was that of a power runner, suggesting an exercise regime that could keep the years at bay. Raine guessed he was an agent or actor. Could he be wearing some sort of foundation? Perhaps Cale moonlighted with bit parts or small roles in adverts on the side.

Raine shrugged inwardly. Or maybe he was Cale's father. Although Cale was still living in David's flat, where a for-sale sign adorned the outside of the building. Which meant Cale was going to need to find somewhere else to live. And even the difficult past was sometimes better than a homeless future. Perhaps this was Cale doing what was needed: rebuilding bridges. The murder of your boyfriend would definitely give perspective.

The man smiled at Cale, briefly touching the back of his hand. The gesture was intimate, his finger sliding over the younger man's skin. Not the father then, or at least not Cale's. The touch was too sensual. Too full of promise. Perhaps this man was the next David. Cale was a good-looking boy. A gym bunny, clearly, and beautifully groomed. Maybe he was playing safe this time when it came to up-fucking. Maybe he didn't mind which door he entered as long as the lodgings were good. Maybe he didn't have a choice. Not going for love, just the security of an older man trying to hang on to his own youth. Raine thought about what it would be like to have all your safety nets removed in one fell swoop. A boyfriend. A place to live. All your sanctuaries from a hard world.

Then she blinked. Not her concern. She'd followed Cale around all day and seen no obvious criminal intent.

He hadn't bought drugs or hung around with anyone shady. He had been to work, to the gym and to a juice bar that appeared to sell only drinks that were radioactive green, but she wouldn't hold that against him. As far as Raine could see, he was clean.

She took a quick photo of the couple with her phone and called it a night. Later she would send in her report to Hume.

On the way home, she caught a glimpse of herself in the reflection of a shop window. Her face looked like it had been run over; the bruising a butterfly wing of blues and yellows.

She stopped and stared at herself for a long moment, the late-night bustle of the city ebbing around her.

It was amazing.

An exact representation of the state of her heart.

'Don't worry, Heather,' she whispered to her reflection. 'I haven't forgotten about you.'

* * *

'I just can't see it. I can't get the connection.'

Echo and Hume were eating out of takeaway boxes and studying the smartboard. The offices around them were dark, the rest of the team assigned to the case long gone. The floors below were still occupied, tied up with problems dealt to a city that didn't even dream, let alone sleep, but theirs was a ghost-floor. After they'd returned from Hammersmith, Echo had hit the Net, trying to decipher the slashes on Alice's broken body. Hume had gone back through the case file, searching for anything that might connect the three victims. Once the police process on Alice had begun, the hospital closed its information stream pending a search warrant, as the records were not directly needed for establishing her death, so she had attempted to track down the young woman's parents. The abuse Alice suffered had started long before today. Just for a moment, Hume had wondered whether the vicar could be involved somehow but quickly realised that Jeremy

Peters would have been a boy himself when half Alice's injuries occurred. Jeremy was thirty-one, and Alice was twenty. The idea that a hard-working young vicar with two primary-school-aged children could systematically abuse the girl, while simultaneously forming a relationship with a gay man prominent on the dating scene, was ridiculous.

The vicar wasn't the connection. Or at least not the professional side of his life. There had to be some other link, something in the victims' lives that drew a line between them. A missing person or place that connected them. Perhaps in the sex trade.

'How are we doing on access to their social media?' she asked, using the plastic spoon to shovel food into her mouth. Echo pointed at the board with his own spoon.

'David's phone is being processed. Cale said that David did everything on his device. All his rendezvous. All through the apps. So there's a good chance that whoever he met that night would be logged in the phone's register.'

Echo saw the look of confusion on Hume's face.

'Even if the phone had been wiped there would be a record on the internal storage. A little like a laptop's hard drive.'

Hume frowned. 'So even if I factory-reset . . .'

Echo shook his head. 'All that does is remove the pathways to the data, not the data itself. That's still stored on the machine's flash memory. But in this case the phone hasn't been reset, as the passwords are still live. We've approached the relevant companies for his access codes but so far no go.'

Hume nodded, delicately placing a sliver of meat in her mouth.

'What about Jeremy Peters' phone?'

'Better. The passwords his wife gave us worked. We have complete access.'

'Brave man,' said Hume. 'I love my husband but even he doesn't have all my passwords.'

'Why not?' said Echo, interested.

Hume looked at him. 'Really?'

Echo glanced away, his face darkening with embarrassment. 'Ah, sorry. It's none of my business.'

Hume laughed, splattering food on her shirt. It felt good to laugh. Echo stared at her, terrified.

'Don't worry. I'm not on the pull for a hot young man!'

'No! I mean, of course not!'

'It's just I don't think he'd be interested in the gynaecological musings of my menopause group chat.'

Echo looked even more uncomfortable. Hume thought she could actually see the fear sweating out of him. She had to put down her carton of food before she spilt its contents on her trousers.

'Stop it!' she snorted, eyes streaming. 'You look like a schoolboy.'

Echo frowned. 'Are you taking the piss?'

'Just a little,' said Hume, getting herself under control. Outside there was a low rumble of thunder. Echo watched the window as drops of rain — part-water and part-dirt from 150 years of pollution — began to hit the window. 'So, what was on the good reverend's Twitter?'

'No Twitter. Facebook, LinkedIn and, surprisingly, Instagram.'

'What was he doing on Instagram?' Hume's tone was hopeful.

'Photographing churches in London. It's a whole thing, apparently. Very interesting but of no concern to us. There are no strange messages. No recently deleted posts that I can find, and no unusual non-vicar-y stuff that sets off any alarms.'

Hume watched the thick rain globules sludge down the glass.

'Anything about his congregation? Criminal activity? The only links between all three attacks so far are sex and drugs. Perhaps one of the reverend's flock . . . ?' Hume raised her eyebrows at him.

He shook his head. 'Nothing obvious. He led the services, gave communion to individuals who were slightly more . . . on the margins; but there's no indication that he was being harassed, or had exposed some sex scandal. Drugs or trafficking or whatever.'

'OK. Did he have a meeting that morning?'

'There's several meetings set up on his calendar app. We're chasing them down but it all looks like normal vicar business. Holy Communion. Counselling. Things like that. We're checking through his messenger apps, too.'

'Good. Now, what the hell am I eating?'

'Suqaar with special sauce. It's Somali street food.' Echo licked his fingers with relish. 'Me and my mum used to travel all the way to Auckland to eat this stuff.'

Hume placed another piece of meat in her mouth. 'And what is it?'

'Lamb.'

'And the special sauce?'

Echo grinned. 'Ketchup.'

Hume wondered if she should hit him.

'What about Alice? Was there anything on her phone?'

'More interesting, although a puzzle. The tech team had no problem accessing it. She didn't really bother with passwords.' Echo said this as if he were talking about someone not bothering with clothes. Hume supposed, for him, that's probably how it seemed. To browse the internet without password protection would be, as far as he was concerned, like walking around holding a big sign that said, 'Rob me!' Hume had heard enough stories from Action Fraud and the NCA to suspect he was probably right.

'And what did you find?'

'Lots of pro-abuse forums.' Echo's voice was hard. 'Places to go for tips on how to self-harm without it showing.'

'That's got to be illegal.'

'For information purposes. Not encouragement, apparently. The chatrooms get closed down but just spring up again elsewhere. There were also links to drapps.'

'What are drapps?' interrupted Hume.

'Drug apps. Snapchat. Telegram. Discord. Kids set up peer-to-peer encrypted accounts just to receive drugs. Because it's done through an app they think it is somehow more secure. Safer. It normalises it.'

'And is it?' enquired Hume. 'Safer?'

Echo shook his head. 'It's still the same dealers: Russian or Albanian mafia. Or one of the postcode gangs if you're down at street-level. Just because something has a nice user interface doesn't alter the base product.'

That made sense. Echo was right. So many people never looked beyond the package. That's why so many scams worked. If something *appeared* legit, people assumed it was legit. It came from a fundamental lack of understanding as to how things actually worked.

'Right. So what have you got? If you have full access to the phone then can you see who Alice was meeting?'

'That's the puzzle. There is a key-trail on her phone to a taxi app, but when I contacted them they had no record of a pick-up.'

'Would they even tell you? Data protection and all that?'

'They could confirm the pick-up, but they said there was no fare for that time in that location.'

Hume frowned.

'Maybe they had no one available and she used a different company? And what the hell is a key-trail, anyway?'

Echo looked at her the way a primary teacher would a child.

'Every phone logs which websites you've visited. And where you, or at least the phone, has been. GPS.'

'I didn't know they logged it, but yes, OK. Why do we care? We already know the route she took.'

'But she might have been dropped off somewhere, maybe to buy drugs. With the phone open we can trace exactly where she went, and for how long.'

'Wow. And you waited until the end of the day to tell me this?'

Echo shook his head again, frustrated.

'Like I said, the phone logs where you have browsed, but it also logs every key you hit; that's how it can do predictive text and stuff.'

'OK,' said Hume doubtfully.

'So I can see the conversation Alice had with the pick-up service, but there's no record of her reaching the company control site. It's like a one-way conversation.'

'Would you expect the other side to be recorded as well, then?'

'Not on her phone, not the actual words. But you'd expect the site to register the connection.'

Hume mulled it over in her head.

'So you're telling me . . . what are you telling me?'

'I don't know. I'll have to do some more checking. But there's something not right.'

Hume nodded, putting down her carton. 'A dead girl with knife slashes on her chest and a man's tooth in her mouth are the giveaways, I think.'

Echo ignored the sarcasm. 'Plus, there's no CCTV. Not outside the church. Not in Hammersmith. Nothing to show anyone leaving or entering.'

Hume leaned back and thought about this.

'Well, if Alice was driven to the abandoned building that makes sense. The killer would know that the place was clean of CCTV.'

'If it was planned.'

'If it was planned, yes. The same goes for the church, unsurprisingly. Having access to CCTV of sex workers, asylum seekers and off-book grey economy workers is something to avoid. Completely understandable the church would not want to put any potential clients off.'

Hume pondered. 'Do you think Alice's phone was hacked in some way? Maybe to manipulate her into getting into a car with the killer?'

Echo shrugged. 'Not sure, but something's nagging at me.'

'What about David?'

'Nothing so far. Given his lifestyle, it's not surprising that he was careful about who could get hold of his data. And you'd think that there'd be CCTV. Some way that he registered who he brought back to the flat. A safety net in case something went wrong. We're checking for any hidden surveillance system he might have set up.'

Hume nodded again.

'Good idea; keep looking. And keep going with the cuts on Alice, as well. If the killer chose that derelict building because of its lack of CCTV, then the wounds must mean something. He gave himself privacy so he could take his time.'

'Except he was disturbed,' said Echo.

'Point taken.'

Hume's phone chimed.

'Text from Raine,' she said, scrolling. 'She says that, as far as she can tell, Cale is clean. No odd behaviour over the day. He might have a new boyfriend already, apparently. She's sent through her report.'

'OK. I'll pick it up from Jonas tomorrow and put it on the board.'

Hume nodded. DC Jonas had been assigned to them full-time to deal with all the data coming in, now that the investigation had been bumped up. 'Good.'

'What's the deal with Raine, anyway?' asked Echo. Perhaps this was the moment to learn more about this curious character his boss was so thick with. 'How come she's working on the case?'

'She isn't. Not anymore. With Alice in the mix there's no way anything can be outsourced from now.' Hume hit her hand against the desk. 'Bollocks! I'll probably have to do a sodding press conference. Did you manage to track down Alice's parents? What did they say?'

'They didn't. She was brought up by the state.'

'Really?' said Hume, suddenly alert.

Echo shook his head. 'Sorry, I checked. They didn't all go to the same orphanage or anything. David was raised in Chelmsford and Jeremy in Hull.'

'Worth a try,' said Hume, standing and putting on her jacket. Outside, the rain had stopped and the darkening sky looked clear. 'It's been a long day, and they're only going to get longer. Let's wrap up for now, and upload all the info onto the board tomorrow. Maybe after a night's sleep something will click.'

CHAPTER 22

Dear Mr and Mrs Salim,

I wanted to write to you to express how very sorry I am about the death of your daughter.

I only met her once, but even in that brief time, I got a glimpse of how special she was. She was warm, brave, funny and clever. I am certain she will be missed by the friends she made here, as well as by those she left behind when she came to London.

The circumstances of her death are terrible and must cause you great anguish but, from what I understand, the nature of her injuries mean that her death would have been instantaneous, and she would not have felt pain.

I am so sorry this has happened to you all, especially as you were so close to being back in touch with her.

If there is anything I can do to help, whether it is assisting the police in their search for whoever killed Heather, or meeting with you and telling you in person about my conversation with your daughter, please, please do not hesitate to ask.

Also, if it is not too much of an imposition, would it be possible for me to attend the funeral? I completely understand if you just want close friends and family, but I would

very much like to come and pay my last respects. In many
ways, I feel I owe it to Heather and yourselves.

Once again, may I say how sorry I am, and if there is
anything I can do then please get in touch.

Yours,
Raine

Raine read back through the email, and then pressed
'send'.

She didn't expect an invite to the funeral. In fact, if she
were Heather's parents, she would definitely not want her
there. After all, she'd failed. Failed to get their daughter back.
Failed to protect her. Failed.

She removed a ginger and turmeric shot from the tabletop fridge and raised the tiny bottle in salute.

'Here's to you, Heather. Sorry you're dead.'

She swallowed the bitter liquid, then placed the bottle in
the recycling bag. Beyond the window, the day was grey and
wet. The rain hit the surface of the canal so hard that it was
creating a thin layer of vapour. The noise inside the houseboat was constant; a steady deep drumming. Raine reopened
the fridge and took out a can of Coke. From the drawer, she
hooked a blister pack of tramadol and popped two pills into
her hand. She made a face. The pills helped with the pain
but made her head a little fuzzy. She took a swig of the Coke
and looked at her laptop. It was exactly the same as her last
one. Raine didn't like change. She had managed to reduce
her life to the absolute basics: living on a boat required it. She
applied it to her wardrobe as well. She had read somewhere
that Einstein had multiple copies of the same shirt and suit
so that he didn't have to think what to wear when he got up.
Raine stuck to the same principle, minimising her clothes
according to environment and job, with no extraneous fash-
ion options required. She also applied it to her hardware. She
spent a long time finding a laptop she liked, and then spent
an even longer time getting used to how it worked. She did

not want to do it again, so when hers was stolen, she replaced it with the same make and model.

Raine's eyes unfocused for a moment as she looked at the laptop. Slipping the tramadol into her cargo stamp pocket, she walked over and lifted the lid. The machine immediately lit up, slipping out of sleep mode, ready for action. Her email client informed her that the message to Heather's parents had been received. Behind the email window, she had other tabs open. Maps. Reports. Personal log.

She shut the lid, waited a few seconds, then opened it again.

The laptop sprang back into life, with all her open tabs ready for perusal.

She had always found this to be one of the advantages of her chosen device: a Pixelbook. The operating system immediately reconnected everything that had been live when the lid was shut. No need to remember passwords. No need to wait for everything to boot.

As long as the machine itself was secure.

'Whoops,' she said softly.

Raine pulled out her phone. It was time to check in with Hume.

'It's me,' she said as her call was answered.

'Raine!' said Hume. 'Good to hear from you. Thanks for the report. Very thorough.'

'Sorry it didn't show anything unusual, but at least you can tick him off the list.'

'Sadly, there isn't a list.' Hume's voice sounded weary and frustrated. 'No suspects. No motive. No connection between the three murder victims—'

'Three?' Raine raised her eyebrows. 'There's been another?'

'Haven't you seen the news?'

'Been busy.' Raine looked at the screen where the email to Heather's parents glowed like an accusation. 'Who was killed this time?'

'Nothing you can help with, Raine, I'm afraid. The investigation is about to come under severe media scrutiny.

Having an outside agent involved, however peripherally, would not be appropriate.'

'Understood,' said Raine.

'Besides, I'm sure you wouldn't want the attention.' Raine could hear the smile coming through the ether. 'A detective who has her face splattered all over the papers can't really do much detective-ing.'

'I think the word you're searching for is "detecting". Anyhow, I wasn't ringing to tout for work,' said Raine, a smile in her own voice. A smile that took her back to different times.

'No?' The smile slipped out of Hume's voice. 'Why, then?' Her tone was interested but cautious.

'Your new underling,' said Raine. Apart from the raindrops bouncing off the roof of her boat, all she could hear was the ticking of her pain. She missed her cat.

'Echo, you mean,' said Hume. 'And he's not my underling, he's a DC.'

'Of course,' said Raine. 'Anyhow, you said he was a technical whizz, yes?'

'No, I said he was a technical whizz compared to me,' corrected Hume.

'And considering you're a Jedi compared to me, that makes him a whizz. Can I ask him a question?'

'He's not here.'

'Meet me for lunch. Both of you. Tell me about the case.'

'Raine, I can't,' said Hume, regret in her voice. 'It was hard enough getting the chief to agree to the surveillance.'

'Not in an official way. Just someone to bounce things off. There's something I need to ask Mr Echo. I'll pay.'

When Hume didn't answer Raine pressed on. 'Look, whatever it is will be all over the media anyway, then online. Nothing can be suppressed these days, just spun.'

There was a longer pause before Hume yielded: 'OK, but I'm not eating anything weird. That egg was practically an embolism on a plate. Then Echo tried to poison me with lamb. At this rate I'm going to be dead before the end of the week.'

'Nothing strange, I promise.'

'OK, I've got to meet a dentist this morning, but I suppose we could squeeze in half an hour, as long as it's close to King's Cross. Where do you suggest?'

CHAPTER 23

'You know, I actually trained on corpses, so this was a bit of a blast from the past for me.'

Hume saw Echo staring at the dentist with morbid fascination, as if wondering whether she might eat him. Hume thought it was not completely off the cards. She had asked Echo to find her a dentist to give a professional perspective on the teeth that had been inserted into the murder victims. He appeared to have managed to find the only goth dentist in London. The raven-haired Dr Arnold.

'Really? Where was that?' enquired Hume politely, concentrating on the woman's eyes. Her make-up definitely had a vampiric quality. Or maybe it was just the black rose tattoo on her neck.

'Dundee University. I was actually one of the first on the pilot scheme back in 2012. We used bodies embalmed by the Thiel method. Allowed for more flexibility.'

Hume could see Echo's jaw drop open like it was weighted down. He actually flinched when the dentist turned towards him, leaning forward to look into his mouth. Hume wondered if he believed she was going to bite him.

'I see your teeth are in tip-top condition, officer. Well done! Maori children are renowned for their dental decay. It used to be put down to their cultural diet choices, but that was just colonial bollocks. It was, and is, just poverty and social deprivation.'

'How did you know I'm Maori?' Echo asked.

The woman tapped the rose on her neck. 'I like tattoos. The Koru in your ear is a beauty.'

Hume was delighted to see her partner blush.

'So why is flexibility important in a cadaver?' she asked.

'It allows the student to move the head and jaw in a more natural manner. Previously, all practice dentistry was done on mannequins and animal skulls, or sometimes simulators. The Thiel bodies gave us the opportunity of transferring skills learned to real-life patients.'

'Right. Well, thank you for seeing us at such short notice. It seems that forensic odontology is somewhat of a specialism. Did you receive all the information?' asked Hume, wondering if the woman had any patients at all, what with the make-up, the tattoos and the swearing. Of course she did, she realised. Having a beautiful goth dentist leaning over you would attract its own clamouring clientele.

The dentist smiled, displaying her own immaculate white teeth. 'Absolutely.'

'And did you form any opinion?'

Dr Arnold opened a drawer and removed a file, flicking it open, all playfulness gone. Hume could see that it contained photographs of David, Alice and the reverend. Close-ups of their mouths, with the foreign teeth in situ, and with them removed.

'There was structural damage to the tooth placed into Alice's mouth. This was due to the means of insertion, which, I suggest, considering the chipping and scarring to the crown, would have involved some form of hammer or metal rod. Enamel is the hardest substance in the human body so it would take some force to knock it in, especially if the subject was conscious.'

'We believe the teeth were inserted when the victims were in a state of drug-induced paralysis,' offered Echo.

Dr Arnold inclined her head slightly. 'So I understand. The first victim, David Webb, is interesting. I'm pretty sure the tooth glued into his mouth is from a woman.'

'How can you tell?' asked Echo.

'There are small differences in morphology, crown size, and root length that can indicate the sex of the host.' Dr Arnold looked at them expectantly. 'Have you confirmed this from any residual genetic material?'

Hume cringed inwardly at the word 'host'. Aloud, she said: 'The lab is working on it. We are searching our records for a likely body but none has shown up so far.'

'The tooth was extracted at least ten years ago. Possibly longer.'

'Wow. You can tell that from the tooth?' said Echo.

The dentist shook her head. 'It's impossible to tell a person's approximate age from a single tooth. If full mineralisation hasn't occurred and the root canal hasn't become closed then one could suppose that it might be a child or young adolescent, but other than that . . .' She shrugged.

'Then how—?' began Echo.

'The dental work,' said Hume. 'You can tell by what's been done to it.'

'Correct,' said the dentist, beaming. She drew out an enlarged image of the tooth. Even in the photograph Hume found it disturbing.

'Once the tooth has reached maturity, as long as it is looked after and a normal diet is maintained, then it is pretty much impossible to give an accurate age. As I said, the enamel is super strong. However, dentistry is not a static science. We move with the times. New treatments and materials are being developed all the time. See here—' Dr Arnold pointed at a slight discolouration on the tooth. Hume realised that it was a filling of some sort, blended to be almost indistinguishable from the tooth itself. 'Our girl has had some expensive work done at some point, and as there is almost no damage to the repair, presumably that point was not long before the tooth was removed.'

'I'm not sure where that gets us,' said Hume.

'The polymeric material in this picture is no longer used, or at least not in this country. It was changed around ten years ago, the acrylic resin formula replaced by a better substance. So the tooth must have been taken out at least ten years ago.'

Echo was absorbed in processing the dentist's words. 'But the tooth could have been removed years after the work was done, surely?'

'Not really. There's no damage to the repair. No abrasion or pocking, which you would expect with a filling that has been in someone's mouth for a longish period. In my professional opinion, this tooth was removed not long after the work was done on it. There's also no sign of wear — the chipping or discolouration one would normally see on an adult tooth — so I would place the woman in her late teens or early twenties. The mesiodistal dimensions of the tooth are fairly standard, so I'm afraid I can't help you much more than that, but see here—' the dentist tapped the enlarged image — 'there are tissue remnants around the base of the root, which suggests forceful removal of a live tooth. There is no way it was extracted by a professional.'

The woman looked up at them, smiling brightly again. 'To sum up, I would say that the body you are looking for will be connected with a cold case, something from at least a decade ago.'

* * *

Seen fleeing the scene. That's what they said on the news.

I knew I shouldn't have been so lenient. I could have come back and killed the prostitute, but I had to get sentimental. Had to leave her standing for old times' sake. Stupid of me.

I'm too fucking soft, that's my problem.

And stupid of me to leave Alice's phone behind.

Not that there's anything on it that can lead to me, but there'll still be something if you know what to search for. And, even in the police, there are people who know what to search for.

At least she didn't scratch me. If she'd scratched me then it would be a different story.

I should have guessed one of them would fight back. It was bound to happen.

I mean, look at Alice's track record. She consumed so many drugs in her life that it was amazing the dose she got from me had any effect at all.

All the heroin and barbiturates. All the antidepressants and stimulants. It's a wonder she didn't just laugh in my face when she took the ketamine.

Like she did when I put the mask on.

I know what you're thinking. Why put on a mask when she'd already seen my face? Good question.

Well, she hadn't, had she? Not my true face. Not my real face.

CHAPTER 24

'All I'm saying is there are 35,000 dentists in London and you have to find me the only one who trained on corpses. Of course you fancy her. You don't do that sort of thing by accident.' Hume planned to milk this situation for all it was worth.

'She was recommended!' Echo protested, his face crimson.

'Who by — Dracula?'

'By Brendon — you know, from the Forensic Investigation team. He said she freelances for the lab on arson cases. He said she has the best—'

'I don't want to know about your strange fantasies. Jesus Christ, you look awful.'

Hume and Echo arrived at the courtyard table and stared down at Raine, who was gently munching her way through a Lebanese lavash wrap. The colours of the bruising on her face had turned from butterfly wing to stagnant pond. The delicate way she was chewing signalled how much it was hurting her. She grinned up at them.

'Lucky I'm not on a date then. Thanks for coming. I'm not even going to ask what you're talking about.'

She indicated the two other seats at the table, and Hume and Echo sat down.

'This is my DC, Echo, who has a dentist fetish. You'll like him, he doesn't bother with a first name, either.' Hume took the seat opposite Raine, with her partner to her right.

'Not a fetish. She's completely making it up,' said Echo, smiling and pulling out a chair. 'Good to meet you. What are we eating?'

The table was by the canal in Coal Drops Yard. The space had been redeveloped from its industrial past and now housed artisan food stalls and craft shops.

'Lavash wraps. Roasted vegetables cooked in honey and chilli without a fried egg in sight.' Raine smiled at Hume. 'As promised. Oh, and I took the liberty of ordering for you two already.'

'Great,' said Echo, taking a huge mouthful of his own wrap. Now that the rain had stopped, the buildings appeared clean, covered by a molecule-thin layer of moisture that made them sparkle in the sunlight. The cobbled floor of the market was grey and green. Hume wondered if the stone had been treated, or whether the variation in colour was natural. She peered at her watch.

'We haven't got long, Raine. What was it you wanted to ask Echo?'

Raine glanced at Echo, who seemed to be hoovering up the sandwich with no discernible chewing.

'Right, and I appreciate it, but before that, I wanted to ask you a favour.'

'What favour?' said Hume, peering suspiciously at her wrap. There appeared to be aubergine in it. The vegetable glistened in the chilli-and-honey glaze.

'Has anything happened with Heather's murder?'

Hume looked up from her sandwich, eyebrows raised.

'I'm not sure. Why, are the parents asking you to look into it?'

Raine shook her head, then winced. 'No, nothing like that. I just need to know. I tried the number Heather gave me but it just ghosts.'

'Ghosts?'

Raine looked at Echo. 'You know. When a message is received, but the sender doesn't get a response.'

Echo's mouth was full of lavash wrap, so his confirmatory remarks were rather muffled. 'Social-media term. Means someone is ignoring you, rather than blocking you.'

Raine turned back to Hume. 'I need to know why her phone is still active. Was it picked up by the parents?'

'No idea,' said Hume. 'Not my case.'

'I know. That's the favour: I want you to put me in touch with whoever is running Heather's investigation. Maybe vouch for me. Ask them to extend the hand of friendship.'

'And why would I do that?'

Raine smiled sweetly. 'Because you love me.'

Hume took a nibble of her wrap. All the moisture evaporated in her mouth.

'How many chillies did they put in this?' she gasped, reaching for her water.

'Just the right amount. Will you do it? I'm happy to trade.'

While day cruisers glided slowly past on the canal, Echo observed the two women. He was uncertain of their relationship. It was clear they knew each other pretty well. He'd heard that Raine used to be on the force but had taken compassionate and, it seemed, permanent leave. He had not been able to ascertain the reasons why. Raine talked to his boss as an equal, he noted — which seemed to suggest a relationship separate from the job.

'Why? What do you have to trade? I told you on the phone that there's no way my boss will accept assistance from an outside agent.'

'Call it intel, then. What was the other drug?'

'What?'

'As well as the ketamine. What was it mixed with?'

Echo intervened. 'What makes you think it was mixed with any other drug?'

Raine turned to him. Her eyes were slate-grey. 'Is it possible to trace a laptop? If it was stolen?'

'Er . . .' The change of direction took him by surprise.

'Is this about your break-in? Because if it is, then—' began Hume.

Raine ignored her. 'I mean, I know you can trace phones. GPS. IMEI. Stuff like that. Is it possible to do that for a computer?'

Echo shook his head. 'Not once it's turned off. It's not like a phone. A phone, even when it's switched off, still sends its location to the Wi-Fi masts. That's why the batteries are non-removable. You think your device is switched off, but in fact it's always on and always being tracked.'

'Well, that's a bit scary,' commented Raine drily.

'Welcome to Big Brother,' said Echo.

'But not with laptops, because they don't have mobile Wi-Fi connectivity?'

'Correct; or at least most don't. People tend to just hook them up to their phones if they're out and about and need the Net.'

Raine nodded. 'What about if the computer is connected, and someone opens an email on it or accesses a website?'

Echo leaned back thoughtfully.

'Ah, well, that's a different matter. If someone uses Gmail or whatever, connected to an unencrypted server, then the computer's access point is logged — whether that is a home network, a public one or tethered to a phone.'

Raine's eyes seemed to turn blank for a second, then she turned back to Hume, switching the conversation yet again.

'Most street drugs are not one thing. They're a mixture of several. Heroin cut with ecstasy. Coke mixed with methadone. The kids expect a multi-layered experience when it comes to their party enhancers.'

Echo took a sip of his water, happy that Raine's gaze had shifted from him. There was something about her undivided attention that was quietly terrifying.

'So?' said Hume, completely unfazed by the latest change of direction.

'So, different suppliers have different mixes. And different areas have different requirements. Uptown socialites don't want something in their cocktail that's going to slow them down on the dance floor, so no smack. Estate gangs, on the other hand, just want to get off their faces. For them, drone-gear, heroin, mixed with PCP will be just the ticket.'

'Different strokes for different folks,' said Hume.

'Which means, depending on the mix, and depending on the intel, then you could narrow down a batch to a certain postcode, or a certain import stream.'

'The mixes are really that different, that bespoke?' said Echo.

'Sure. Like black-market cigarettes or trafficked people. Ports in different parts of the country get different brands. Same with drugs.'

'And you have this knowledge?' said Hume, dubiously.

Raine shrugged. 'I'm connected. Closer to the street than Vice. I know some people who might give me information.'

Her smile looked to Hume like petals falling off a rose, the skin still wounded and discoloured from the beating. Raine switched her attention back to Echo.

'What if the computer wasn't turned off?'

Echo blinked rapidly, trying to keep up. 'What do you mean?'

'Where is this going, Raine? Because—' began Hume, but Raine wasn't listening.

'What if, for the sake of argument, the laptop was only in sleep mode? If it hadn't been turned off, just the lid closed?'

'Ah,' said Hume, connecting the dots. 'You never signed out, did you?'

Echo looked at Hume, then addressed Raine.

'Well,' he began slowly, 'if the machine was never properly shut down then as soon as the lid was lifted the next user would have full access to whatever tabs were still running.'

'That's what I thought. And if I gave you my password? Could you track it? If the device was still live?'

'If Gmail was open, or Dropbox. Something like that. Then you'd need to log in to admin and get the IP address of the user. That would be time-stamped. You could follow a trail of IPs, which would link to real-world locations. So long as the thief isn't using a VPN — a virtual private network . . . But are you really telling me you didn't shut down your laptop before you left home?' Echo was incredulous.

'I closed the lid,' said Raine. 'What more does it want?'

Echo appeared personally offended. 'You could install something like Prey, which when activated would open up your webcam and capture an image of the thief, as well as providing an address for the IP, for a start. Or maybe, I don't know, you could do something radical like turn it off when you've finished.'

'Get her details,' Hume sighed. 'Look into it when you have time.'

'Thank you,' said Raine.

Hume shrugged. 'Dezolam. That's the other drug. Apparently it heightens the ketamine; adds to the other-worldly effect.'

A couple at another table paused in their conversation to stare at the trio. Raine smiled sweetly at them. They took in her battered face and quickly looked away.

'Dezolam. Got it.'

'But just on the quiet, yes?'

Raine spread her hands wide and stood up, ready to leave. 'Am I anything but the soul of discretion?'

Hume thought about this. 'Yes,' she said, finally. 'You are anything *but* the soul of discretion.'

'Exactly. I'll let you know if I turn anything up. You'll get me the name of whoever's running Heather's case?'

'I'll do my best.'

Raine leaned down and kissed Hume on the cheek.

'Thank you,' she said, then turned to Echo, handing him a card she removed from a pocket in her combats. 'Here are my details. The food's on my tab, so knock yourselves out.'

Echo watched as she walked away, across the wet cobbles and out of sight.

'Wow,' he said, putting the card in his wallet. 'I bet she's high-maintenance.'

'Finish your sandwich, dentist-boy,' said Hume, her eyes still fixed on the corner Raine had walked around. Her expression was unreadable. 'We've got a psychologist to visit next.'

CHAPTER 25

Raine was hurting inside. By the time she got back to her boat, she was barely holding it together. It was only the pain in her face that was keeping her grounded.

Echo had basically told her that whoever had stolen her laptop had access to not only her emails, but potentially all the case files that she stored remotely.

And all her personal stuff.

'Stupid!' she muttered, unlocking the new padlock and opening the hatch. As soon as she unlatched it the alarm countdown began, giving her fifteen seconds to disable it before it was triggered, sending a message to the security firm it was connected to. Reaching in, she punched in the code. The countdown ceased, replaced by silence.

She waited for the feel of Melania rubbing round her ankles. But no one greeted her as she descended the few steps into her home.

Putting the kettle on, she lifted the lid of her new laptop. Immediately the screen lit up, displaying the last thing she had looked at before closing it: her email account. Behind that, indicated by the tab above, was her virtual office. She tapped on it, bringing it to the front. The landing page listed her indexing system, formatted by date and client. She scanned through the titles, trying to see if perhaps there was someone listed here who might have had reason to take her laptop. There was information concerning a selection of figures from London's underworld. How might it be used in the right, or wrong, hands? Since leaving the Met she had worked almost exclusively in London, specialising in finding people who were unfindable. Runaways and hideaways. People who lived in the shadows of the capital. People who frequented the places civilians didn't tend to go or have access to.

Locations. Contacts. People who could feed her information.

'Shit!' she whispered. Why the hell hadn't she encrypted any of this stuff? If someone had stolen the laptop to order, then certain people could be in real danger.

But the question was: how? Very few people knew where she lived. Certainly none of the people she was trailing, and certainly none of the criminals she occasionally had to deal with.

She thought of Luke, the gang leader who had threatened Heather.

Just want to know who to look for, when it's time to come calling.

That was what he'd said, just before he ran.

'No,' she muttered to herself. 'There's no way he could find me.'

Then she thought about her clients. The people who employed her. Maybe her address could be traced through a bill or payment? She made a mental note to follow up on her recent jobs. To check no one had been asking about her.

She changed her password to the virtual office, and sent the new password to Hume, asking if Echo could see if her files had been accessed somehow.

Next, she googled Dezolam. Etizolam, also known as Dezolam, was a psychoactive drug, licensed in Japan. It was used to treat anxiety and panic attacks. It wasn't licensed in the UK. So no chance it had been prescribed to any of the victims legitimately.

Among its known effects was a slowing down of body and brain function, causing a sense of calm and sleepiness.

Mixed with the ketamine, Raine guessed it would produce a completely compliant and possibly silent victim. And then, when the drug-induced paralysis manifested, it would be simplicity itself to do what needed to be done.

Raine closed her eyes a moment, trying to put herself in the victim's place. Trying to feel the imprint. Every action left an imprint that connected itself to the primary source. She'd always believed that. It was just a matter of finding the key.

She opened her eyes and called up the London newsfeeds. She scanned the stories until she found a piece about the latest killing. It didn't take long. Alice was all over it.

Alice Watkins, a troubled young woman barely twenty. A history of mental health and social disruption. Found by a sex worker in an abandoned rubber factory in Hammersmith. The witness said she saw the assailant running away when they were disturbed.

'It was a devil,' the sex worker told the police as they arrived at the scene of the carnage. 'A devil! It was pulling guts out of the poor girl's mouth, and then it flew away screaming.'

The woman in question, the piece gleefully detailed, *has a history of substance abuse and was believed to be under the influence at the time she first spoke to the police.*

'Wankers,' muttered Raine. Without overtly saying so, the reporter had painted both Alice and the woman who found her as somehow worthless, not legitimate citizens. As if how they'd ended up was their own fault.

Raine continued calling up reports from other sources.

Alice was found with blood in her mouth, as if she'd bitten her attacker.

The assailant was described as a devil with wings.

The witness was a sex worker, with a long arrest sheet.

The victim was a victim long before she was murdered.

Had she gone to that cold and abandoned building for sex?

Or drugs?

Could all the murders be gang-related?

Many of the sources also pointed out that David was gay and liked to pick up men on the internet.

Also, that Reverend Peters was known to give communion to criminals and prostitutes.

Raine wondered who had leaked the connection between the murders. As well as the legitimate news feeds there were all the hashtag haters; the tributaries in the information stream that the internet thrived on.

#kink-killers
#devil-sacrifice
#sadisticserialsexscene

That it had happened was not surprising. Three was the magic number. That's when it became the work of a serial killer.

'There's no smoke without fire' was the subtext.

Raine reached for her phone and sent Hume a quick message. Then, as an afterthought, she messaged again, asking what code-carving had been left this time.

A minute later she got a message back, along with the name of the officer in charge of Heather's case.

Raine smiled.

'I always thought you needed to see a shrink,' she said to Hume's ident picture.

CHAPTER 26

Professor Flynn looked like he got dressed in front of the type of mirror that had bulbs around the outside. Everything about his appearance was immaculate and perfectly put-together. Hume wondered if it was part of his psychology training, perhaps a special module near the end when students were close to having actual patients. *How to project a sense of superiority through the sartorial.*

'So, what you're saying is it could be something that occurred in the killer's childhood,' she said.

The professor shook his head of perfectly coiffed hair as if he were astonished at her stupidity. 'No, officer, I'm merely pointing out that there are certain markers.'

He extended one digit, topped off with an immaculately manicured fingernail. Hume could see a slight sheen to its surface and wondered if it was achieved through buffing or clear polish.

'The most recent murder victim was a young woman damaged emotionally from a young age, if I have understood you. The second,' he raised a second elegant finger, 'was a vicar?'

'Yes.'

Flynn grunted. 'Someone who had it within his power to offer understanding without judgement and, ultimately, the ability to forgive.'

'Forgive what?' asked Echo.

Flynn looked at him benignly. 'That's the question, isn't it? What could our killer need forgiveness for?'

'And the first victim? David Webb?' Hume tried to sound neutral, professional.

'Well, he was gay, and active in the casual sex scene, yes?'

'So?'

'Perhaps, to our killer, the vicar and the first victim represent two extremes. A kind of reversal of the popular female tropes.'

'What extremes, what tropes?' said Hume.

Flynn's tone was smug, superior. 'The virgin and the whore. The vicar stands for the virgin. The other victims stand for the whore.'

'And the teeth?' said Echo. 'How do they fit into your theory?'

The professor gazed at the young detective over his half-moon spectacles.

'Yes, that is interesting. And you say the first victim you found, David, had a molar inserted which was taken from a female? Not yet identified?'

'Yes. The forensic dentist believes that it's from someone who died at least ten years ago.'

'How can he know that?' Flynn was clearly intrigued.

'She,' corrected Hume. 'Apparently there are radiological and morphological markers.'

Flynn absorbed this. 'I suspect you'll find that the victim was a teenager.'

'What makes you say that?' said Echo. 'All the other victims have been adults. Alice was the youngest at twenty.'

'The youngest so far. As poor Alice's tooth has been taken, I think we can assume the sequence has not concluded. That there will be more killings.'

A chill silence filled the space as the professor's words sank in.

'Which is why we need to understand the motivation, Professor,' said Hume. 'So we can stop them before anybody else dies.'

Professor Flynn nodded soberly.

'Why do you think the tooth found in David Webb's mouth might belong to a young adult?' repeated Hume after a moment. Dr Arnold had said the same, but Hume was interested in the professor's reasoning.

'Because of the lack of a body,' said Flynn.

'You'll have to explain, please.'

'I understand that the murderer has made no attempt to conceal his victims' bodies. So it's likely that, if the tooth belonged to someone who had been killed recently, you would already have found her. It's reasonable to assume then that the first tooth was taken quite some years ago. Perhaps from someone the killer knew as a teenager or when he was in his early twenties. One of their *peers*. Most psychological abnormalities develop or become evident either in childhood or early adulthood.'

Professor Flynn paused for a few seconds. Hume supposed it was for dramatic effect. And then he continued, with every word precisely enunciated. 'I believe adult teeth come through in late childhood, and are full-sized. I would suggest that, when you establish whose tooth it is, you may also find that your killer knew the tooth's owner. They could even have been friends.'

He smiled at them and glanced out of the window.

Any minute now he's going to steeple his fingers, Hume thought with mild horror.

They were in the office of the professor of criminal psychology, on the third floor of the UCL building in Bloomsbury. The world outside was kept at bay by a window that could be opened, Hume noted, only a few inches. In a moment of childishness, she wondered how many visitors wanted to jump out of that window after meeting Professor Flynn.

When the professor turned back to them, his fingers were steepled in a scholarly church. Hume shuddered inwardly.

'What do you know about the victims' childhoods?' he enquired.

Echo shook his head. 'We checked, sir. The victims were of different ages and backgrounds. There is no crossover between them.'

'Detective Echo, when it comes to connections there are two main directions. From the murdered—' he separated his hands and held them in front of him, palms up — 'and from the murderer. Did the unfortunate victims actually have something in common, or were they merely triggers? The removal and replacement of the teeth suggests they *are* connected in some way; either the victims themselves or by the process. Is the common factor in the real world — a shared teacher, perhaps; a club or institution they all belonged to? Or is it something perceived only in the mind of our mystery assailant?' Flynn leaned forward. 'If, on the other hand, the connection is from the killer — something only he could know — then we have to work in the other direction. Extrapolate the flesh from the bones of the clues. It is possible that the teeth represent a kind of fundamental pre-birth cycle, or perhaps even rebirth.'

'I'm sorry, sir, but you're losing me,' said Echo.

'Did you know that teeth, or at least their buds, are already present in the foetus?' asked the professor brightly. 'First there are the baby teeth, which are discarded, then come the adult teeth. Planting the teeth of his previous victim into the next body might be seen as a sort of rebirth. A second chance, if you will.'

'A second chance?' said Echo incredulously. 'They're dead!'

Flynn raised an amused eyebrow. 'Well, I didn't say the killer was sane, now did I, officer? It is possible that, as far as he is concerned, the version of the human he has killed is wrong. Hence the removal of the adult signifier.'

'Adult signifier?'

'The tooth, officer, the tooth. It not only contains the genetic code of the victim, but was within the body before birth. Before the corruption that occurs through living.' Flynn raised his chin and addressed the ceiling. 'Because being born is where the problem begins. Prior to that the code is untouched. Our killer thinks those he is targeting are mistakes. Somewhere in their lives, an error has occurred. Hence the dissociative code on the victims' chests, embellishing the flesh with his own meaning. Giving each of them a marker, as it were. The scarification as a framing reference.'

The professor lowered his chin and peered at Echo. 'You said it was text speech?'

'The first one, yes. A code used back in the '80s. The second was a calculator gimmick. When the numbers are read upside down they spell out a word.'

'Then clearly you should be looking for someone with technological knowledge and skills. It's likely that the knife marks on the third victim — Alice — are also some kind of code. I would be examining pictograms or computer languages. Something the lines could represent.'

'You keep referring to the killer as "he",' said Hume softly. 'Why?'

Flynn looked pleased. 'Very good. There is no guarantee, of course, but I should think the penetrative nature of the replacement of the teeth is significant. It has distinct phallocentric overtones.'

'Are you saying the attacks have a sexual dimension?' said Hume. 'Because there was no sign—'

Flynn held his hand up. 'No, not at all. If anything it is *pre-sexual*. Hence the use of the tooth rather than genitalia. The attacker could still be in a mental state of prepubescence, or not connect procreation with sex at all. Sexually neutral, if you will.'

'How can the crimes be pre-sexual *and* have phallocentric overtones?' asked Echo.

'It is possible that the killer took the social identifiers of sexual control — penetration, submission, etcetera, without the sexual aspect. Applying the structural meaning as he sees it, without sexualising it. Like being able to enunciate the words of a language without grasping their meaning.'

The professor appeared suddenly weary as if his analysis caused him pain. Hume felt a slow tide of warmth for him. 'Well, thank you for your insight, sir. You've been very helpful.'

Hume rose, ready to depart, but Professor Flynn had some parting words for them: 'Count on it: your killer has a link to his victims in the past, or the victims' past has a link to the killer in the present.'

'I'll definitely bear it in mind, sir,' said Hume, as she and Echo headed for the door.

In the lift back down to the ground floor, Echo repeated the professor's last statement.

'Do you think he knows he sounds like a bad version of Yoda?' he mused.

'Look at the code again,' was all Hume said. 'The professor isn't a fool. No way are those cuts on Alice random. Everything else is so meticulous; the cuts must be too.'

'And the teeth?'

'God knows. I barely understood a word he said about those. I'll have to read his report and process.'

From inside her jacket, her phone pinged. A message from Raine. Frowning, she looked up at Echo.

'Were there any buttons found near Alice's body?'

CHAPTER 27

The name Raine had been given by Hume was not one she recognised, which was good. Although she had left the force some years ago, echoes of her remained. If the detective didn't know her history, then there would be no preconceptions. She waited for her call to be answered.

'Hello, Conner here.'

The voice on the line was rich and warm. Raine imagined a man with brown eyes and a soft embrace. Someone used to hugging his children, maybe. She closed her eyes.

'Detective Inspector Conner,' she said brightly, opening them again. Outside the window a swan glided past. 'Good to speak with you. My name is Raine. DI Hume gave me your number.'

'Miss Raine, of course. Mary mentioned that you might call. You were working a misper for the parents of Heather Salim, yes?'

'That's it. I wonder if you can help me out?'

'I'm afraid I can't discuss anything to do with the case, Miss Raine,' said DI Conner. 'As a civilian, you—'

'That's OK, Detective Inspector,' said Raine. 'I wouldn't ask you to tell me anything that isn't, or won't soon, be in the public domain. I was just hoping you could save me a bit of legwork.'

'OK,' said Conner cautiously. 'I could probably do that. Mary says you've helped her on a few cases in the past.'

'You bet. I wonder if you can tell me if Heather's body has been picked up yet?'

'I'm not sure. She's had a DA, and there were no anomalies in the initial diagnosis.'

'DA?'

'Digital autopsy. Heather's parents requested that she not have an intrusive post-mortem. Obviously, because of the nature of her death, an investigation was necessary. A non-invasive post-mortem was the compromise. Actually,' Conner's voice lightened, 'DAs are being trialled nationwide. They're becoming more and more accepted as a diagnostic tool. A way to determine cause of death.'

Raine understood Conner's enthusiasm. Attending post-mortems was one of the more unpleasant duties a detective had to undergo. The number of times Raine had been sick after seeing some poor body being prised apart, and the organs weighed and measured, was something she chose to forget. If there was a high-tech answer that involved less of that then she could see the attraction.

'Got it. So the cause of death was definitely the bullet to the face?'

'Yes. Then she was run over by the shooter's vehicle, but she was already dead by then. Blood splatter at the scene confirmed this.'

Raine knew that the blood pattern produced by rupture to a body in which the heart wasn't pumping would be different from the pattern produced where the victim was still alive when the vehicle ran over them.

'CCTV?'

'Some. Not of the event itself, but of Heather leaving the building, and the van arriving and leaving the scene. There were multiple cameras around the square. Piecing them together gives us a pretty comprehensive picture. There is audio of the shot, with a scream just before. Also footage after the incident from various mobile phones.'

'Would it be possible to have copies of all this?'

There was a pause, while Conner thought about it.

'I don't see why not,' he said eventually. 'Most of the feeds have already made it into the public domain.'

Raine nodded and the swan nodded back at her. She'd already seen footage that had found its way onto the web. Not just screen-grabbed shots from the various security cameras, but from the phones of bystanders, quick to sell a story and get their fifteen seconds of fame. Or just uploaded for kicks.

'I'd appreciate that. And you think it was a gang misfire?'

'Mistaken identity,' Conner confirmed. 'That's the current line of enquiry.' His voice suddenly took on a more official tone. 'Unless you have any intel to add? The parents said that you met up with Heather. Followed her, even. Is there anything about her that you think might be useful for us to know?'

If you can give me your number, I'll ring you in a day or two. Just to check you're not having a panic attack or anything.

That was what she'd said to Heather, back in the cafe. And when she'd phoned the number all she got was ghosted. Not wrong-numbered, or unavailable. Ignored.

'Nothing,' she said. 'I just need to fill in some details about the case for my report. I keep an indexed databank about all my cases. You know how it is. You never know when you'll get an overlap in this city.'

Raine could hear the answering smile all the way down the line.

'Tell me about it! I once had what looked like a '56 in an abandoned chicken farm where the frayed end of the rope around the guy's neck was a direct match with the restraints used in a gang assassination from a decade before.'

10-56. Police code for a suicide. Except, in this instance, if the rope was connected, the deaths were connected. So maybe not a suicide after all.

'So what was the thinking: a guilty conscience or *fowl* play?'

It took Conner a moment to get the joke, but the pay-off was a deep laugh, straight from the gut.

'Give me your email. I'll send you through the video files.'

'Much appreciated, Detective Inspector.'

Raine gave Conner her details then, after the obligatory wind-down, ended the call and turned her attention to her laptop screen.

A few taps on her computer pulled up Heather's face, scared, with Luke leering at her. Raine studied the gangster, then the woman she had failed.

'Sorry I let you down,' said Raine softly. 'But I promise I'll find out who killed you.'

Outside, on the canal, the swan glided silently by.

CHAPTER 28

Echo looked at the image of the cuts on Alice's body. He was sitting on his tiny balcony in the last rays of the day's sun, sipping a glass of 42Below vodka poured from the bottle he kept in the tiny fridge by his bed. He was viewing the image on his tablet and getting nowhere. The professor had said the cuts must signify a language or code, but he wasn't seeing it.

Using a stylus, he traced over the cuts and opened the image on another page. Now all he had was the graphology of the ripped skin on a blank screen.

Echo took another sip of vodka and used the stylus again to bubble the possible symbols. He did an image search. No matches were found. The nearest he got was an article on the Nazca Lines in Peru: ancient geoglyphs that could be seen from space. Echo smiled. He was fairly certain that the killer, whoever they were, was not an extraterrestrial.

Next, he straightened the lines, making them more uniform. After a few minutes he was happy with the result.

$= I) I - I$

He put the results through the search engine.

Your search - $= I) I - I$ - did not match any documents.

Nothing. He sighed, and looked out over London. When he'd first arrived here from Aotearoa New Zealand he'd been desperately lonely. He'd missed his family. Not just his mother and siblings, but his extended family. His cultural family. The way they all fitted together. Pieces of a jigsaw in the landscape of life. All through his upbringing he had been taught about the connectedness of everything. About how the land and the people were inseparable. And then he had moved here, to this ancient city, and had never felt so disconnected in his life. It had taken him months to begin to feel the pulse of the capital. To work out its strange tides. The way it seemed to ebb and flow like an ever-changing sea, with currents moving the inhabitants around as if they were weeds.

But once you hit its rhythm there was nothing like it. The sheer variety of what was on offer was mind-boggling. Hundreds of languages and cultures, constantly changing and evolving. It was dizzying, and if you slipped out of the current, the loneliest place on earth.

He jumped as his door flew open and the girl with the spider-bite lip crashed in.

'Don't you ever knock, Bitz?' said Echo.

'I do. You just haven't heard it yet,' she said.

'Come again?'

Bitz smiled at him, then gently knocked on the door.

'See? Quantum knocking. Chapter two of *A Brief History of Time*. Me and Stephanie Hawkins go way back.'

'I think he was called Stephen.' Echo smiled as the woman opened his fridge and helped herself to the vodka bottle. She was dressed in a pair of baggy shorts and a muscle shirt, proclaiming 'NO I DIDN'T'.

'If you like. Fancy a game of Pac-Man?' Bitz grinned at him. 'I'll let you nearly win and everything.'

Echo smiled back and shook his head.

'I can't, sorry. I'm trying to work something out.'

Bitz looked past him at the tablet in his hand. Echo was glad he'd taken the graphology of the image before she'd barged in. Sharing close-up pictures of a mutilated dead body was not the way to win friends and meet nice girls who didn't have to be from Aotearoa

'That?' she said.

'Yep. I can't work out what it might mean. I thought it was a representation of something, but I can't figure it out. It's not any syntactical structure I can find.'

'Sure it is. It's just upside down.'

Echo looked at her, then at the lines on his tablet. 'What do you mean? It doesn't matter what way up they are. They're not letters or numbers. They're just lines.'

Bitz shook her head. 'No, they're not. It's a form of leet-speak. See?' She took the tablet out of his hands and flipped it round.

I - I (I =

Echo looked, and shook his head. 'I still don't see it.'

'The first two vertical marks with the horizontal line between them?'

'What about them?'

'That's an "H".'

Bitz traced a black-nailed finger over the tablet, illustrating.

'Fuck me,' said Echo.

'Nice offer, but I'd rather play Pac-Man,' Bitz dead-panned, then pointed at the screen. 'The second one, with the curve—'

'Is a "C",' said Echo, staring. 'Why didn't I see that?'

'You're not meant to. Not unless you do it all the time. It's coder's speke. Elite speke. It's kind of a secret language.'

'Right, yes. Like replacing numbers with letters. I remember now. It was popular with all the skateboarders back home.'

'I've got a skateboard!' said Bitz indignantly. 'And any-way the sk8te community—' Bitz drew a figure eight in the air as she talked — 'was often also the gaming community.

And some of those people went into coding and became zillionaires.'

'If you're a billionaire you have my permission to marry me,' said Echo. 'So what's the next one: the straight line? An "L" or an "I"?'

'No, the line and the equals sign are all one thing. An "F".'

'Right. *HCF*.'

'Halt and catch fire. It's an old computer execution code.'

At the mention of execution, Echo felt a chill. He looked at the girl next to him, studying the screen.

'An execution code?'

'Sure. If something has gone wrong with the program or whatever. It's the code to shut the system down.'

She turned and gazed straight at him, her smile wide, the setting sun glinting off her lip piercings.

'It's the kill code.'

CHAPTER 29

Luke scanned the street. Years of living by his wits had made him fine-tuned to everything and everyone in his environment. With a final look at the empty thoroughfare, he slipped into a tiny alley between two council houses. In the warm night, the streetlights were barely visible, just a weak glow against the background of the toxic air. Luke didn't care. He was just pleased it wasn't raining and the garden outside the council house was dry. Because dry meant no footprints. Footprints left by his trainers. Trainers that could be identified by distinguishing nicks and areas where the soles had worn down.

Always thinking.

He opened the side gate and entered the garden, glancing first at the dead eyes of the house's windows, then at the pink-and-yellow plastic playhouse set against the fence at the end of the garden. Inside was a plastic bag full of drugs worth more than Luke's life. The first time he'd done this run he'd been in bits. Wondering if anyone from the house would see him. Or from a neighbouring house. Wondering what would happen if one of the kids who lived there ever found the drugs. Took them, maybe, if they were nice-coloured pills and looked like sweeties.

But then he'd got wise. There were no kids. The whole thing was a beard — a shell house with the paying tenants set up somewhere else. Whatever. Not his concern.

All he ever did was pick-ups and deliveries. The drugs were left in the playhouse, and his job was to scope out the area and, if it was safe, to take the stash and distribute to all the postcodes on the schedule. Business was so good that it was easier for rival gangs to let a neutral roadman be the postboy than fight among themselves. Everybody happy.

As Luke reached down for the playhouse door, he could hear, several streets away, the tannoy of the DLR station announcing the arrival of one of its Noddy trains.

He opened the plastic door, crouched down and stepped in, letting the door close behind him. Inside the tiny house, his large frame felt claustrophobic. Closed in. Luke didn't like enclosed spaces. That's why he spent most of his time on the road. That was why, once he'd got enough coin, he was going to sack London and move to somewhere wide open. Australia, possibly. Or Canada. Somewhere he wasn't known. Somewhere he had no history.

He lifted the lid of the little play-desk in front of him. Inside were tightly wrapped bricks of plastic, containing thousands of pounds' worth of pills and powders. Snake remedies of the modern world. Instant karma. Immediate salvation. Do not pass go, do not collect any fucking experience that is real.

Luke sucked air in between his teeth and shrugged off his backpack. Not his problem. Everybody happy.

He began transferring everything to his backpack, careful to preserve the order. Each package was marked with a code. As he packed, he kept a mental image of the route he would take. Which packages would be dropped off where. No point in taking out more product than was necessary at each stop. That was a sure-fire way to get killed.

When he was finished, Luke pulled the rucksack back on and listened at the door.

The night was still and silent. Not even the streetlights buzzed anymore since they had moved over to LEDs.

Luke smiled. Once this delivery was done and paid for, he was well on his way to getting the fuck out of London. Silently, he opened the Wendy-house door.

The fist that smashed into his throat was hard and fast and holding a roll of coins for added strength. The pain was incredible and Luke felt his lungs paralyse.

'Hello, Luke. I'd told you I'd make you pay for cracking my tooth.'

Raine stepped forward, punched Luke in the throat again, and drove her knee hard into his balls, causing him to vomit. Two seconds of excruciating pain later and he passed out.

CHAPTER 30

Hume gazed out across the Thames. The river was dark in the night, an absence of light that seemed to pull at her gaze. To the left, on the far-off shore, was the Shard, a metal-and-glass finger piercing the sky. It always made her think of the Snow Queen. When she had read the tale as a child she had suffered from nightmares for weeks. She used to think the witch would visit her when she was asleep and slide her finger through her skin and into her heart, freezing it. The Shard, with its tapering top and crystal sides, brought it all back. She shivered.

'Cold, love?'

Robert wrapped an arm around her. They were sitting outside the Sail Loft, a gastropub off Victoria Parade in Greenwich. It wasn't really Hume's scene, but the views of London from its balcony were spectacular. Her job often broke the city into small patches of brutality, so it was good for her to see a bigger picture from time to time. A reminder to look out from the gutter and up at the stars.

'How much electricity do you think it takes to light up a whole city?' she mused. Below them, the tide had receded, and the new mudlarks — amateur archaeologists and environmentalists with torches strapped to their heads — were down at the river's shore, searching for treasures.

'No idea,' said her husband amicably. 'Less than it used to, that's for sure.' He took a swig from his glass of red wine.

'How do you work that out?' she asked, turning away from the glittering lights to observe him. There were a lot more lines on his face nowadays. But she supposed there would be. You don't walk through life without leaving a map of your progress behind. Laughter lines. Worry lines. Deep cuts of joy and sadness like ruts in the landscape of living.

'Different systems,' he said, pulling her back from her thoughts. 'It used to be neon. Or incandescent. Now it's all LED. Uses a fraction of the electricity.'

'I didn't know that,' said Hume. She put her arm around her husband, snaking it over his back and resting her hand on his hip.

'That's why they're so cold to look at. When they first came out you could only get white, but even now there are other colours available, there's no warmth to them.' He sighed. 'I miss the old lights. It was like having tiny fires everywhere. LEDs are just . . . not as real. Like the ghosts of lights. Emotionless.'

'Very poetic,' Hume murmured.

Her husband smiled, raising his glass.

'That's why you let me drink so much wine. To oil my poetic heart.'

Before Hume could reply, her phone vibrated in her pocket. She had turned off the ringer so as not to disturb their evening, but she couldn't turn it off completely. During a live investigation, she always needed to be contactable.

'Sorry,' she said, slipping it out of her pocket. 'It's Echo.'

Her husband smiled his understanding and got up from their table. He walked away a few steps, giving her space. She felt a keen spike of love for him, then swiped her phone, answering the call.

'Echo, what's the news?'

'I've deciphered the code. On Alice. The cuts.' His voice was low, urgent.

Hume gripped the phone tighter, feeling the excitement.

'Great! How did—'

'Actually it wasn't me. It was a friend of mine. She's a coder for one of the Fintech companies in Shoreditch. Don't worry — I didn't show her anything,' he quickly added before Hume could reprimand him for involving a civilian. 'I had transposed the cuts into lines on my tablet and was playing around. She doesn't know they're from a body.'

'Are you stepping out with a coder, Echo?' said Hume. 'Isn't that a bit insular? What about the dentist?'

'She's not my girlfriend,' said Echo. Hume could feel the heat of his blush all the way across the river. 'And I'm not a coder. Nothing like her, anyway. I can use computers, assimilate data, stuff like that. She's the real deal. She looks at computers like she can see the Matrix.'

'I have absolutely no idea what you're talking about, Echo. What does the code say?'

'HCF,' he said. 'It stands for "halt and catch fire". It's an idiom referring to machine code.'

'Still no idea,' said Hume. She watched her husband as he leaned against the rail and took a sip of his wine.

'A kill code, if you like,' said Echo bluntly. 'You punch the kill code into a computer that's malfunctioning and it closes it down. Permanently.'

Hume stared at the lights of Canary Wharf opposite. The towers of Canada Square were thick and Lego-like compared to the Shard but somehow seemed more classic.

'So that's what our killer believed he was doing to Alice — shutting her down?' murmured Hume, a coldness spreading inside her. 'Like an infected computer.'

'That's got to be what it means. He's a coder, or at least he was, back in the day. That's what I'm thinking,' said Echo, excited. 'And he must know Alice, or at least have access to her history.'

'What history? To her medical records, you mean?' said Hume sceptical. 'I think that's a reach.'

'I know it sounds that way, but it must be that. He must've known she was damaged for the code to make sense. Plus, I've been thinking . . .'

'And what have you thought?'

There was a pause. Hume knew what he was going to say. She smiled at her husband, who had turned to look at her, eyebrows raised in a question. She shook her head, mouthing 'sorry'. He rolled his eyes, shrugged, and drained his wine.

'Actually, hold those thoughts and meet me in the office,' she said. 'I'm on my way.'

Hume ended the call, linked her arm through her husband's, and began searching for a taxi.

* * *

Lately I've been thinking about my past. All the shit I've tucked away over the years. My son doesn't know about any of it. Nothing. As far as he's concerned, I'm just ordinary.

Well, as ordinary as anyone else in this fucked-up society. Enough to fool him and the school and all the little ants. They don't know a thing.

Nothing about the prostitution. Nothing about the drugs. And absolutely nothing about the other stuff. Not even his mother knew about that.

And of course, when I say 'son', It's a bit of a loaded term. I only met his mother after he was born. When he was a baby.

He doesn't know that, either.

Stepson? It sounds old-fashioned, like something out of a fairy tale. Probably not the right term, anyhow.

Maybe it's just 'son' now. Or maybe people just go with first names. Everything is fluid these days, isn't it? Including life.

That's what they found out. What I've always known.

I think I'll just stick with 'son'.

Life. Love. The day-to-day shit you get caught up in. Like a dream that covers the real world.

Well, it's uncovered now.

I watch them on my phone.

Alice living her half-life. Bad programming from the start.

Jeremy in his collar and cross. Believing in the ghost in the machine.

David in his bubble of choice. Letting nature determine lifestyle.

All of them frozen inside the K-hole. Watching me fix them. Deprogram them.

Really, they were all waiting for me. Waiting for me to set them free.

I have a list. It wasn't hard to get. You'd think somewhere like that would be more careful, wouldn't you?

Fucking imbeciles.

It was so easy for me to get the list, and now that I've started on it I have never felt so alive. I should have got it years ago.

It's as if each one is giving me their spark. Their unused potential. Flames to the fire.

I look at the names on my phone. Two left.

Which one next, I wonder?

I know where one of them is. Of course I do.

But I think I'll go for the other one first.

CHAPTER 31

When Luke regained consciousness, he entered a world of pain. That was OK. In fact, it was better than OK. Pain was life. Pain meant he wasn't dead.

Carefully, he opened his eyes. He was propped up against the wall of the Wendy house. He'd been dragged inside, presumably by the woman, and the door closed behind him.

Which meant she didn't want him dead. If she'd left him outside in plain view he'd be carrion by now. The street vultures would have stripped him clean. Taken his phone and his money and his drugs.

His drugs.

Panicking, Luke reached around for his backpack, the movement almost causing him to black out again. His breath rasped from his damaged throat as he tried not to vomit. There was a deep well of pain in his groin where the bitch had rammed her knee into him, but worst of all was the freezing fear that enveloped his brain when he realised the backpack wasn't there.

He flicked his gaze around the space, hoping that perhaps she'd taken it off him and left it against the wall.

Nothing.

Luke swallowed, causing another spasm of pain.

He was fucked. Double-fucked with bells on.

If he was late making his deliveries then that would be difficult, but not a shutdown. He could explain his way out of it. Especially with his injuries. But if he didn't have the drugs at all . . .

Luke tried to move, to pull himself into a crouch, but all he did was blur his vision and fill his mouth with bile. He blinked away his tears and spat. His phlegm was flecked with blood, suggesting some serious damage to the inside of his throat.

'Fucking bitch,' he croaked, fighting through the pain and dragging himself to his knees.

She'd taken his backpack of drugs. She'd taken them and, in doing so, signed his ticket. There would be nowhere safe for him in London. No postcode. No estate. It wouldn't matter what he said or how beaten-up he was. They'd think he'd sold them. Or even if they didn't, it wouldn't matter. The whole deal was he was an independent. Not affiliated, not protected. He'd have to pay.

Whichever way he looked at it he was a dead man walking, and he couldn't even fucking walk.

He reached for the door, sucking air down through his broken throat. It was like breathing broken glass. If he ever saw that detective again he was going to rip her head off.

The business card stuck to the door was off-white, with a dark-blue border. Luke squinted at it in the dark.

Raine
Private Detective

Underneath was scrawled:

Call me if you want your drugs back!

Under that was a hand-drawn smiley face.

Luke stared at it for a long beat, then tapped his pocket. He could feel the reassuring slab of glass and metal through the fabric of his jeans.

She hadn't taken his phone. Gritting his teeth, Luke took out the device, swiped it awake, and punched in the number on the card. It was answered before the first ring.

'Luke!' said the voice down the line. It was light and playful, and Luke wanted to reach through the mobile and rip out her vocal chords. 'How lovely to hear from you! Have you called me a bitch yet? I bet you have.'

'If you don't give me my bag back I'm going to fucking kill you!' hissed Luke, his fingers white with the pressure. 'I'm going to fuck you up so hard you'll wish—'

'Get over yourself, Luke!' said the detective, her laughter clear in his ear. 'You're not going to fuck anyone, possibly ever again. How are the balls, by the way?'

Luke said nothing, just gripped the mobile tighter.

'Thought so. Here's how it's going to work. You're going to meet me at this lovely late-night cafe I've found and we're going to have a nice chat about what you owe me.'

'What the fuck are you talking about?'

'And just in case you were thinking of getting some of your comically dressed friends to come with you, the drugs aren't here. I've given them to a colleague for safekeeping, and should I even get a whiff of something wrong, she will set fire to them and have herself the highest BBQ in the world. Are we clear?'

'What do you want?' said Luke, hate and fear jostling for attention in his voice.

'I want a new life-logger, Luke, and I want you to pick up my dental bill.'

'What?' Confusion swept over him. Was that what this was all about? Because he'd trashed her stupid video camera? He felt the phone vibrate against his head.

'I've just sent you the address of the cafe. It's not too far away, so you should be able to hobble here quite quickly.'

'If you don't give me my drugs . . .' Luke couldn't think of anything else to say. The woman seemed impervious to threats. 'What do you want? This can't be just about the logger.'

'I want to know who trashed my house and killed Heather,' said Raine. 'Was it you?'

'What?' Luke thought he might throw up again. His balls felt as though they were the size of mangoes and seemed to be generating their own heat. 'I haven't got a fucking clue what you're talking about—'

'See you in ten, Luke. If you're not here I'm leaving and you can kiss your drugs — and therefore, I suspect, your life — goodbye.' There was a click as she ended the call.

He stared at his phone in disbelief, then opened up the message the detective, Raine, had sent. It contained an address and a Google Maps pin.

Slowly, Luke left the Wendy house and began shuffling towards the road.

CHAPTER 32

Hume kissed her husband goodbye outside the police building and watched as the TX5 taxi drove silently away, carrying him back to their home.

She always kissed him. Always stayed watching. Just in case it was the last time. Because you never knew.

Once the taxi had turned the corner, its tail lights danger-red in the dark, she entered the building. Her office was on the fourth floor and as the lift carried her up, she pulled out her phone and sent a text to Raine. She had tried calling to thank her for the tip about the buttons, but Raine's phone seemed to be switched off. Although not seriously concerned, she was aware of a thin wire of worry at the back of her brain.

The lift stopped with barely a jolt and the doors opened. Hume stepped out into the main office space, causing a few of the overhead lights to wake. She could see the lights on in her office, partitioned off from the main room, and walked over past empty desks and even emptier chairs. When she entered, Echo was adding to the smartboard the information he had given her over the phone.

'I think we need to revisit David Webb,' he said before she even sat down. 'The reverend, too.'

'OK,' said Hume, pushing the chair away and leaning against her desk. 'Shoot.'

When Echo turned towards her, she could see the excitement dancing at the back of his eyes, like tiny fires. 'HCF. The code on Alice's chest—' he began.

Hume broke in impatiently. 'Halt and catch fire. You told me. Some sort of kill code for a faulty computer.'

'Not for the hardware, the *program*. A way of shutting it down before it can cause any damage.'

'OK,' said Hume again. 'So where does that get us?'

'Well, for one thing, I think we can now say for certain that the killer must know his way around computers. Or at least he did. Leetspeak — the text code he carved into Alice — is not something the average person would know about.'

'So he's a computer geek?'

'It's more than that. It's like . . .' Echo shook his head. 'What if he viewed her as a faulty piece of software?'

'What on earth are you talking about?'

'Halt and catch fire. What if he thought she was corrupted? Not in a moral way but . . . functionally. What if Alice's psychological and emotional problems offended him on . . . on a computational level? Like she was programmed wrong.'

Hume frowned but Echo was on a roll now: 'And he shut her down before she could infect him? Because she triggered something in him? Creepy, but not a million miles away from what Professor Flynn suggested. Something in Alice's make-up, or something in her past, could have reminded him of himself. Something that needed to be corrected, or wiped away completely.'

Echo looked expectantly at Hume, eager for a response, but she took her time. Eventually, she murmured: 'Maybe that's how the teeth tie in. They're like a USB stick or something? Injecting new DNA. Like a computer code?'

Echo seemed unsure, but Hume was already switching course. 'OK. Why do we need to look at David Webb again?'

'Remember I said there was something off about Alice's phone?'

'The taxi app. You said the company had no record of her last journey.'

'Well, now we know that, in all probability, the killer is seriously computer-literate, maybe even at a coding level, then I think I know how he might have done it. How he might have got her into his car.'

'Really?' said Hume, leaning forward. 'How?'

'I think he used an MITM attack.'

'Yes,' said Hume, nodding. 'That's what I was thinking too.'

'Oh,' said Echo, surprised. 'I didn't know you—'

'I have absolutely no fucking idea what you're talking about, Echo. What's an MITM attack?'

'Ah, you're taking the piss out of me again, aren't you?'

Hume stared hard at him. 'I was having a lovely evening with my husband, Echo, that had a good chance of ending in some experimental yoga, so I don't want you to gabble in geek-speak or whatever. Just tell me what you know.'

Echo didn't know what experimental yoga was, and absolutely didn't want to find out. He swallowed and continued cautiously.

'MITM stands for "man in the middle". It's a cyber-attack term, like phishing. It means exactly what it says. Someone puts themselves digitally in the middle of a connection between two parties. Each of the parties believes they are talking to the other, when in fact they are talking to a hacker.'

'And that's possible, is it?' said Hume, amazed.

'It's more than possible. It's actually easy. You could just use SHODAN and a packet sniffer and— *Ow!*'

Hume had thrown a ball of paper at him. 'Speak English!'

Echo glared at her, then relaxed. 'Fine. All you have to do is get the encryption key off the victim's phone and you can position yourself between them and whoever they are trying to connect to. As long as you know what you're doing and the phone isn't secure — and most people's aren't — then it's not hard. You can look it up.'

'That's what I've got you for. So when Alice ordered a cab . . .'

'She wasn't speaking to the cab firm. She was speaking to the killer. Then he spoke to the cab firm as if he was Alice, getting the quote.'

'Jesus,' whispered Hume. She made a mental note to bring up communication security with her commander.

'And I think the same thing happened to David,' said Echo softly.

Hume looked at Echo. She noticed he was in his civvies and fleetingly wondered what he did with his evenings.

'Explain.'

'We checked David's phone for dating apps, right? And checked with the providers to see if he'd hooked up with anybody that night.'

'Yes, but they wouldn't release any information. Data protection. We're still waiting for the court to bring pressure to bear.'

'I don't think their info will help. If David hooked up with the killer through an app, it might not have been legit.'

This time Hume quickly picked up on his train of thought. 'You think it might have been another man-in-the-middle thing? A set-up to get David to trust his killer?'

Echo shrugged. 'If you're using these dating apps you trust them. People don't understand how easy it is to get phished. As far as David would know, him and his date were put together by the app. He wouldn't have thought twice.'

'And thinking he's on a real date, he takes the killer back for some no-strings sex and it only gets better when he's offered a party drug,' Hume added. 'Makes sense. What about the priest — Jeremy?'

'Same thing, perhaps. The killer could have got in the middle of a conversation and arranged a meeting. I'm not sure how it would work in detail, but . . . It's got to be worth a look, no?'

Hume thought about it, then pointed at Echo. 'OK. Arrange for the reverend's regular flock from the streets to be re-interviewed first thing. Get the team to ask if anybody tried to message the reverend and got an odd reply within the time-frame we have for his murder. I bet some of his congregation like to text him first — make sure they're safe.'

Echo began tapping at his tablet while Hume's thoughts turned to the reverend. His ministry of sex workers and homeless people — throwaways from society. She felt the weight of their plight like a stone in her stomach.

'And if this played out the way you think, then the killer must have had prior knowledge of each of the victims. And quite a lot of it. Which would suggest that he already knows what he's looking for. That he's not just being triggered by people he randomly sees in the street or whatever.'

Echo nodded. 'That's what I mean about him knowing them. He must've tracked them down specifically.'

Hume glanced back up at the board, at the names and faces and details of three snuffed-out lives.

'Which suggests there must be a connection between them that we're missing. And that either he knows them all personally, or he's searched them out.'

Hume could feel it in her gut; the twist of pressure that meant she was close to something. She tapped her fingernails on her desk. Finally, she looked at her young colleague.

'Computers,' she said. 'You think he's good with them, yes?'

'Got to be.'

'You said you thought he must have had access to Alice's medical records. To know where she would be. Maybe how to manipulate the situation to get her where he wanted.'

'It's what makes sense.'

'Agreed,' Hume said. 'So that's where we need to look. That's where we'll find the connection.' She pointed at the board. 'Jeremy, David and Alice. They must all be on a data-base somewhere. A club. Or a holiday destination. An online health-food shop. Something. Something that connects them all in cyberland.'

'Cyberland?'

'The internet. Online. Whatever you want to call it.'

'I actually like cyberland. Has a nice tone.'

'Good.' Hume shot him a sarcastic smile. 'I'm happy to help. Check out their history. There's got to be something there.' Hume had another thought. 'And see if there are any records of . . . leetspeak being used in any crimes. Go back as far as, say 1980. And don't forget the tooth angle. Maybe start with what your dentist said. Check out people in their twenties and late teens.'

'That's a big ask,' said Echo. 'A lot of stuff from that time won't have been digitised and put into the database. Plus she's not my dentist. I don't even like dentists.'

Hume shrugged.

'But you have got really nice teeth. See what you can find. We might get lucky. I'll ask the CI to allocate a couple of number crunchers to you. This feels like it's speeding up. We need to shut it down before it all goes south.'

She stood up and started walking to the door. 'That's it for tonight. I'm going home.'

Just before she left the office she turned and smiled at her partner. 'That was good work, tonight, Echo,' she said, softly.

He smiled tiredly back at her. 'Thanks.'

Hume suddenly realised it might have been the first time she had given him praise — and there was no mistaking the excitement dancing behind his eyes again.

'Go on then, tell me. I know you're dying to,' said Hume, raising her eyebrows.

'Tell you what?'

'What SHODAN stands for.'

Echo lit up. 'Sentient hyper optimized data access network. It—'

Hume held up her hand. Echo stopped speaking.

'There. I've let you say it. Now never repeat it. If you ever repeat it again, you're fired.'

Before he could answer she closed the office door. She was smiling all the way to the lift.

CHAPTER 33

Luke sat opposite Raine in the booth of the tiny cafe. Their seats were at the back of the room so there was no one to overhear their conversation.

'Where are my drugs?' hissed Luke. 'If I don't deliver them tonight then I'm a dead man.'

'Did you break into my place?' said Raine. 'Did you break into my place and kill my cat?'

'What the fuck are you talking about?' Luke looked genuinely confused.

'What about Heather?'

'Who's Heather?'

'The woman you assaulted in the alley. The woman you were going to rob. Did you kill her too?'

'What are you even saying here?' Luke's gaze slid around the cafe, checking to see if they could be overheard. 'I've never killed anyone.'

They were the only customers, and the owner was playing on his phone by the counter. Luke leaned forward.

'Look, lady, I—'

'Raine. My name is Raine. Like the weather, but with an "e" at the end.'

'Whatever. Raine. I was shaking down the woman in the lane, but that's all it was. A shakedown. Easy money until you turned up. I don't know nothing about your fucking cat. And I don't know nothing about no dead girl. Shit!'

Raine gazed at him for a long beat, unblinking. Luke felt his swollen balls trying to contract. There was something about the way she looked at him that made him want to run. He held her gaze for another beat then glanced away. Even then he could still feel her eyes boring into him.

'I believe you, Luke,' she said finally. 'Now tell me about the drugs.'

'They're not mine. I'm just UPS, man.'

'UPS?'

Luke turned back and stared at her like she was stupid. 'Yeah, UPS. Like the delivery van. And if I don't deliver them soon then it's game over, you get me?'

Raine nodded again. 'Where to?'

'Everywhere, man!' said Luke. 'All the postcodes this side of the river. Now, are you going to tell me where they are?'

Raine ignored his question and continued asking her own. 'And what are they?'

'What do you mean?'

'Don't fuck with me, Luke. What are they? Hardcore junky drugs? Party drugs? What?'

'Oh, right. Party. The lifers get their gear from other places.'

By 'lifers' he meant addicts. The people who weren't in it for the parties or as maintenance for their life choices. For the addicts, it *was* their life. Nothing else mattered until they stopped breathing.

'What are we talking? Coke? Molly?' said Raine. 'Speed?'

Luke sucked air through his teeth, clocking the manager again, lowering his voice to be sure the man couldn't hear.

'Like that, yeah. And if I don't deliver them—'

'What about ketamine? Special K?'

Luke shrugged again. 'Sure. Whatever makes the night bright, man.'

'I'm not a man, Luke,' Raine said patiently like she was talking to a child. 'I've told you that before, remember?'

The woman was deranged, that much was obvious. But whatever he had to do to get his drugs back he would do. After that, though . . . Luke felt a hard ball of anger growing in his stomach, but kept his face serene. 'I remember. Sorry.'

'And what about cocktails?'

'What do you mean?'

'Drug mixes. Do they come premixed, or is that something that happens down the line?'

'They're cut, yeah, but not mixed. Not in the way you mean.'

'So who mixes them?'

'The postcodes, lady. Before they hit the street. Different areas like different highs, if you get my drift.'

Raine noted that the road-ganger was saying almost exactly what she herself had said to Hume: that different demographics used drugs in different ways. She leaned forward, placing her hands palm-down on the scarred table, and grinned at Luke.

'Right, and which postcode mixes ketamine with Dezolam?'

Luke's eyes narrowed. He was coming to the conclusion that this wasn't about the woman's recording hardware, or the robbery in her crib, or even the murdered Muslim woman.

'Why do you want to know?'

'Just answer the question, Luke. Which postcode mixes ketamine with Dezolam? Is that a party cocktail? Big on the gay scene? What?'

Luke stared at her, calculating. 'Where are my drugs?'

'About five minutes from going up in flames if you don't answer my questions, road-boy. Who uses those particular combinations?'

'Can I get you guys anything else?'

Raine looked up and smiled at the manager. 'No thanks, James,' she said, reading the name off his tag. 'We're just finishing off here then we'll be out of your hair.'

The young man smiled back, then returned to his spot by the serving counter.

'Donkey Kong,' said Luke softly, watching the broad back of the manager as he retreated.

'What?'

'Dezolam and ketamine. Donkey Kong. That's what the kids call it. The mix. D for Dezolam; K for ketamine.'

'Right. And what kids are these? Gang kids?'

'Schoolkids.'

The tilt of Raine's head, coupled with the hardness in her gaze, sent a new shiver of fear through Luke.

'You sell drugs to schoolchildren?'

Luke shook his head quickly, causing the pain in his throat to flare. 'No, no. I'm just a delivery guy. I take the product to the 'codes and they distribute it. I don't have anything to do with the customers.'

'But you know who they are? You know which post-codes sell to the children?'

Luke shrugged his shoulders. 'They all sell to the kids, yeah? There's not a school in London that don't have a connection to gear. Fuck, half the kids are on Ritalin or some shit anyhow!'

'This particular combination, though — this isn't normal kiddie stuff, is it? Dezolam isn't just made in some smacker lab in the suburbs. It comes all the way from Japan.'

'Yeah. Donkey Kong is fairly exclusive,' Luke agreed. 'Just the plated schools. Wimbledon. Kingston. Places like that.'

'And which postcode gang covers Kingston, Luke?'

Luke licked his lips. 'What are you going to do?'

Raine smiled at him radiantly. 'I'm going to phone every contact in your mobile unless you tell me the name, Luke. I'm going to phone them all and tell them you've been working for the feds. I'm going to tell them you're snuggling so close to the boys and girls in blue that you're thinking of exchanging rings.'

'That would be like killing me,' said Luke, simply. 'That would be like cutting me up yourself.'

'Well, let that be a lesson to you. Never hit a lady. Last chance, Luke: which postcode gang?'

Luke saw the hardness in her eyes and wondered why he'd not noticed it that first night. All he'd seen was the young woman and the smile and the chance of some free fun. Had he seen what was behind the smile that night he'd have run a mile.

'Tick tock,' said Raine.

Luke blinked. And told her.

'Now that wasn't too hard, was it?' she said, standing up.

'Wait a minute,' said Luke hurriedly. 'We had a deal! Where's my—'

'We all good here?' The manager was back, hovering by the edge of the table.

Luke turned to tell him to fuck off, but stopped. The man was staring straight at him. In his hand was a short length of wood, planed and polished and stained with dark smudges that sent alarm bells ringing through Luke's already battered body.

'Hey, James,' said Raine softly. 'Yes, we're all good here.' She turned and looked at Luke. 'Luke, I'd like you to meet ex-police constable James. He runs this little cafe now, but previously he was a complete wrecking ball in the Met. Sadly, he got thrown out for his inability to fully grasp the command structure.'

James smiled. His teeth were straight and white and somehow terrifying.

Raine was talking again. 'Now, being an interesting gender-non-conformist kind of person, I don't normally rely on stereotypes, but on this occasion, I'm going to make an exception. Big, strong, manly James here is going to watch over you when I leave, so that you don't do anything silly. Then, in a few hours, when I've got the information I need, he's going to let you go.'

Raine leaned forward. 'And that's when it's going to get super interesting.'

'What are you going to do?' Luke felt his world slipping away. Everything he had so carefully constructed.

175

'I'm going to set a fire, Luke. I'm going to light a match under those dealers that'll be seen right across London.'

'You're killing me,' he said, his voice flat. 'If I don't supply the package—'

'I'm not going to give you the drugs back, Luke,' she said. 'I was never going to give you the drugs back. Sorry if you thought I was. Drugs kill people. What I am going to do, however, is give you a choice.'

Luke just gazed at her. It was like looking through a tunnel, he was so far inside himself. Back in the cave he used to hide in when he was five and being beaten by one of his 'uncles'.

'This is no life, Luke. Selling drugs. Jostling for a place on the pole. It will only end in jail or the morgue. Or, if you do manage to live on, having no soul.'

'It's my life, not yours,' said Luke.

Raine shook her head. 'Not anymore. Not by the morning. As you said, if you stay here, you're dead.' Raine took out a business card from her waistcoat and put it on the table. 'And like I said, you've got a choice.' She tapped the card. 'This is Detective Inspector Hume's number. A man like you, Luke, who delivers to all the postcodes in London, would have some very interesting information for her.'

Luke sucked in air between his teeth. 'Not going to happen.'

Raine shook her head slowly. 'You're still not getting it. Your old life is over. Without the drugs, no one in it is your friend. There is no loyalty because you have no future. Even if you say nothing and end up in jail you'll be dead within a week. People don't like their drugs being stolen.'

Luke knew she was right. He was trapped.

'However, if you provide enough information, the feds will set you up somewhere else. You'll have a chance to start again. Go to college, maybe. Become a painter or a poet or a carpenter. Some life that has a future.'

Raine was curious to see how Luke would respond. She didn't know if he had the strength to see past his present and imagine better things beyond. She hoped so.

'Alternatively, when I give him a call, James here will let you go and you can do what you like — run to your drug-bunnies or leg it out to the sticks. I really don't care.'

She looked down at him from where she was standing. Luke felt as if he were a child again.

'Whatever you decide, I hope you've told me the truth, because if I turn up and it's not like you say it is, then James is going to double the number of bones in your body by breaking them all in half.'

She smiled and pointed two fingers at him, her thumb in the air. She shot him with an imaginary bullet. 'And you still owe me a life-logger.'

CHAPTER 34

Hume was woken by her phone. She stabbed at it with a finger before it made its second ring, slipping out of bed as she did so.

'Hume,' she whispered into the mouthpiece, walking quickly into the next room, hoping Robert's sleep hadn't been disturbed. The early morning sun had tried to beat its way through the cloud cover, but only a few shards had made it, streaking the day outside her window with smudges of grey.

'We've had confirmation back from the lab. The buttons found at the scene of Alice's murder weren't part of the general detritus. Plus the lack of any dirt on them suggests they were deposited there recently.'

'Meaning?'

'Meaning there's a strong possibility the buttons are from the killer. How could Raine have known that?' Echo's voice was full of wonder.

'Echo? What time is it? Have you even been home?'

'I stayed in the bunk. How could she know about the buttons? All she had to go on were the media feeds.'

Hume looked at her watch. It was just before six. The 'bunk' was the name for the small dorm in the basement where officers could get some sleep if they were on double shifts.

'I don't know,' she said, scanning her phone for messages. 'She still hasn't got back to me.' Hume felt a twinge of worry, like a strum on a guitar string. She had left several messages for Raine. Since the death of her misper, Heather, Raine seemed to be coming slightly unhinged. Then there had been the canal-boat break-in and the bludgeoning of her cat. Hume sighed.

Or maybe not. Raine had always been slightly unhinged. Even before . . . Hume felt the strum again and shut it away.

'So what else did the lab say? About the buttons?'

There was silence for a few seconds, and Hume imagined Echo swiping and tapping his tablet.

'Three buttons were found in a disturbed area of the floor fifteen metres to the south of Alice's body. Forensics point to this being the area where Alice was murdered, and then the body was moved to where we found it. The buttons are black plastic resin, with frayed ends of thread still attached.'

'Which could mean Alice put up a fight,' said Hume, feeling the excitement build, the grey day outside forgotten. 'Was there anything under her fingernails? DNA? Fibres?'

'Nothing. It seems that whatever the buttons were attached to was smooth, with no purchase for fibre transfer.'

'Like they were wearing a protective coat or something. Plastic, maybe.'

'The lab is thinking raincoat. Something synthetic that wouldn't allow for any snagging.'

Hume nodded. 'Check the tooth. Maybe we'll find something on that. In fact, check all the teeth and cross-reference them. Was Alice given a different mix of drugs? Is that why she was able to fight back?'

'The working hypothesis is that she was somewhat acclimatised. She was already on some fairly strong stimulants for her own medical conditions. Possibly just enough to keep her on the right side of comatose. Just enough for her to fight back.'

Hume pictured the young girl, stripped and pliant, suddenly lashing out at her murderer, grabbing hold of him. Ripping his raincoat open.

'Hang on a minute. If she had enough in her to fight back, and was near enough and strong enough to tear buttons off his coat, how come she didn't go for his face? You'd expect at least a slash. Some blood or DNA somewhere.'

'That was my question, too. The lab has taken the entire floor apart and they haven't found a thing.'

There was a tone in Echo's voice — as if he couldn't quite believe it. Outside Hume's window, London was pulling itself out of its slumber. She could see street cleaners and gym-jumpers on the pavement below her. She felt slightly groggy. She'd like to go to the gym herself before work. Maybe have a swim. She looked at her husband. They had been together for such a long time, but she knew it would never be long enough. Even if she lived to be a hundred, it would never be long enough.

A devil with wings.

That's what the sex worker, Miss Frane, had told them she'd seen in that abandoned factory.

'What about the databases? Has anything turned up?'

'What? The thing we discussed four hours ago?' Echo's voice was incredulous. 'You think I've had time to set all that up?'

Hume smiled, walking through her apartment towards the shower room. 'Sleeping in the bunkroom, Echo? Rubbish. It's such a giveaway. You've been tip-tapping away all night.'

She heard a sigh slip down the phone.

'Fair enough. I've set up some meta-searches.' Before Hume could say anything, he forestalled her. 'Don't worry. I'm not going to tech you out. All you need to know is that I've rigged up a program with all the info we have from the three victims and set a search going. All public records. PNC. Adoption services. Facebook. Anything in the public domain.'

'Facebook?' queried Hume doubtfully.

'2.6 billion monthly users. Biggest database in the world. Plus another God knows how many shadow profiles.'

'I don't even want to know what a shadow profile is,' said Hume.

'Look it up. It'll scare you to death.'

'I'll take your word for it.'

'One thing. I was doing research on the chemical make-up of the buttons. To see if I could narrow them down to a source . . .'

'Yes,' said Hume, switching on the bathroom light. 'Anything?'

'Did you know over half the world's buttons are made in one town in China? It's called Qiaotou. Isn't that amazing?'

Hume pictured Echo, hunched over his tablet, excited by his discovery. She imagined a Red Bull energy drink next to him. Possibly some computer game open in another tab. Then she wiped the image, replacing it with a tired police officer who was so involved with his case he was prepared to stay up all night working on it.

'Go and actually *use* the bunk, Echo. Get some sleep. Meet me in the office in two hours and we'll review.'

Hume ended the call, stripped, and got in the shower.

CHAPTER 35

Raine sipped her coffee, scanning the video, reviewing all the footage DI Conner had sent through to her. He had split it into private and professional groups. The private footage came from bystanders' mobiles. The professional stuff was mainly CCTV from the various offices around the square where the murder had occurred.

She glanced up and checked the clubhouse in the flat light of the early morning. Luke hadn't given her bad information; the place was clearly a distribution centre. She had observed mopeds and pushbikes coming and going throughout the night. Even the odd electric scooter. Boys and girls just under the age to go to big jail, taking satchels of drugs to wherever they needed to go. If they got caught, so what? They wouldn't do any serious time in custody. And by the time they were old enough to work on more dangerous stuff they were already so deep in the life that they would never flip. Never give up the people they'd worked for. Because they knew nothing else. It was a closed circuit of hopelessness, with no way out offered except a knife, or surviving long enough to become an OG. A gang leader.

Raine wondered when it had happened. When the life choices of young people like Luke had become so predestined.

Poverty was one rod. And a lack of attention in the education sector — systemically failing the people it was meant to emancipate — was another. But mainly, she suspected, it was just prejudice and racism. The system grinding up the meat of the city to grease its own wheels.

Right now, though, it was a ghost-house. Nothing moving inside or out.

'Another five minutes,' she muttered, then turned her attention back to the phone.

Heather's murder crouched inside her like a spider, eating its way through her. Gnawing at her thoughts until there was a permanent itch in her head. She watched the feeds. Saw the body of Heather on the ground, her head just a smudge. None of the footage actually showed the kill-shot but the screams came through in high fidelity. As did the van speeding away. Conner had said the vehicle had been found abandoned near Vauxhall. No prints, meaning it had been wiped down, adding to the theory that it was a mistaken gang hit.

Raine had texted back, thanking him and asking if they had any intel as to where the van had been stolen from, and when?

Seeing Heather's body twisted something inside her. The young woman's skirt had ridden up her body when she had been thrown off her feet to the concrete, exposing her legs. Raine found that more upsetting than the blown-off face. The face was just meat, impossible to rationally relate to anything Heather had been before. But the exposed legs, pale brown and not meant to be seen without permission, were somehow more shocking. As if Heather had been discarded by life, thrown aside as if she didn't matter.

Raine spent a few more minutes randomly searching through the footage. Hearing the gunshot and the screams. Watching the van drive away, its wheels bouncing over the dead woman like she was nothing.

Raine's eyes blanked for a moment, then she played the footage again.

And again.

As the van drove away, just for a moment, she caught a glimpse of something that jarred in her. She paused the video and framed it back until she saw what it was.

On the opposite side of the square was a builder's skip, full of cardboard and rubbish bags. And the shape of a man.

Raine swiped, expanding the image. The man in the skip, presumably homeless, was unidentifiable, grainy and blurred and out of focus. But Raine could tell one thing: he was looking straight at the van.

'Well, well,' she muttered, screenshotting the image and sending it to Conner with a brief explanation. Then she put her phone away and drained the last of her coffee. 'Five minutes are up.' She tossed her cup in an overflowing green bin next to her.

The time to walk into a drug depot was not in the middle of the night. The night was when it did business. The night was the worst time. Just after dawn was best. When the party was dying down and everybody was tired. When the drugs that had kept them going through the night were wearing off and all that was left was the vodka that they'd used to knock off the edges of the amphetamines. No time like the present, then.

Raine didn't know what she was about to do but she knew it wouldn't be very sensible. She shook her head, trying to clear the image of Heather from her mind. If the murder of the woman was a drug hit gone wrong then, for all Raine knew, it might be this one. Two birds with one stone.

She waited until she saw a roadman slouch his way out of the clubhouse and up the street. He was tall and, despite the lateness of his working day, moved like oil. Even from her vantage point, she could tell he was dangerous. Good. Dangerous was what she needed.

She took a slow breath, then stepped out of the alley where she'd been hiding. She was wearing her best steel-toe-capped Docs and grasped a telescoping police baton in her right hand. She didn't have a knife or a gun because she wasn't stupid. PI or not, if she was stopped with anything other than personal protection on her, then she would be losing her licence as well as her liberty. She started crossing the road to fall in behind the man ahead of her. She held the baton in place by her sleeve, ready to be released when needed. She wasn't kidding herself. She would get only one opportunity to take him down. He wasn't Luke, all bluster and cock-modelling. He was the real deal: dead-eyed and in it for life. She could see the ink on the back of his neck, dark and angry and clearly done on the lo-fi — tattoos stamped by hand with a knife or a steel pin. Half ink and half scarification. No-turning-back markers that said you were in with both feet.

Raine felt her chest tightening, and gripped the baton a little harder. The roadman ran a bony hand through his hair and clocked a half glance in a window he was passing. Raine was fairly sure he was checking her out. That he had felt her presence. She wondered if Luke had managed to overpower James and warn them in some way, then immediately dismissed the thought. The man was just good at his job. Professional paranoia mixed with a killer instinct. It was now or never. If she gave him anymore time he might turn and stick her before she could do anything.

Because it was one hundred per cent certain he would have a knife. They all had knives.

Around the corner, in front of them, a youth appeared. He had headphones on and his eyes were cast down. When Raine saw him she immediately changed her plans. She took out her phone and held it to her ear.

'Beth!' she said to the dead silence of her mobile. 'I can't find the bagel place anywhere!' She crossed the road, feeling the roadman's eyes on her. 'What? Oh, I think I must've gone past it. Hang on.' She started walking back the way she had come, not turning around. With the youth there, even with his downward stare and his headphones, she felt the roadman wouldn't push. He would think she was just another hipster chick, out in the slums looking for a cheap new property or whatever. A future customer, maybe. Getting the drop on the early bird.

She didn't care. By the time she'd passed the clubhouse on the other side of the road, chatting to the non-existent Beth about muffins, she didn't feel his eyes on her, and she turned into the alley, immediately spinning round and peering back along her route.

The roadman was gone. The only person on the street was the youth. Which was perfect, because it was the youth she wanted.

Donkey Kong is fairly exclusive. Just the plated schools. Wimbledon. Kingston. Places like that.

That's what Luke had said.

The boy was wearing a generic black hoodie, but Raine could see his school uniform underneath. She didn't know much about which schools wore what, but she was fairly certain that the boy was not from any school in this neighbourhood. He was too clean-cut and un-street. No one in their right mind would be caught walking around here with their head down, wearing an expensive pair of headphones. Headphones like that would be attached to an expensive phone, for sure. In fact, the only way the schoolboy hadn't been stripped of his expensive toys already was either because he was extremely lucky — or extremely protected.

Raine watched as the boy turned into the clubhouse. He didn't look furtively round to check he wasn't being observed. Raine smiled humourlessly. *Protected it was.*

He didn't look round because he wasn't here to buy drugs. He was here to pick them up and sell them. He was the last link in the chain.

If you wanted to sell drugs to the middle-class boys and girls in their middle-class school you didn't plant a scary roadman at the school gates. You planted a nice middle-class boy who needed extra cash. You got an inside man.

Raine's smile widened as the boy disappeared inside the clubhouse.

CHAPTER 36

Hume's phone buzzed just as her car was crossing Westminster Bridge. She checked the ident: Raine. The picture that accompanied it was an old one, from back when she was still on the force. Hume had not yet updated it.

'Raine. I've been trying to reach you.'

'Sorry, I've been tidying up some loose ends.'

'Concerning the break-in?'

'No, but while we're on the subject, did Techno-boy manage to do anything with my laptop?'

'I don't think he'd like to be called Techno-boy,' grinned Hume.

'Hotpants?' Raine offered. 'I bet he's a hit in the romance department. Slim. Young. Just the right side of indie. You've seen the tattoo in his ear, right?'

'Yes. I think it's tribal.'

'I think it's woofy. If only I was that way inclined I might try to lick it.'

Hume sighed. She was too tired for banter. 'I'll ask him about the laptop. How did you get to the buttons, by the way?'

'Buttons?'

'Alice Watkins. The girl in the abandoned factory.'

'Right. It was the devil with wings.'

Raine kept her eyes on the door of the clubhouse. The schoolboy had been in there for five minutes. If he wasn't out in another two, she was going to hand it over to Hume. She might be a little wired but she wasn't mad enough to attempt a home invasion on a gang clubhouse.

'The witness statement?' Hume was saying.

'The sex worker, yes. The media made her out to be stupid, but she wasn't young. She was middle-aged.'

'So?'

'So, you don't survive that long out on the street by being stupid.'

Silently, Hume agreed. At the roadside, the pavement was blocked by concrete barriers. After the terrorist attack on Westminster, they had been installed to make sure no car could mount the pedestrian walkway. Hume thought they were ugly. She thought it would be better to just ban cars. Maybe have trams instead.

'So, you're saying she's not delusional. She's in shock. But what did she see if it wasn't wings?'

'A flapping coat — maybe made out of something shiny. Maybe lightweight and very mobile as he ran. It probably wouldn't have been open when he attacked his victim, but it was when he ran away. Hence the buttons.'

Hume pictured it. The gloom of the empty warehouse. The sight of a sinister figure running through it. It was entirely possible that Raine was right.

'And the devil part? Did she conjure up some horns, too?'

'What time is it?' said Raine.

Hume peered out of the car, up at Big Ben.

'Just gone seven. Why?'

'Bit early to go to school, then, do you suppose?'

'What are you talking about, Raine?'

'Nothing. I don't know about the devil bit. Maybe the killer is badly scarred? Something that made him seem demonic in the half-light, anyway.'

'Where are you?' said Hume. 'You sound like you're outside. Are you on a case?'

'Just tying up loose ends, as I said. By the way, would you like to come to my boat on Saturday? I'll have Melania's ashes back by then, and I'm going to scatter them in the canal.'

'Is that legal?'

'Irrelevant. It's what I'm doing and I'd like you to come. Robert, too, if he wants.'

Hume looked back at the clock looming overhead. Hearing Raine mention her husband left a tight band across her chest.

'I'm not sure, Raine.'

'No worries. I'll ping the address over anyway. I'll do it via Maps because there's no way you'll find it by a postcode.'

'I wasn't aware boats even had postcodes.'

'How are you getting on with finding a connection between your victims?'

Hume frowned. Raine was sounding even more manic than usual. 'Have you been to bed yet?' she enquired, concern in her voice.

'Only I might have a lead on the drug angle.'

'Raine! I've expressly asked you not to—'

'I've got to boogie,' said Raine abruptly, ending the call.

* * *

From her hiding place in the alley, Raine watched as the boy in the school uniform came out of the clubhouse. He turned and said something to whomever was inside. Raine saw that he had a backpack on, not dissimilar to the one she had taken from Luke. The boy shut the door and started walking back the way he had come. Raine snapped a photo on her phone as he walked away.

CHAPTER 37

As soon as Hume walked into the office Echo broke off his conversation with DC Jonas, the data technician assigned to the team, and hurried over to her. The dark circles under his eyes told Hume he hadn't taken her advice to grab a couple of hours' rest, instead remaining at his desk, working.

'It's the same thing! We've checked David and Jeremy's phones again. Even without full access it's clear. They both have classic MITM signifiers.'

'The attack thing?' asked Hume, shutting the door.

Echo nodded.

'So there's our connection.' Hume took off her jacket and hung it behind the door. 'The killer knows the victims. Enough to collect the information he needs from their phones, anyhow. And enough to know he wants them dead.' She stopped, suddenly struck by something. 'Did we get anything back on other similar crimes? Other murders with the code thing . . . ?' she looked at Echo inquiringly.

'Leetspeak,' he offered.

'With a leetspeak connection? Or any sort of text code?'

'Nothing yet,' said Echo. Tiny lines were forming around his eyes that no amount of coffee could hide. 'But it's only been a few hours. Plenty about teeth, but nothing that matches our demographic.'

'What about teeth?'

Echo grimaced. 'Let's just say amateur dentistry plays a part in certain gangland negotiations.'

Hume grimaced in return. 'Right. Don't tell me any more.'

Echo yawned, showing his perfectly uniform, non-English, apparently better-than-average Maori teeth.

'You didn't use the bunk, did you?' reprimanded Hume. 'All you did was drink more coffee, or Red Bull.'

'Both,' grinned Echo. When he smiled, he looked about ten. Hume suspected he would break some girl's heart. Possibly the coder he'd mentioned. Or the dentist. Probably not the dentist. She'd just cocoon him in her web and save him for a snack.

'You'll regret it by this afternoon. Here's a question for you. Why now?'

'What do you mean?'

'Why start now? Assuming he hasn't been quietly doing it forever. What started him off? What's the catalyst?'

Echo shrugged. 'The professor thought it was something from the killer's past. Something he recognised in the people he killed. Some code only he could see.'

Hume shook her head, beginning to pace around the small office. 'But that doesn't work, does it? To do the phone-attack thing he has to have already singled them out. Has to already be familiar with their routine, so that when he commits the murder he knows he can get away with it.'

'Right. So, unless each of the victims triggered the same response in him, which seems unlikely, there must be some other connection.'

Hume sat on the edge of her desk.

'It was the flapping of the wings, by the way. That's what alerted Raine to the buttons.'

Echo glanced at her, confused, then his face cleared. 'Alice.'

'When the murderer fled the scene, his coat trailed behind him, because Alice Watkins had ripped the buttons off.'

'Of course.' Echo clicked his fingers. 'That makes sense, but how did—'

'How did Raine make the connection?' smiled Hume. Echo nodded.

'That's what she does. What she's always done. She makes connections. Joins up dots before the rest of us have even realised they're there.'

Hume's smile slipped into something else. It took Echo a moment to recognise what it was. Loss.

'That's what made her want to leave the force, in the end.' Her gaze went somewhere else, then snapped back. 'Right. I need to go and brief the chief on all this. While I do that, you can see if anything new has come in from the lab, or if we're on a roll and hit any jackpots connecting databases with our victims.'

Hume glanced up at the smartboard, then walked out of the office. Two seconds later, just as Echo was reaching into his desk for an emergency Red Bull, she walked back in.

'Oh, and Raine asked if you'd managed to do anything with her laptop?'

'Actually,' said Echo, trying to surreptitiously hide the energy drink behind his tablet, 'I have. It was just a matter—'

'Not interested in the technical. Send her what you've got, will you?'

'OK, boss.'

'And stop drinking that shit. Your heart will explode and your skin will erupt. Then how are you going to marry the coder?'

Echo opened his mouth to protest, but Hume had already disappeared. He stared at the empty doorway for a beat, then reached for his phone.

CHAPTER 38

Lucy was so excited she felt it in every atom in her body. Fizzing and whizzing and making her brain froth with anticipation.

She was getting married! She still couldn't believe it. The question had finally been asked and she had said yes.

She looked at herself in the mirror, although her image kept on jumping about as though her eyeballs were vibrating, and she couldn't concentrate. The excitement was dizzying.

At twenty-nine, soon to be knocking on the door of thirty, she had thought she'd be single for ever. That she would end up living by herself, doing some shitty job, then dying alone and being eaten by her cat. She'd read about it. Old people who snuff it and don't get found for months. Sometimes years.

Lucy blinked and slowly began cleaning the make-up off her face. She didn't know why she was thinking about lonely people now, when what she should be thinking about was hot young people, or more specifically, one hot young person.

Well, not that young, but definitely hot. Most definitely hot.

The man of her dreams. Older than her, yes, but that was a good thing. He'd been around the block a few times.

Quite a few times. He knew what was what; what he wanted. And what he wanted was Lucy.

Smiling, she messaged her dressmaker. She knew it was an unnecessary expense, going the designer route, but she'd waited so long for this to happen, there was no way she was going to have an off-the-rack number. As soon as he had popped the question she had gone tip-tapping online, searching for a company in her area and price range who could make her something bespoke. Something that would make the whole wedding unique. She had been incredibly lucky. One of the companies she'd approached seemed to understand exactly what she wanted, as if they already knew what she was thinking. And the person they'd assigned to be her dressmaker . . . well, they were perfect.

Hi. It's me. Are you on your way? she typed.

She put the phone down and examined herself in the mirror; looked at her eyes that were now crowed with fine lines and her nose, broken two years ago on a skiing holiday in the Alps. Her brows, which she fully intended to Botox the hell out of before the big day, and her slightly yellow teeth — she wondered if she could somehow afford to get them veneered.

Her phone buzzed, indicating a message.

Unique dresses.
Because no two people are cut from the same cloth.

Lucy beamed.

You see, that's what you paid for, as much as the dress itself. The personal touch. You didn't get that from sodding Primark. She swiped the message open.

Hi Lucy. I've got something special for you. Are you alone?
It's a bit saucy and I/we wouldn't want the future Mr Lucy
to see!

Lucy read through the message and laughed. She'd also asked her dressmaker to design something for the honeymoon. Something . . . exotic. Because the future Mr Lucy had been round the block a few times. Quite a few times. He'd already seen most things. Lucy was going to have to think out of the box if she was going to make the wedding night something memorable.

Feeling excited, Lucy tapped back:

Just me and the cat! Let me know when you're here and I'll buzz you in. x

She put the phone back on the side and smiled shyly into the mirror. The bulbs around the edges, washing her face in warm light like a 1940s film star. Maybe she'd have a little drink? If her dressmaker had made her something a little kinky she might need a teeny-tiny bit of wine just to get over her nerves. She felt a gentle pressure on her bare shin and smiled down at her cat.

'What do you think, Mittens? Shall we have a teeny-tiny drink?'

Mittens purred and wove between her ankles like a salamander. Lucy nodded.

'You're so right, Mittens. We don't need a teeny-tiny drink. We need a massive one.'

CHAPTER 39

Raine felt her phone vibrate as she watched the boy enter through the gates of the school. Almost immediately he was surrounded by fellow students. She noted that it wasn't just kids in his year. Some were clearly older, some younger. Some stepped around him like guards while others vied for his attention, laughing and jostling, happy to be in his ambit. The boy himself seemed to revel in the attention, joking and low-fiving his crew.

Raine sighed. She'd give the boy five years before he was in jail, dead or buried in the business.

Because he already had 'drug dealer' written all over him. The fact that he was not living on some estate in a tracksuit with street-eyes didn't mean a thing. The people from whom he got his supplies would kill him in a snap if he stepped out of line. And the kids he was selling to would be just as prone to addiction, no matter what sort of house they lived in. No matter how many societies their parents were members of. Maybe more so, because they assumed that nothing could touch them.

Her eyes never leaving the boy, Raine took the buzzing phone out of her pocket.

'Raine, it's Echo.'

The boy disappeared into the building.

'Echo, how's it going?'

'Good. Look, I got your number off DI Hume. She said—'

'Have you managed to find my laptop yet?'

Raine began walking down the street. Even though it was a nice neighbourhood she kept her senses on full. The boy had just strolled into school with a backpack probably full of drugs and worth a lot of money. It was entirely possible that whoever he was dealing for would have put a ghost on him. Someone to make sure he went exactly where he was meant to go, without any unscheduled stop-offs.

'Actually, that's why I'm calling. You were right; you'd left the laptop hot. Just in sleep mode. I've been able to data-trail it through the telemetry. Once I had the IP address of the Wi-Fi it was connected to, I phished it. Even when they moved it—'

'Echo, what does Hume do when you start talking techno-porn to her?' interrupted Raine.

There was a pause.

'She throws things at me.'

Raine grinned. 'Consider something thrown. What's the takeaway?'

'I've found your laptop.'

'Wow, that's fantastic!'

'Or at least I know where it was.'

Raine slid into the doorway of a solicitors' office. The windows were boarded up and the door had a padlock on it. Even in the well-to-do areas of South London, the economy was tanking. Amid the middle-class cleanliness, there were closed shops and grimy-looking alleys, like little tumours waiting to turn malignant.

'Where?'

'Well, using the email client you gave me I was able to triangulate—'

'Throwing something, Echo.'

'Come on! You've got to let me show off a little bit! I've been up all night on the code murders and need a boost.'

'How's that going?'

Raine checked out the street. On the other side of the road, a tall youth walked by, his earphones disconnecting him from the outside world. No threat.

'We're actually making progress, I think,' said Echo cautiously. He knew Raine had some sort of special relationship with his boss but didn't want to compromise any aspect of the case. 'Good call on the buttons, by the way. That was quite a . . . leap to get there from the description of the wings.'

'Thanks. So what about the laptop?'

There was another pause as Echo adjusted.

'Right. Well, I've tracked it from your address and across London. It was opened and used at several locations in the capital before being transported somewhere else. The last data point I have for it is a motorway service station on the M1. Since then, it's been dead.'

'Dead?'

'Maybe the thief turned the machine off, or it ran out of power. Maybe it hasn't been opened again. Whatever, it hasn't connected to the internet since yesterday.'

'Right. Thank you. Very impressive. No wonder Hume sings your praises.'

Raine mulled over what Echo had said.

'What do you think? Why was it stolen?' she asked, vaguely watching a young mother pushing an expensive-looking pram but engrossed in the screen of her phone. Raine wondered if she'd notice if the baby in the pram were swapped.

'The laptop? Judging by the jumps around London, then the possible trip up north, I imagine it's a gang. Possibly from Birmingham or Manchester. Going on a burglary spree across London, collecting any hardware, laptops, phones, things like that, then selling them. Maybe mining them for data first. Any phone with a payment app: it's as good as stealing a bank card.'

'And the last hit was on the motorway?'

'The M1, yes. Heading north.'

'Can you send me the trail? Of where it went after it left me?'

'Sure, but all it will be is a red line on Google Maps with time-stamps.'

'Sure. Ping it over to me, please. And Echo . . . ?'

'Yes?'

'Thanks. I really appreciate it.'

'No problem.'

Even through the tiredness in his voice Raine could hear the warmth.

'Have you found the mask yet?' she asked.

There was another pause, longer this time.

'What mask? What are we talking about now?'

From somewhere inside the school a bell rang, indicating the beginning of lessons. Or maybe a pre-lesson breakfast club. The boy she had followed seemed to get to school super early. But then, she surmised, he probably had a fair amount of business to do before lessons began.

'What time does school finish?' said Raine.

'Sorry? What school?'

'Secondary school. What do you think? Three? Three thirty?'

'I have absolutely no idea, Raine. What's that got to do with masks?'

'Nothing. It's just something I'm working on.' Raine did not want to mention her conversation with Luke yet. She wasn't even sure what it meant. There were probably a hundred schools in South London alone that had in-house dealers. But maybe not that many selling Donkey Kong.

'So, what did you mean about the mask?' Echo repeated.

Raine closed her eyes momentarily. When she opened them, the woman pushing the pram had gone.

'It's just the way the sex worker reported what she saw. Or maybe it was the way she was reported in the paper. Like she was dumb or something. People never really pay attention to people they don't respect, do they?'

'I'm not sure—'

'Like with the wings. If she'd been a "regular" person they wouldn't have written her off as an unreliable witness. They would have searched for another interpretation of what she said.'

There was another silence.

'Look, Raine—' began Echo.

'Don't worry; I'm not criticising you. It's just the way it was reported. It really makes me angry. Everyone deserves respect.'

'Even the killer?' said Echo softly.

'Fair point,' acknowledged Raine.

'What were you saying about a mask?'

'The witness said she saw a devil with wings, yes?'

'Yes.'

'And they really looked like wings to her. In the gloom and the fear.'

'Yes,' said Echo again.

'So?'

'So what?'

'We know what gave her the idea of the wings, but what about the face of the devil? Either the killer is really ugly, or . . .'

'Or he wore a mask,' said Echo, hooking onto her drift. The tiredness that had clogged his voice was completely gone. 'DNA on the inside of it. Jesus, Raine! If we can find the mask—'

'Which he might have dumped somewhere.'

She expected Echo to answer her, maybe share something else, but instead there was silence. 'Echo? Are you still there?'

Still no answer. Frowning, Raine peered at her phone to check she was still connected.

'Echo?'

'It can't be . . .' His voice was faint, like it was coming from far inside of him.

'What? What is it?'

'Sorry, Raine. I've got to go. I'll ping you over the laptop info. I need to find my DI.'

'What is it, Echo? What have you found?'

'Something impossible. Just come through from the lab.'

'What?'

There was no answer. Echo had ended the call.

CHAPTER 40

'I don't believe it,' Echo whispered, looking at the latest lab report. The sounds of the building ramping up for the day seemed to fade away as he took in the information. He couldn't make sense of what he was seeing. Almost on auto-pilot, he opened another tab and cross-referenced the new information with the data they already had. Then he grabbed his phone and began dialling. Half an hour later he sat back and gazed into space.

Eventually, he stood up and scanned the open office beyond the glass walls, searching for Hume. Then he remembered that she had gone to brief the chief inspector. After quickly forwarding to Raine the data he had mined from her laptop, he grabbed his jacket and left the office. On the way out, he tapped on Hume's ident. She answered on the first ring.

'Guv, where are you?' he said before she had a chance to say anything.

'I'm just with the chief,' she said, picking up the urgency in his voice. 'Why, what's the problem?'

'Not over the phone. I'll come to you.'

'Has something happened?' Hume's voice was suddenly full of concern. 'Has there been another victim? What—'

'No time. I know the link between the murders.'

'Really?' The concern in Hume's voice changed to excitement. 'What is it?'

'Two minutes. I'm in the lift.'

As the lift door closed, Echo lost connection. He put the phone away and stared at his distorted reflection in the lift doors. He was alone in the space and his image made him feel dislocated from himself. As if he was looking at his reflection, but there was something wrong. He was blurred and somehow out of proportion. He wondered vaguely if it was his reflection that was wrong or something in him.

Then his image split in two as the doors opened and he stepped out.

'Echo!'

Hume was standing outside the CI's office. The CI was with her. Both looked alarmed by the sight of him. Echo wasn't surprised. He had been up all night and was surviving on coffee and adrenaline. He probably, *definitely* looked like shit.

'Sir,' he said, nodding at the CI as he approached, then turned his attention to his boss.

'We've had a comparison report back from the lab. You remember we asked to have the blood-at-scene analysed to see if the killer had left anything behind. Perhaps via cross-contamination with the knife or scalpel?'

Hume nodded. Especially after learning that Alice had been conscious enough to fight back, she had hoped that there might be some DNA evidence.

'Then you asked me to DNA the teeth for cross-reference.'

'Yes?'

Echo took a deep breath. 'Well, we've found a match.'

'That's great news,' said the chief inspector, beaming. 'And are we lucky enough to have him in our system?'

Echo shook his head, his eyes still fixed on Hume. 'No, not a match to the killer. The match we've found is between the victims — all the victims. The teeth.'

Hume gazed back at him. 'What do you mean? A DNA match? But we already know who the teeth belong to, except the first one.'

'It gets weirder. The report's just come in. There is a high probability that all the victims are related.'

'What?' Hume's voice rose with surprise, attracting a few glances their way. The CI placed a hand on Echo's shoulder.

'In my office, I think, DC Echo.'

When the door was closed Echo explained. 'The report shows a comprehensive DNA analysis of the victims. As you know, this needs to be done to reveal any material that doesn't belong to them. The analyses are cross-checked to reveal any DNA evidence which might be present in or on *all* the victims' bodies, and at the location of each murder. So anything that shows up at each of the murder scenes must come from the murderer, yes?'

Hume and the CI nodded in unison.

'Unless,' continued Echo, 'there's a connection between the DNA of the three victims.' He took a breath. 'Turns out there's a 99 per cent probability they all have the same father.'

Hume shook her head. 'Not possible. We traced the parents. There is no family link. The ages alone don't work!'

Echo stayed calm, sure of the facts now. 'After I got the information I checked back through the follow-up reports. We had contacted the parents of Jeremy Peters, but not those of Alice Watkins or David Webb. Alice was given up for adoption shortly after she was born and David's parents are dead.'

'So what are you saying?' asked the CI, obviously confused. 'That all three victims are the children of the vicar's father?'

'No,' said Echo, shaking his head. 'I've just spoken to them. Jeremy's father is not the father of all the victims. In fact, he's not even Jeremy's biological father, even though his name is on the birth certificate.'

Hume's face was tight with excitement at the implications of what Echo was saying.

The CI looked even more confused. 'I don't understand. Was the Reverend Peters adopted too, then?'

'The man Jeremy Peters knew as his father was unable to have children. Some medical problem from a childhood illness left him with damaged sperm,' said Echo. 'They tried several treatments through a private fertility clinic, before finally deciding to use donor sperm.'

There was a long silence as this information sank in.

'And what about Alice and David?' Hume asked finally.

'Alice's birth certificate doesn't list a father. I haven't managed to track down David's yet. Not all of them have been digitised.'

'But if they all have the DNA signifiers, that means they're related . . .' Hume said.

'Absolutely. They must all have the same donor father. I tried HFEA — the Human Fertilisation and Embryology Association. They have records of all official sperm donors in the UK post-1991.'

'And?' This from the CI, who had finally caught up.

Echo shook his head. 'Not open yet, but their office is only down the road—' Echo glanced at his tablet — 'Spring Gardens, St James. I thought we could . . . ?'

'Come on. You can fill me in on everything else on the way.' Hume was already heading for the door. Finally, they seemed to have got a break.

CHAPTER 41

Raine sat in the empty scrub-park sipping her coffee, and eating bubble and squeak from a plastic tray. It was one of those hidden spaces that were scattered throughout London. The fact that it hadn't been developed probably meant there was a plague pit under it, or some ancient river just below the surface that wouldn't allow for construction. She'd bought her breakfast from a burger van, suddenly feeling faint with hunger after the long night. As she forked fried onion and cabbage into her mouth, she leaned back against a stunted tree and studied the information Echo had sent to her phone. It consisted of a timeline of her laptop's travels from her boathouse to where the trail had gone dead on the M1. She tried to see a pattern in the lines that had been drawn on the map. From far away, as if in a different world, the day progressed without her.

Her laptop had been stolen around midday. Echo had managed, with the information and passcodes she had given him, to pinpoint the exact time it had disconnected from her Wi-Fi. The next time it had reconnected to the web was on a public network: a free access point at King's Cross station. According to Echo, her email had been viewed, and her files accessed. She cursed herself again for her shoddy security measures, then she blinked and pushed the thought from her mind. Fretting over the past was pointless. Always had been. Instead, she concentrated on the task in hand. After King's Cross, the next access point was a private house in Lewisham. Echo had noted that the property was part of a social housing scheme. He suspected that the northern gangs might recruit from ex-cons, staying in such houses before being offered permanent accommodation.

Raine understood Echo's reasoning. People on parole were prime targets for such activity. Either they were recruited in prison with jobs already set up, or the sort of accommodation offered to them bred such work. Either way, it was a closed system. Once you were on the penal treadmill it was hard to get off. Getting hooked up with a gang and pulling the type of crime that was rarely investigated was an easy 'in'.

Except Raine didn't think that was what this was about. A burglary sweep would not necessitate a stop at King's Cross to see what was on the laptop. And an ex-con would not have left behind her tramadol, which was worth far more than her skanky old computer. Raine could think of only one reason why the laptop would have been fired up again at a service station on the M1.

To check if she'd changed the codes. And if she hadn't, to see what she'd been looking at. Or what she had been working on.

And since then, nothing. No more spying.

Which meant maybe they had what they needed. Or that she didn't have what they wanted.

Raine shook her head in frustration and sent a message to Echo, asking him to confirm which files had been accessed, and if any stood out in any way. Then she texted James, the ex-policeman at the cafe, to say she would be along soon, and to keep Luke safe and tidy until she arrived to deal with him. She drained the coffee cup, then stood up, searching for a bin in the overgrown space. There wasn't one. The scrappy grass was covered in kebab wrappers and nose whippits — used balloons that had once contained nitrous oxide. Raine sighed. You didn't have to step far off the main roads to hit the darker side of London. She pocketed her phone and started walking toward the rusty railings of the park's perimeter.

'Where's my drugs?'

The voice was low and hoarse, as if it cost the speaker a lot of effort to speak above a whisper. Maybe their throat was scarred from too much crystal. Maybe it had been damaged in a fight. Whoever had spoken was close behind her and very good. She hadn't heard them coming.

Raine stopped moving. There was no one in front of her; just an abandoned piece of London scrubland. Which meant there would be no one coming if she were to cry out. Or if she were, say, to be stabbed. The pressure against her side was sharp and hard and almost certainly caused by the point of a knife.

'Well, I've been a bit stupid,' said Raine cheerily, slowly raising her hands in the air to head height. 'I should have guessed that you'd have eyes on Luke; all that product he picked up. How did you find me?'

'It was easy, bitch,' said the man, his voice almost a whisper in her ear as he leaned in. 'Now where's my—'

Raine let go of the coffee cup and thrust her raised right arm back, spinning away from the knife and smashing her elbow into where she judged the face attached to the voice to be. She felt a satisfying crunch as she made contact, the force jarring the full length of her forearm. When she turned and looked at the man on the ground, his face a bloody horror show. Even with the devastating damage to his nose Raine recognised him as the youth who had passed her outside the drug den.

'Never lean in to whisper in a person's ear because they'll know exactly where your head is,' she advised him, while rubbing her elbow. Then she reached into her jacket and pulled out the telescopic baton. 'Did you steal my laptop and kill Heather? I shouldn't think you did, but no harm in asking.'

The youth started to get up and Raine slammed the baton down. The bones breaking in his wrist made a wet snapping sound in the empty park. A high whistle of air emerged from his mouth.

'And how many times must I say this? Using "bitch" just isn't acceptable. It's not only demeaning to me, but stereotyping to you. And lazy! Really, you should be able to come up with something better.'

Raine grabbed hold of his hoodie and hauled him along until his back was against a tree. She smiled brightly at him. 'Now, do I need to knock you unconscious while I phone the feds, or are you going to be reasonable?'

The youth spat on the ground. Bits of brown mixed with the blood. Her elbow had broken off shards of rotten tooth. 'You broke my fucking teeth, you bitch. I'm—'

Raine slapped him open-handed, all signs of levity absent from her face now. 'I told you. Don't call me bitch. Tell me who sent you. And how did you know to follow me?'

Raine grabbed his broken wrist and held it gently in her hand. The skin felt tight and hot. He breathed in sharply but said nothing.

'Fair enough.' Raine squeezed.

The man passed out.

* * *

'Do you mind if I ask you something, boss?'

Hume and Echo were walking past Trafalgar Square, where a scattering of tourists were taking photographs of the lions, and municipal workers were power-spraying the pavement in a futile attempt to remove hundreds of years' worth of pigeon shit.

'What is it?'

'About Raine.'

Hume kept her pace steady. It was a trick she'd learned when she first joined the force, walking the beat in Soho. Never too fast and never too slow. It somehow created a separation from everything around you. Subconsciously, the public recognised that, as if the action itself denoted respect or power. A lion never ran until it was chasing down its kill. The rest of the time it walked.

'What about her?'

'Well, if you don't mind me saying, she seems a little manic.'

Hume smiled. 'You're probably right, but not in the way you think. She just doesn't fit easily into a box.'

'Is that why she left the force?'

Hume kept her face expressionless. Her pace didn't change.

'Technically she didn't leave the force. Not in the resigning sense, anyway. She took a leave of absence and . . . just never came back. After a while the absence became an official dismissal, but it was made clear she could reapply and return to work whenever she felt ready.' They left the square and stepped onto Cockspur Street. The morning sun had burned off the early mist and the day was beginning to heat up. 'Depending on a medical exam, of course,' Hume finished.

'So was she . . .' Echo didn't know how to continue. 'Was there an incident or something? PTSD?'

'Why do you want to know?' Hume said mildly.

'It's just that she . . . that you seem to cut her a lot of slack. In fact, I'm not even sure why she's connected to the case.'

'We often use outside assets, Echo. You know that.'

'Yes, but this seems more . . . personal. And that stuff with the buttons and mask.' On the way out of headquarters, Echo had told Hume about Raine's theory that the killer could have been wearing a mask. Hume had agreed it was possible, that it could also explain why Alice had failed to scratch the killer's face and no DNA had been found under her fingernails.

'She could always find connections no one else could. That's why she was such an exceptional officer. But it was also what got her into trouble.'

'How d'you mean?'

Hume guided them left into Spring Gardens. Ahead of them was the building housing the HFEA.

'All you need to know is that she's good at her job, and I trust her.'

'OK,' said Echo, sounding slightly frustrated.

'Plus,' added Hume as they reached the building, 'Raine gives off this aura of kookiness, but it's all an act. You know how it feels when you've just bitten down on a piece of tinfoil? Like everything is wrong and there's a pain in the middle of your head?'

'Yes?'

'Well, don't bite down on Raine.'

'Because she's like tinfoil?' said Echo, smiling slightly.

'No, because she's like the factory that makes the tinfoil,' said Hume, not smiling at all. 'She's *all* the tinfoil.'

Without another word Hume entered the building. After a moment's hesitation, Echo followed.

* * *

Raine slapped the youth again, pulling him back from unconsciousness. When he finally opened his eyes, she raised his chin with her baton.

'Welcome back. How did you find me?'

The youth said nothing, just glared hate at her. She shook her head, put down the baton and held his broken wrist.

'Last chance,' she said.

'All right! Luke messaged me. Told me what you did. Stealing the gear. He gave me a description and I clocked you in the street.' He spat the words out like bullets.

If Luke had warned the drug cartel, then he must have escaped from James. Which might mean the ex-policeman was hurt, or worse. She took out her phone and began to swipe one-handed, then stopped. She looked at the youth enquiringly.

'What's your name?'

The youth glowered back but said nothing. Raine squeezed his wrist again. The scream that erupted from him sounded like a boiling kettle.

'Name?'

Raine stopped squeezing.

'Blade,' he croaked through his broken mouth.

Raine's smile was radiant. 'Excellent! So street! Your mother must be delighted. Now, Blade, what is Luke expecting to happen here?'

'Go fuck yourself,' said Blade. Raine squeezed his wrist again. She could feel the broken bones crunch together under her grip. She was quite impressed Blade didn't pass out this time.

'OK! Jesus! Once I spoked you I was going to message him. Set up an exchange—'

'What the hell does "spoked" mean?'

Blade looked from his wrist to her face. There were beads of sweat on his brow. 'You know. Got you running smoothly. So you could be pedalled.'

'Ridden like a bike. Beautiful image, Blade. Then you were going to exchange my freedom for the drugs, yes?'

Blade nodded. 'And the copper, yeah.'

'James.'

'Whatever.'

Raine squeezed his wrist a third time, with slightly more force. Blade's eyes fluttered backwards in his head for a second.

'Don't fuck with me, Blade. I'm having a really shitty week and am not in the mood. Where is this exchange supposed to take place?'

Blade breathed through his mouth and squeezed the tears out of his eyes.

'At Dee's.'

'Dee's? Where's Dee's?'

Blade dead-eyed her. 'You'll never know unless you let go of my wrist.'

Raine sighed. 'Come on, Blade. I'm trying to be nice here.'

'You're so dead,' said Blade. 'Those drugs belong to some serious people.'

'Don't feel dead,' she said, not only squeezing the wrist again but rotating it. The noise Blade emitted this time was somewhere between a gasp and a whisper. Raine suspected he didn't have any scream left in him. 'Now for the very last time . . .'

'She's at the clubhouse!'

'What clubhouse?'

'The one on the street where I clocked you following the boy.'

'Thank you.'

Raine kept hold of the wrist as she swiped at her phone, bringing up Hume's number. She let it ring for twenty seconds before cutting the call. She thought for a moment, then swiped again. This time the call was answered almost immediately.

'Conner here.'

'Inspector, it's Raine. Do you remember who I am?'

'Yes, of course, Miss Raine. Thank you for the still from the video footage. I'm not sure if we'll be able to track the person down, but—'

'No problem, and it's just Raine, but that's not why I'm calling you. When we talked, you said you thought Heather's death might have been a mistaken drug hit. Does that mean you have connections to SOCA?'

'What's this about?' The DI's tone was cautious, but interested. The Serious Organised Crime Agency dealt with all the major drug-related crimes nationwide, coordinating with local drug squads.

Raine looked down at Blade. 'I've got intel that a major drug deal is about to go down. I'm not sure how much gear it entails exactly, but enough to give the whole of South London a hell of a night.'

Suddenly Conner's tone was all business. 'Where?'

'Not sure yet but it's going to be at a gang clubhouse. If I gave you the name of the crew, would you be able to find it?'

'As long as they're active, sure,' said Conner.

'Oh, they're active, all right. Delivery, storage and distribution.'

'What's the name?'

'I should know in about half an hour. Do you think you can have some people ready to hustle by then? Might be worth bringing some AFOs.'

At the mention of authorised firearms officers, Conner's tone switched to urgent.

'Look, Raine, if there is a chance guns are involved—'

'And if you could let DI Hume know that the clubhouse is probably where her drugs originated that would be cool. Tell her the street name for the mix is Donkey Kong.'

'Donkey Kong? Raine, I really think you should—'

'Gotta boogie. Get your people ready.'

Raine ended the call and turned her attention back to Blade.

'Take out your phone and send a message to Luke telling him that you have me, or I'll break your other wrist in so many places you'll never be able to pick up a phone again.'

Blade held out a moment longer, then slowly pulled out his mobile. When he had finished messaging, Raine took it and placed it in her pocket.

'Thank you. Now, do you think you can come with me quietly to the clubhouse or will you need to wait here?'

'I'm going to kill you when—'

Raine smashed the baton against the side of his head, knocking him out cold.

'Wait here it is, then.'

CHAPTER 42

'I know it's an unusual request, but we already have DNA confirmation that the victims had the same father. The evidence suggests sperm donation was involved, and they were all born after 1991, which means you'll have records, yes?'

The man sitting in front of Hume and Echo seemed extremely uncomfortable. He was in his early thirties, with a fade cut to de-accentuate his baldness and the kind of skin texture normally found in playdough. Hume felt the urge to poke him to see if an indentation would remain.

'If I understand you correctly, detectives, the information you require pertains to people who have not actually committed any crime, nor are they the victims of any crime?'

'As far as we know, Mr Porter,' agreed Hume. 'But if our information is correct, they may be in danger.'

Mr Porter pressed his hands together, a regretful look on his face.

'I understand. And as you know there have been occasions when we have shared data with law enforcement, but this has normally required a court warrant. The information we keep here is private. Sometimes the media get wind that a celebrity was conceived using sperm or ovum donation and . . .' Mr Porter separated his hands and gave a tiny shrug.

'Completely understandable, sir,' said Echo. 'Which is why our chief inspector has started that particular process. Our worry is that if the donor has other children whom he's targeting, and has somehow got hold of the names—'

'Impossible,' said Mr Porter firmly. 'All those names are encrypted. Our systems are most robust.'

'I'm sure that's true,' said Hume softly. Inside her shoes, she scrunched up her toes until they hurt. 'But even if you can't share the actual names until we have the correct paperwork, could you at least check that your system hasn't been compromised? We have reason to believe that the suspect may have some technical expertise in computers. Perhaps even some hacking experience.

'We also have reason to believe that the person we're looking for has not completed what he set out to do. It's vital that we get as much information as we can on him. We need to find him. Fast.'

The man sighed, but turned to his computer and tapped in his password.

'What did you say the names of the offspring were?'

'Alice Watkins, David Webb and Jeremy Peters,' said Echo.

Mr Porter tapped in the names. After a moment or two he declared: 'They were all conceived using sperm collected in 1991.'

'How come they are all different ages, then?' asked Echo.

'Sperm can be kept for up to twenty years, although fifteen is the more accepted commercial ceiling, with no degradation, as long as it is stored correctly,' said Mr Porter, still looking at the screen. 'It is not uncommon to find vast age differences among siblings conceived by sperm or ovum donation.'

'What criteria do most people base their choice of sperm on?' said Hume, interested.

'It really varies,' shrugged Porter. 'The donors are profiled in a database these days. Height. Eye colour. Ethnicity. Education. You name it — we'll have it on record.'

'So even if you can't give us the donor's name, could you give us a description?' said Hume eagerly.

'Well,' said Porter, doubtfully, 'I think that might infringe data protection.'

'At least tell us if all the sperm came from the same batch or whatever you call it,' said Echo.

Porter nodded.

'The donor made several deposits, back in 1991, to a single clinic. That would be quite normal.'

'And the three names we've given you,' said Hume, 'is that the sum total of children conceived from his sperm, or were there more?'

'Two more,' said Porter.

Two more, thought Hume gloomily. Two more possible victims — if the killer had his way.

'Can you at least tell us if the donor has been in touch. Tried to contact his offspring or whatever the term is?'

Porter thought for a moment then did some more tapping.

'The donor has not tried to get in touch,' he said after a moment. 'But one of the children did reach out to us to find out who their donor was.'

'Which one?' asked Echo, reaching for his tablet.

'David Webb. Three weeks ago.'

That was it, thought Hume. The spark that started the fire.

'Do you have CCTV footage of his visit?' said Hume.

'Data protection—'

'He's dead,' said Hume flatly. 'I don't think data protection is an issue. Could you confirm whether the donor is alive and responded to David's request?'

Despite looking concerned, Porter started tapping again. After a moment his concerned expression morphed into confusion.

'What?' said Hume. 'What is it?'

'Strange,' said Porter, viewing the screen. 'There must be some technical error.'

'Why? What makes you say that?'

'Well, there's no donor listed for David Webb,' said Porter. He tapped a few more buttons then turned to Hume and Echo, looking confused. Confused and seriously worried. 'Or for the other two. That's just not possible.'

Hume was gripped by a curious mixture of alarm and exhilaration. 'So, are you saying you have no record of the donor?'

Echo's phone chimed. 'Sorry,' he said, standing and reaching into his jacket. He turned away and spoke quietly while walking to a corner of the room. Hume ignored him.

'There must be some sort of technical glitch,' insisted Porter.

'Are records kept elsewhere?' said Hume. 'Back-ups, maybe. Or at the original clinic?'

Porter's face registered relief. 'Yes. Yes, of course. Give me a minute, I'll try to find . . .'

'Guv?'

Hume looked up at Echo, who was pocketing his phone. 'What is it?'

'That was DI Conner. The one in charge of the Heather Salim murder case — the girl Raine was hired to find.'

'Right, yes. Heather. What did he want?'

'He wants to know if Raine is on the level.'

Hume grimaced. 'A bit of a loaded question. Did he say why he was asking?'

'Apparently she's got intel on some sort of massive drugs set-up and wants him to organise an armed response team to liaise with her.'

Alarm bells began to ring in Hume's head. She took out her own phone to see if Raine had been in touch, and frowned when she saw her battery icon. It had dropped under 20 per cent, meaning it had gone into power-save mode and would not automatically announce messages. 'What sort of drugs set-up?'

'That's the other thing. She told him to tell us that the drug cocktail used in our case has the street name of Donkey

Kong: a mixture of ketamine and Dezolam put together in a South London drugs ring.'

Hume bit her lip, thinking. Finally, she turned to Mr Porter. 'You said there were two more? Two more people whose names are on the donor list?'

'Well, it's not a donor list but—'

'I need those names. Three dead means he's not going to stop, Mr Porter. Which means we need to get to them before he does.'

Porter looked at her a moment, his eyes frightened in his putty face. Then he nodded and began to type.

* * *

Back outside, Hume plugged her phone into her emergency power bank. Too many vital calls had been lost by phone batteries running out of charge, so now all officers were required to carry a replacement power supply.

'Pass the names on to one of the team. I want them chased down and under police protection as soon as possible. Everything tells me this is speeding up.'

'Boss.' Echo pulled out his own phone and began tapping.

'How come your phone never runs out of charge?' she asked.

'Custom OS,' he said, not looking up. 'Removes all spyware and stops apps working in the background. Increases battery life by up to thirty—'

'It was a rhetorical question, Echo.'

'Oh.'

'Come on. While we're waiting, we need to pay another visit to Professor Flynn. See if he can suggest anything fresh with the new information we've got.'

* * *

The thing about Lucy is — she's pregnant.

Isn't that wonderful news? She is so happy as she tells me, practically glowing. Only nine weeks, so nothing's showing yet, which is good, she says. Otherwise, it might affect the wedding dress. I might have to let it out a bit to accommodate the bump, she says. Plus, it might have an impact on the wedding night. The evening of erotic extravagance Lucy has planned for her soon-to-be husband.

I laugh and refill her glass of bubbly. I tell her congrats, and that she'll make a wonderful mum, even though she's having a glass of wine right in front of me. I tell her not to worry because there is no way she will be showing by the wedding day. I tell her that she'll be absolutely fine for the wedding night. Possibly better, as she'll be able to tell hubby about the little miracle he has helped create when they are lying in each other's arms after the nuptials.

What I don't tell her, as we clink our glasses together, is that she'll be absolutely fine because there isn't going to be a wedding. She needn't worry about her baby interfering with their lovemaking because there isn't going to be any sex. Or any baby. Because there isn't going to be any Lucy. Lucy is going to be shut down by then.

I smile and laugh with her. Lucy's eyes are shining with happiness, but I don't know if that is true joy or a result of the drugs I put in her champagne. I'd say we've got about five minutes before it's time for me to open my special bag. It's sitting by my feet. Lucy keeps glancing at it. She thinks it's got a special outfit in it. Something risqué for her wedding night.

I'm actually enjoying myself. My daughter is good company. And so excited! Even though she's thirty, she's like a little child. I can almost picture what she must have been like when she was younger. A girl. I bet she used to love Christmas. I bet she used to look out at the night sky and try hard as hard to see Santa Claus.

Well, I say 'daughter', but I only mean that in a biological sense. She contains my DNA.

My code.

And of course, what she doesn't realise is that the code is wrong. Corrupted. That there's something wrong with the programming. Which is why I need to shut it down. Why I need to daisy-chain them. File-share.

I watch as the glass slips from Lucy's hand.

'Whoops!' I say, laughing. I put down my own glass and pick hers up.

'No harm done,' I say. 'Why don't you lie down on the sofa for a few minutes while I get the special surprise from my bag?'

She laughs and does as I say. I open the bag and pull out my face. The face I wear when I correct the code. My real face. She looks at it, puzzled.

'Oh, no,' she says. 'I don't think that will work. That doesn't say lots of hot sex.'

I smile and say that she'll understand better when she sees it on. I place it over my face to show her, then I strike a little pose. Her eyes are muddied now, unable to focus, and her head is lolling. I think she's about ready. I tell her it's time to prepare her and begin unbuttoning her dress. I take my time. After all, there's no hurry.

She doesn't stop me. I know she understands, deep down. She must. Even when I pull out the scalpel and the pliers she doesn't struggle. After all, why would she? It's in her DNA.

Lucy, she was made wrong.

CHAPTER 43

Dee hated her life, which was just as well, as it was about to alter forever. She had been a gang pass-around since she was fourteen and had turned her first trick for a pipe of crystal. Now, at eighteen, she was used up and just about ready for the dump. Four years of being the postcode-fuck had emptied her out. If she could somehow find a way to kill herself that didn't require courage, she would. All she had to live for was collapsed veins, a battered soul, and a monkey on her shoulder so greedy it was a daily struggle just to feed it. When the woman walked into the clubhouse, Dee had been up all night and it took her frazzled brain a few seconds to realise that she wasn't local.

'Sorry, we're closed today,' said Dee, thinking the woman must be here to score.

'That's OK. I'm not buying,' said Raine, smiling a smile that, had Dee been more together, would have sent her running for the hills. Raine shrugged off her backpack and placed it on the table. 'I'm just here to deliver a message from Blade.'

Dee relaxed. If this woman knew Blade, then she had to be legit.

'Yeah? What is it?'

'He's had an existential crisis, and has decided to leave the drugs-selling business. Permanently.'

Dee gazed at her in bewilderment. Raine opened her backpack and pulled out the phone and knife. Dee's eyes widened. 'Those belong to Blade.'

'What I'm saying is he's given all the information about this place and his operation to the police. The feds. They'll be along any minute, I imagine, to arrest everyone, and seize all the drugs and money.'

Raine looked around the shabby room. There was a wicked-looking sword leaning against the wall and a selection of paint aerosols, presumably for gang-tagging.

'And the weapons,' she added.

Dee's brain couldn't process what Raine was saying.

'There's no one here. Everyone's out on delivery.'

'Delivering to where?'

Dee shrugged. She was feeling dislocated from her body. This woman was insane. Or possibly not real; just a figment of the drugs she had taken. Any minute now one of the boys would be back from their drop and all hell would break loose.

'Everywhere.'

'And what about the Donkey Kong? Where is that being delivered to? Blade said it was just the one school, but that can't be right, can it? Surely there must be more?'

She smiled winningly at Dee. Dee's own smile slipped. The way the woman was grinning was cutting through her chemical barrier.

'I don't know, lady. You'd have to ask Blade.'

Raine stepped forward, still smiling. 'I have asked Blade. I kept on asking him until he fell unconscious. And now I'm asking you. How many schools is Donkey Kong sold to?'

Dee took a step back, stumbling a little.

'I don't know. I think it was just the one, like Blade said. Like a depot or something.'

'A depot? What, to sell on?'

Dee nodded. She had retreated as far as she could. Her back was against the clubhouse wall. Her nice morning buzz had worn off, leaving her with nothing but a hard headache drilling behind her eyes.

'OK,' said Raine. 'That makes sense. Do you know who broke into my boat? Do you think it has something to do with Heather? Because I'm really beginning to think it might have.'

'What?' said Dee, thinking she might have misheard. 'What boat? Who's Heather?'

'Worth an ask,' said Raine. 'What's the name of this club?'

'Name?'

'Your gang name! What's the name you all go under?'

'Oh, right,' said Dee. She was on safer ground here. 'The Nightingales. It's the name of the estate.'

'Of course it is,' said Raine, tapping the name of the crew and their address into her phone to pass on to Conner.

'And what's your name?'

'Dee.'

'Then I suggest you leave, Dee, and never come back. By now Blade has turned over everything he knows to the cops. It won't be long until they start raiding all the addresses, including this one. If you've got anything incriminating at home then I suggest you get rid of it. Preferably not by swallowing it.'

Raine waited while the young woman fled. Two seconds after the door closed, she started emptying the contents of Luke's backpack, spreading the drugs around the clubhouse.

* * *

'Detective Inspector Conner?'

'Raine? Is that you?'

'Who else sounds this sexy in the morning? Did you get my message?'

'Yes. We're—' there was a pause and a muffled conversation — 'approximately two minutes away.'

'You're coming yourself? I'm flattered.'

'Raine, I don't know what—'

At that moment James turned the corner, with Luke pressed up close behind him, presumably to hide the knife. Raine wondered what Luke had said to the ex-policeman to make him come with so little fuss. That Blade had her held captive? That if he didn't come quietly they'd kill her?

She whispered into her phone. 'There'll be two men on-site: a roadman called Luke, with at least one knife, possibly more, and a hostage.'

'Is the hostage a civilian?'

'Ex-police. Not part of the gang.'

Raine gave brief descriptions of the two men, along with the layout of the clubhouse and the exit points.

'Where are you?'

'Safe. Remind Luke about Hume.'

Raine ended the call before Conner could reply, and watched as Luke and James entered the building. A minute later a police van arrived and silently pulled up outside the clubhouse. The doors to the van opened and seven figures dressed in body armour emerged. One — Raine guessed Conner — directed three of the officers round to the back of the building while the other three took up positions at the front entrance. There was a lull while everybody got themselves into position, then Conner spoke briefly into a collar mike and the officers entered the building.

Two minutes later she observed Luke being marched out, handcuffed to one of the officers. Taking out her phone, she sent a text to Conner, detailing where he could find Luke's accomplice, Blade. She stayed just long enough to witness James exiting under his own steam, then slipped away.

CHAPTER 44

'Fascinating,' said Professor Flynn, rubbing his hands together in excitement. 'And all the messages are left in some sort of computer code?'

'Yes,' said Hume. She couldn't seem to stop staring at the professor's hands. She had an image of them bursting into flames as they slid back and forth against each other. 'And with the information on the shared DNA, they seem to have gathered new significance.'

'*I don't love you. Go to hell. Halt and catch fire,*' the Professor read aloud. He looked at Echo. 'And this last one is a program directive, you say?'

'Yes, sir. From the '80s. It's a kill code to render a computer inactive when its program has gone wrong.'

'And had it?'

Echo's brow creased. 'I'm sorry?'

'The girl, Alice — had her programming gone wrong?'

'You could put it that way,' said Hume. 'According to her records, she had been in and out of mental-health institutions since she was a child. Personality disorders. Eating disorders. Drug dependency.'

The professor was still rubbing his hands, but much more slowly. Contemplatively. To Hume it now looked like he was trying to grate them.

'And do we know anything at all about the donor? Who he was?'

'The records have been removed somehow, possibly by the killer. The only information we have is that the sperm donations were performed, if that is the right word, at a clinic in Leicester in 1991, and that five children were conceived using his sperm.'

'Why didn't he remove the records of the children?'

'Stored in a different way, apparently. Donors' records are sandboxed — kept separate — from information on their children. So that no cross-contamination of the information can occur. The only information about any offspring that can be given to the donor is number, age and gender.'

'So how did he find out?'

'As I say, he must have some serious computer hacker skills.'

'Or perhaps he works there,' said the professor. 'But that's not what I mean.'

'What do you mean?' asked Hume.

'I mean, how did he even know who to start looking for if the two sides are kept so separate? How did he even know he had any offspring?'

Hume eyed him thoughtfully.

'That's a good question,' she said, finally. 'The institute was visited by one of the victims three weeks ago.'

'So that was the lighted match,' said the professor. 'That was what alerted the killer. But who struck the match?'

'I'm not following.'

The professor glanced out of the window, then directly at Hume. She realised that she had made a mistake. The man wasn't some dry academic, hiding in his ivory tower. Those were just the clothes he wore. His disguise.

Really, he was razor-sharp.

'David — I'm guessing David because he was the first of the victims — came looking for a father and found a killer. But why did he come looking? What did he want? And when he found him, what did he find? What pieces came together to form murder?'

'What can you tell us about him now? Psychologically, I mean,' said Echo. 'We know from the people he murdered that—'

'His children,' said Hume bluntly.

The temperature in the room seemed to notch down a degree. There was something so fundamentally wrong about killing your own children.

'Indeed,' agreed Flynn. 'His children. If the donor files were missing, what information did the clinic still possess?'

Echo swiped his tablet. 'Profiles of every donor are kept separate from their personal details — name, address, date of birth, etcetera — so that even if the child does not wish to know the identity of their parent, they still have access to any relevant biological and culture-specific information.'

'And . . .' queried the professor.

Echo consulted his device.

'He's Caucasian. And we know he must be a minimum of forty-eight and probably older, as you have to be at least eighteen to donate sperm in the UK.'

'And you said the donations were made in 1991. Are there no records at the clinic where it all happened?'

'The Leicester clinic went out of business in 2000 but, in any case, all records are centralised,' said Echo. 'We also know that he is blue-eyed, five foot nine inches tall, and has fair hair.'

'Unless he changed those details to lead you off the scent,' said the professor. 'Because he sounds like a planner.'

Hume and Echo stayed silent. If that was the case then they had learned practically nothing about their suspect, and that was too dismal to contemplate right now.

The professor turned in his chair and looked out of the window once more. Beyond the dirty pane, the sunny day had given way to London greyness.

'And you believe he wore some sort of costume each time he did the actual . . . um, deed?'

'A coat or jacket. Something shiny and sheer that won't allow purchase. Possibly a mask of some kind too. We're almost certain this was the case for Alice and, judging by the lack of DNA evidence at the other sites — no material or skin fragments under the fingernails — we're working on the assumption that it is the case for all three murders.'

Professor Flynn steepled his fingers. 'And you don't think it's to hide his identity?'

'No. The way he's operating seems to suggest that he is not known to his victims. At least, not for long. He uses a digital subterfuge to get them alone before . . .'

'Correcting their code,' finished the professor.

'Precisely,' said Hume.

'And inserting a tooth. Fascinating.'

'I thought the tooth might be a sort of surrogate USB,' said Hume.

'Or a way of short-circuiting the DNA.' The professor appeared to be looking at an interior blackboard. 'Feeding it back on itself.'

Echo squinted, trying to grasp the professor's meaning. 'So, what do you think? Do you have any insights?'

'Well, the mask hypothesis is very interesting, for a start. He might be disfigured in some way.'

Echo was doubtful. 'If he was hideously scarred or something, then he would have worn the mask when he first met his victims, surely?'

'No, not disfigured in the eyes of others, not to the victims. To himself. The mask wouldn't be for them. It's for him.'

'I don't understand,' said Hume.

'It's all about his identity, don't you see?' said the professor, excitement bubbling beneath his urbanity. 'The DNA that is somehow corrupt. He feeds it back to the victims like it is a closed loop or something. As if it is not part of him. He converts them into the snake that eats itself. The ouroboros.'

'Is that the one that swallows its own tail?' said Hume.

Echo gasped. 'Bloody hell! I never saw the connection.'

Under Hume's stern eye, Echo flushed. 'Sorry,' he said. 'It was just a shock hearing the professor mention the ouroboros.'

'You've heard of it, then?' the professor enquired.

'Every computer graduate has. I just never made the link to this case.'

'But how?' said Hume, her voice now full of energy. Everything seemed to be coming together. 'How is it used?'

'It's used as a metaphor to explain meta-programming and recursive constructs.' Echo couldn't help himself.

'Echo.' Hume shot him a warning look. Echo held up his hands.

'It's a way of reducing code by making the program replicate itself. Once set off, the program becomes self-learning, cannibalising parts of itself to adapt to new situations or realities.' Echo's face glowed with excitement. 'This just confirms that he is computer-literate to a high degree!'

'Goodness,' said Professor Flynn mildly.

Before Echo could continue, Hume's phone rang. She apologised to the professor and turned away to answer the call.

'Hume.' She listened for a few moments, then stood up. 'Brilliant. We're on our way.'

She ended the call and turned to Professor Flynn. 'I'm sorry, sir, but we have to go. Thank you for your time. If you can think of anything, any other interpretation of the information we've given you that might help, please do get in touch.'

She shook his offered hand, then walked briskly to the door, Echo behind her.

'Inspector,' said the professor, just as she was turning the handle. Hume paused and looked back at him.

'Yes?'

'One thing springs to mind. If you believe the murderer was only in his late teens or early twenties when he donated . . .'

'Yes?' Hume repeated.

Professor Flynn spread his hands, palms up. 'Well, Leicester's a university town. I believe you said the sperm was donated there? You may want to check the university records. Perhaps the computing department.'

Hume looked at him a moment, then nodded. 'A good suggestion. Thank you, Professor.'

'Who was on the phone?' asked Echo as the door closed.

'It was Jonas. They've tracked down one of the surviving donor children. She lives in South London.'

'That's great!'

'They're sending a couple of officers there now to check on her. If we get a boogie on, we can rendezvous and meet them. Assuming she's in.' Hume's face was more animated than Echo had seen it in days. 'With any luck we'll finally start getting some answers instead of more questions.'

CHAPTER 45

Raine studied the block of flats opposite her. Strung across many of the balconies were brightly coloured lines of clothing, drying in the heat and dust of the city. Although the sky was grey, the air was greyer, particulates from traffic fumes turning it thick and sticky.

She was in Lewisham. Outside the building Echo had pinned as the last place her laptop had been active in London. Echo had mentioned it being a halfway house for people just released from prison, but the people entering and leaving the building didn't seem like recently released criminals. They looked like recent immigrants, perhaps refugees. Specifically, they looked like refugees from West Asian countries. Raine's knowledge of the proxy conflict between Saudi Arabia and Iran, and its effects on Iraq and Yemen was sketchy, to say the least. The same with the Allied interventions, and the cultural disruption they had caused. She was aware of some tension between the Sunni and Shia Muslim traditions but was not sure of the reasons. She had seen the pictures of vast refugee camps in Afghanistan and Pakistan but had only a vague grasp of the history of those countries and people. She had watched the exodus of migrants across Europe on the news and understood that a world shift was occurring, but her own life required her attention, so she had not delved deeper. The plight of millions of people became a background colour in the picture of her home city. Protests and marches. An increase in slavery and street poverty. An increasing richness to the cultural fabric of London. New sounds and smells and customs.

And new tensions, struggles and clashes.

Men and women came and left the building. Raine noticed that the sexes remained, for the most part, separate. She wondered what they thought of their new country. Whether they considered the long, dangerous journey and handing every penny they owned over to the traffickers had been worth it. If the death and destruction of their history was something they could bear, or if it would ultimately crush them.

She thought she needed to get some sleep soon.

Inside her jacket pocket, her phone buzzed.

'Inspector Conner, how lovely to hear from you. Sounds like a productive morning. Is James, the ex-cop, OK?'

Outside the flats, two men lounged in folding chairs and were sharing a shisha pipe.

'Just bruising and a stab wound to his right hand.'

'Ouch.'

'Done with his own fork at the cafe, apparently. He's quite embarrassed about it.'

'I'll bet,' smiled Raine. 'What about the drugs?'

'The thug, Luke, totally denies the drugs are his.'

'Of course he does.'

'Says he has nothing to do with them and was just delivering James as a service to Blade.'

'How is Blade, by the way?'

The friendliness in Conner's voice increased. 'Extremely angry, with a very nasty fracture to his wrist and a sore head — which he claims you administered before tying him to a tree.'

'What? He's telling you he was beaten up in broad daylight by a woman who's about a foot shorter than he is?' Raine sounded incredulous.

'Doesn't sound likely,' agreed Conner cheerfully.

'He was probably climbing the tree for fun. Then fell out of it and broke his wrist when he hit the ground.'

'Climbing the tree for fun?'

'Yes. Then tied himself up for safety,' finished Raine firmly.

'Anyhow, he also denies having anything to do with the drugs.'

'OK. I had Luke under surveillance and have photographs of him picking up the drugs from a Wendy house if that's any help?'

'A Wendy house?'

'That's what they were using as a drop-off point.'

'Like a child's Wendy house?' Conner's voice was a mixture of disbelief and disgust.

'What can I say? They're lovely people. As I mentioned, I have photos, and the bag used to store the drugs is clearly visible. Luke's prints should be all over it as well. I also have a recording of a conversation between me and Luke in the cafe where he clearly says the drugs are his. I'll send them through when we finish.'

'And what about the other one — Blade?'

'It's entirely possible that you might have found his phone in the bag of drugs, with a message on it telling Luke that he kidnapped me. Also, there are probably quite a few other conversations regarding dealings of a nefarious nature.'

'And just how would you know that?' said Conner, but Raine could hear the smile in his voice.

'Lucky guess?'

'The luckiest.'

'Have you let Inspector Hume know about the party-drug mix?' said Raine, watching as a man walked a woman into the building, his hand tight on her arm. The woman grimaced like she was in pain.

'Donkey Kong? Sure.'

'Great. I've not been able to get hold of her.'

'Can I ask you something, Miss Raine?'

'Just "Raine", Inspector. Like the weather but with an "e" at the end. Shoot.'

Conner's voice was tentative. 'I've asked around about you. I thought it best. It's not every day a civilian gives you intel on a drugs op this size.'

'That's not a question, Inspector.'

Raine's body ached. From lack of sleep and lack of food and too much caffeine. From lack of care and lack of love and the overwhelming weight of the past. She closed her eyes for a second and leaned back against the brick wall.

'As far as anyone can tell me, you signed yourself off the force for personal reasons, but then never returned.'

'Still not a question.'

She opened her eyes. Women wearing hijabs hurried in and out of the building. Almost none of them were alone.

'OK, here's my question.'

Raine's hand tightened on the handset. She really didn't need this now.

'Is there anything I can do to help?'

Raine's eyes widened slightly. 'Well, that wasn't the question I expected.'

'Nevertheless.'

Raine smiled. She liked this man.

'OK. Can you tell me if the family has picked up Heather's body yet?'

'That wasn't what I—'

'I know, but that's the help I need, Inspector. Somebody shot the young woman whom I was paid to find. You think it might be gang-related but there's no evidence of that as yet. Maybe something might turn up in the clubhouse, but the chances of it being the same gang are slim. Can you tell me if the family has arranged for her body to be collected from the morgue yet?'

Conner sounded hesitant again. 'Why do you want to know?'

Raine took a deep breath. 'I've done all I can with this, Inspector. I've nowhere else to go with it. I just need closure now. So I can move on to the next thing. It would help me if I knew that Heather was being looked after. That she was home.'

There was a pause, then Connor's voice came back firm and strong. 'I'll find out for you.'

'Thank you.'

As the call ended Raine saw there was a text message from Echo.

The only file that was opened more than once was your report on Heather.
Hope that helps.
Echo

'Well, well,' Raine murmured, and looked across at the people coming in and out of the building across the street. 'I wonder if anybody you knew lives here, Heather? Or maybe not someone you knew. Maybe someone your parents know.'

She let thoughts tick through her brain for a few moments, then looked down at the clock on her phone. She had just enough time to grab a couple of hours' sleep and some food before school finished.

CHAPTER 46

Everything about the little flat above the launderette said 'lonely'. From the cat meowing in the corner to the cuddly toys on the windowsill. From the mirror with its dusty edges to the electric heater and the cheery magnets on the fridge that contained sad food: one-person ready meals that had their calories blazoned on the lids next to pots of chocolate pudding, like a yin and yang of body-hate. Cans of cat food. Upmarket bottled water so expensive it was a life statement. In this case, one that no one else would ever see.

'How long?' said Hume. She looked at the wedding dress on its hanger by the full-length mirror. It was pearl white, with feathers sewn into the bodice as if the wearer was meant to represent a swan.

'Not long. The first on-scene knocked but got no answer. He was going to wait but heard the cat meowing and decided to investigate.'

Hume raised her eyebrows. 'Over a cat mewing?'

Echo shrugged. 'Apparently the officer was a cat person. Thought the animal sounded distressed.'

Hume glanced at the door. 'And it was unlocked?'

'Yes. The officer had the foresight to put on gloves.'

'Good. Get it dusted. You never know.'

Hume stared down at the empty wine glass. On the table next to it was another, half full. 'And the glasses. Check them for DNA, too. We're certain it's Lucy?'

'Lucy Briar, yes. One of the two names Porter gave us,' said Echo quietly.

'Fuck,' muttered Hume. It should have been simplicity itself to find her. The killer obviously had. After leaving the HFEA building earlier that morning Hume had set up a search. The address had come back only as they were approaching the property, responding to the murder-call. Too late. Far too late.

'Do we have any details on the remaining child yet?'

'No. Other than his gender. Apparently, he is male. All other information has been wiped. I'm getting the data technicians to deep sweep the system's registry. See if he left anything behind.'

'Right. Do we know what the cat's called?'

'Eric,' said Echo.

Hume looked at him. 'Eric? Eric the cat?'

'Definitely. There's, like, a billion pictures of him, including his own scrapbook.' Echo reached down and picked up a photo album. Hume peered at it.

Eric's and his mummy's life journey.

Below the writing was a picture of Lucy with a big smile on her face, holding Eric up with one hand. Her other hand was out of shot, presumably holding the camera. A selfie.

'Jesus,' said Hume. 'I think I'm going to cry. Where's the body?'

'In the bedroom,' said Echo. As if on cue, a flash of light came from the room to their left, presumably from a camera bulb. Hume walked through. Lucy's body was lying facedown on the bed. In the harsh glare of the police lighting, it looked like she was made from papier-mâché. She had clearly gone on a crash diet for the big day: her skin didn't seem to quite fit her body.

'Have we seen what he's left for us yet?'

The SOCO looked up. 'We were waiting for you, ma'am.'

'Do we know how he got to her this time? Was it a man-in-the-middle thing again?'

The SOCO appeared confused, but Echo cut in, eager to tell what he'd learned so far. 'The dress is handmade. Lucy has a company in her contacts that makes dresses.'

'And they've never heard of her, yes?'

'They gave her a quote a few weeks ago. That's it.'

'And after that, our killer took over, I suppose. Said he was the dressmaker or whatever.'

Echo scrolled down his tablet. 'Seems like it. In the last text she received he asks if she's alone. Says he has some wedding apparel to show her.'

'And she invites him in, no doubt telling him they won't be disturbed. Jesus.'

'We've tracked down the fiancé from her phone. He has an alibi.'

Hume glanced around the bedroom. The cuddly-toy motif from the front room was repeated here, along with more pictures of the cat. An additional twist of guilt and sadness hit her.

'OK, roll her over. Let's see what he left us.'

Echo nodded to the SOCOs and they turned the body. A mixture of vomit and blood dribbled from Lucy's mouth. Even though Hume couldn't see the tooth, she imagined it. Imagined the intimacy of the act. The removal and replacement. The invasion. The sheer weirdness of it.

She studied the symbols carved on Lucy's chest, viewing them from every angle.

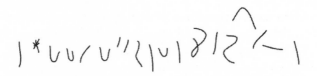

Finally she turned to Echo.

'OK. What the hell does it say?'

Echo was scribbling madly on his tablet. He looked up confidently. 'Now I know what to search for, it's easy.'

239

He handed over the tablet. The horrendous slashes and cuts had been turned into lines and numbers:

| *\/\/ | V | =20 | \/ | 8127 | - |

Hume gazed at them, then at Echo. 'Right. Pretend I'm me and tell me what I'm looking at.'

'Sorry.' Echo took the tablet back and began separating the symbols. 'Do you see these first two?'

Hume eyed the symbols Echo had isolated.

'A straight vertical line and a star.'

'That's a "p". And the next two, "v" and "v", make a "w".'

Hume could see it now. 'Right,' she said again, feeling the excitement. 'What's next?'

'The line with the "v" makes an "n". The next two make an "F", like last time — on Alice's body.'

Hume remembered the symbols carved into the flesh of Alice Watkins. Now it had been pointed out to her she could see it. 'And what's the whole message?'

'*Owned from birth*,' said Echo.

'Weird!' whispered the SOCO quietly.

'Like the professor said,' Echo gazed at Lucy with equal measures of pity and horror in his eyes, 'the killer makes it a closed circuit. The DNA of their sibling is fed back into them through their mouths. Which is the corrupted DNA of the killer. So the code is self-referencing.'

'But what is it supposed to mean?' said Hume, frustrated. 'That he owns them? Because it's his code? That no matter what they have done in life, it doesn't matter? Everything is determined by the original DNA? Then why kill them? Why "delete" them if he created them?'

Echo shook his head. He didn't have an answer for her.

'May I ask you something?'

Both the detectives turned to the SOCO. She had her hand up like she was at school.

'What?' said Hume.

'The code? That you translated?'

'Yes?'

'Well, it doesn't say "own", does it? It says "pwn".'

Echo shook his head. 'But it means own, or control. It's just the way it's spelled in leet.'

'Why?'

'Because the "p" is next to the "o" on a keyboard. Somebody hit the key wrong once, then thought it looked cool. They used it and it caught on.'

'Seriously odd.' The SOCO frowned.

'Leet is all about hiding. Being better than the ordinary drones, as it were. Hence the name. "Leet". EL-E-E-T. PWN is big in the gaming industry. It's kind of like, "Game over". Like, "I own you because I've won."'

Hume was struggling to absorb all this. 'So, it's a game to him,' she said, half in disbelief. She focused again on the crudely disfigured body of Lucy, never to be married or held or loved. From the other room, she heard the mewling of the dead woman's cat.

'Why did you do it?' she whispered. 'Why murder your own daughter and then mutilate her as if she were just a toy?'

Then she turned to Echo, a fierce look in her eyes. 'One child left. We need to find him, Echo. And we need to find the father before he kills again.'

CHAPTER 47

When Raine woke up she didn't know where she was. She kept her eyes closed for several long seconds, trying to reinsert herself into her life. Images flashed by.

On the shooting range, straight out of Hendon.

Her father setting up the rigging for an M25 field party.

Her first kiss with Clara.

Then she opened her eyes and stared up at the ceiling of her boat. The wood was smooth, with a patina of swirls and lines made by varnish reapplied many times. Without looking away, she reached her arm up behind her head, under her pillow, and pulled out the photograph she kept there. The only photograph on the entire boat.

Because you only need one, don't you?

She stared at the picture. It was of her and Clara, both in uniform. They were holding hands and giving the thumbs-up to whoever had taken the photograph. Raine pressed two fingers to her lips and transferred a kiss to the picture.

'I miss you,' she whispered.

The girl in the picture didn't answer, just stayed smiling from the safety of the past.

Raine's phone buzzed. She reached for the device sitting on the table by her bed, laying the picture face-down on her chest as she did so.

'Inspector Conner!' she said. 'So many times in one day; people will talk.'

'That's what people do,' said Conner. Raine recognised it as a line from a show, but she couldn't remember which.

'What's the news?' she said.

'Heather Salim's body has been collected from the morgue. You asked me to let you know.'

'Oh, right. Thanks.' Perversely, Raine felt angry with herself at not seeing the girl for a final time. That she hadn't offered her respects and her apologies.

'No problem. The autopsy was straightforward, apparently, and there was no need to keep her. Her body was picked up earlier this afternoon.'

Raine had an image of Heather's parents travelling slowly behind the hearse. Or maybe it would just be Mr Salim riding in the car. Or a younger relative.

'OK, well, that's case closed.' There was a rumble of thunder. Raine sat up and peered outside her window. Although it wasn't raining there was a definite storm on its way. The air was even heavier than earlier. 'I hope they have a decent journey back up north. It looks like it's going to tent it down any minute.'

'Tent it down? I don't think I've heard that expression.'

Raine grinned despite herself. 'It's like lashing it down, only including the whole canvas.'

Conner chuckled. His laugh was chest-deep and full of sunshine. 'Right.'

'Thanks again for letting me know. I really appreciate it.'

'No problem. Anyhow, I don't think the weather will matter. It's not as if she's going very far.'

Raine blinked. 'Sorry?'

'Well, her parents used a direct-to-cremation service here in London. So she won't have far to travel.'

Outside her window, a Thames swan, all ripped feathers and dead eyes, glided past.

'What do you mean, a direct-to-cremation service?'

'You know. One of those places where you don't have a service or whatever. They're quite popular these days. They just do the business then deliver the ashes to wherever. I guess the family will have a life-celebration later.'

'Inspector, Heather was a Muslim.'

There was a pause as Conner took this in.

'Called Heather?' he said, finally.

'Sure. Problem?' said Raine.

'No; just quite unusual,' said Conner quickly.

'Point being,' continued Raine, 'Heather was a Muslim and, as I understand it, Muslims do not go in for cremation. In fact, I'd go so far as to say that it would be a kind of sin to them.'

'Maybe she wasn't religious?'

'But her parents are. And her extended family. Not to have a formal burial . . . to have her anonymously cremated . . .'

Raine slid the photograph back under her pillow and reached for her shirt.

'What?' said Conner.

'Well,' said Raine, cradling the phone against her neck, 'to do that suggests to me that they must have really hated her — unless they were simply honouring her own wishes for a quick cremation.' She paused. 'But then again, what healthy person under thirty-five thinks far enough ahead to tell their parents what kind of funeral they want? Did you say she had undergone a digital autopsy?'

'Yes, the parents said they didn't— Shit! I should have clocked that there was a religious reason. Sorry, Raine.'

'No worries. There's no reason why you should have done, especially as they didn't make any other special requests. And then they opted for a cremation.'

Raine's eyes lost their focus for a moment, then she blinked. 'Did you get anywhere with the guy in the skip, the witness?'

'No. The skip has been removed, and there's no sign of the man in any of the normal night-stops around there. I've had an officer ask around, but you know how it is.'

Raine knew. The chances of finding her man were slim to nil. Unless he had a regular haunt, he would be invisible, below the radar of any agency or charity in the city.

'That's fine, but I would suggest getting the pathologist to have a look at the autopsy results again.'

'For digital autopsies it's a radiologist. And why might another look be a good idea?'

Raine shifted her shoulders, feeling the tension-pops. Her body hurt from too many blows and not enough caresses. Her brain hurt from too much thinking and not enough sleep. And her heart hurt from too much past and not enough future.

'Because if you come from a culture where cremation is prohibited and yet you insist on it for your daughter, you have either disowned her or have something you wish to hide.'

CHAPTER 48

It was a new experience for Raine watching students file out of school gates. She herself had never attended a formal school. She had either been home schooled, no-schooled, or something in between, on the converted barge. Looking at the unhappiness on the faces of most of the students, in their badly fitting uniforms, humping identical bags, she felt privileged.

It was interesting to observe the different groups. Girls and boys seemed to be quite separated. There were clearly popular and unpopular cliques. Watching the popular girls, with their uniforms subtly altered to accentuate their new sexual awareness, Raine felt a stab of sorrow. They thought they were so grown-up, but the only grown-up traits they were displaying were the shit ones. Selfishness. Superiority. Envy.

It wasn't a large school. Private funding allowed the intake to be kept to a manageable level. Raine supposed the thinking was that it would improve the pupils' prospects in life. That they would stand a better chance of going to a top university, getting set on the right financial path. But in Raine's eyes, all it did was perpetuate the status quo, and the status quo was rotten. Most of the kids were white, and of those that weren't, hardly any were black. Almost all of them exuded the sort of confidence that came with privilege.

Raine spotted her boy leaning against the main building. She grimaced.

Doesn't stop them fucking up their lives with drugs, though.

She kept her eyes on him as he laughed and joked, jostled and let his little gang collect the money. He was good; she had to give him that. He knew his trade. He was friendly to everybody and kept a group of kids around him of different ages, so that no one felt they couldn't approach. Because drugs were an equal-opportunities hobby. No one was excluded.

She couldn't see any product changing hands, just money. She guessed the drugs had already been distributed. Into lockers or coat pockets or desks. What was happening now was payment. Smart. Most people would assume it would be the other way round: get the payment first, then give out the drugs.

Wrong. Get rid of the drugs as quickly as possible. Take orders one day. Pick up and distribute the drugs. Then take payment, or better still get someone else to take payment. Getting caught with drugs and a ton of money screams dealer. Getting caught collecting money could be arranging an outing, in these circles.

As the crowd of students leaving school began to thin, the boy started winding things up. Staying late would only attract suspicion, although Raine reckoned a boy this cocky probably had a few staff members in his pocket as well. Because nothing corrupts like power, and this boy had power.

Something caught the boy's attention. He gave a little wave and said a few words to his gang. They laughed and began to disperse. Raine followed his gaze. Perhaps the person he had waved at was coming to replenish his supply or take their cut of the money.

Then she smiled. If it was a distributor, they had the best disguise in the world. Whoever the boy had waved at was in a Fiat Punto. Raine guessed it was his mother or father. Maybe an older sister. Raine couldn't see for sure from her angle.

247

As the boy strolled out of the gates and began to cross the road, she turned away and dialled Hume. The phone went straight to voicemail. Frowning, Raine left a short message, attaching the photo she had snapped of the schoolboy outside the clubhouse earlier.

CHAPTER 49

Hume took out her phone to try Raine again, only to find she had several missed calls from her. Cursing, she punched redial but was diverted straight to voicemail.

'I think I've found something,' said Echo excitedly. They were back at the office, and Echo was following up on Professor Flynn's tip about Leicester University.

'What?' asked Hume. She was worried about Raine and only half paying attention.

'Well, firstly, Leicester University has a shit-hot computing faculty — has done for decades, apparently — so if our man went there, he's defo the real deal.'

'OK.' Hume saw that she had three new messages. She swiped through to the number and dialled.

'Secondly, they are famous for the discovery of genetic fingerprinting.' Echo read from his screen: 'DNA fingerprinting was invented here at the University of Leicester by Professor Sir Alec Jeffreys in 1984. It was first used as evidence in 1987—'

'Wow,' said Hume, interrupting. 'As fascinating as that is . . . ?'

'It's a bit of a coincidence, isn't it? That the hub of DNA identity analysis was—'

'Do something computer-y,' said Hume. 'Check local papers online. Find out if there was any trouble at the university around 1991.'

Echo nodded and began tapping. Hume pressed her phone to her ear and listened to her messages. Most of them were from Raine.

The first was clearly from some hours before, informing her that she'd found the drugs, but was unable to get in contact with her. Hume guessed that was when she went into the HFEA building — and her phone switched itself to power-saving mode. The second was something about Raine's last case.

'I'm chasing down Heather's murderer and your Inspector Conner is being super helpful. I think he's feeling the love. Bell me, yeah? Oh, and don't forget Melania's ashes ceremony. Bring Robert. Really, I mean it. There's going to be nibbles.'

Hume smiled.

There was also an attachment: a picture of a schoolboy. Hume frowned.

'Bingo,' said Echo.

Hume paused the last message.

'What?'

'The *Leicester Chronicle*, 1990. There's a story about a student, Laura French. She was moonlighting as a prostitute and got caught up in a suspected revenge attack. Apparently she was walking home late at night and was dragged into a park—'

Hume interrupted impatiently. 'That doesn't sound like our guy.'

'No, but get this. She was found by some kids on their way back from a party. Her top had been ripped off and her chest written on with lipstick. Here, I've got the police photograph.'

Echo handed over his tablet. He had split the screen; on the right was the article from the *Chronicle*, and on the left was a stark photo, taken in an ambulance. The girl — she couldn't have been older than eighteen — was staring straight at the camera. Her heavy make-up was smeared across her face. She had a blanket around her shoulders and a thin arm covering her breasts. Clearly visible above the arm were the words:

ꟼ ᕼMƎOᑌƎƧ

ⵉOO

Hume turned the tablet upside down, so that the girl's head was at the bottom.

'Game over?'

Echo nodded. 'But how the gamers used to write it back in the day. And the skaters. Bitz still does.'

'Your coder girl?'

Echo blushed. 'She's not my girl. She's not anyone's girl. We sometimes play video games. To relax.'

'What sort of video games?'

'You know. Pac-Man. Space Invaders. Things like that.'

'Space Invaders,' said Hume, deadpan. 'Like the game for kids from the last century?'

'Bitz says that they have a coding purity about them.'

'Of course. Coding purity. That's what I think, too. How old is Bitz, by the way?'

'Look, the point is, she is really into heritage gaming speech. And skateboard language.'

'So, what does the code underneath mean? *F00?*'

'It means "fool". Or, in gaming terms, "unskilful player".'

'Unskilful player, as in "not good at the game"?'

'Yeah.'

Hume eyed the photograph. There was something there, something relevant, but just out of her reach. Game over. 'On the game' had long been slang for sex-working.

And considering the context of the article, from so long ago, before the information dumping ground that was today's media, certain details were bound to have been withheld. Not for the public domain.

She glanced up at Echo. 'Could this be a warning tag? A way of saying "no more prostitution"?'

'Yeah, could be. No one made the connection at the time, but maybe the killer was telling her to get out of the game because she wasn't any good at it.'

Hume stood up, her face suddenly animated. 'Maybe meaning he won because he was better at it than her. Which means he might have been on the game too.'

CHAPTER 50

As the boy got in the car and was driven away, Raine scanned the crowd of students, searching for one face in particular. A girl who had been hanging around the dealer. After a few moments, Raine spotted her by herself, walking away up the road. Raine followed her at a safe distance, placing her phone to her ear as if mid-call.

'Jack? I want to order some prosecco for tonight's little bash. I wonder if you could be a miracle-bunny and help me out? Franco has run out of the good stuff, and you know what it's like if you serve her up any old shit.' Raine paused as if listening to what the imaginary Jack was saying, then laughed. 'Waitrose, I know! What a poser!'

Raine had no idea if anyone around her was listening, but she thought she gave a pretty good impression of one of the mothers who might live in the area. Then she looked down and saw what was wearing, realised she couldn't pass for a local without a style lobotomy, and pocketed the phone. Ahead of her, the girl turned into a little park. Raine gave it a few minutes, then followed her in. The girl was sitting by herself on a bench. Raine sat down next to her.

'Shouldn't you wait until you're home before you take your drugs?' she said brightly.

The girl started, nearly dropping the half-hidden wrap in her hand. 'I'm sorry?'

Raine wondered what drove this girl to take drugs straight out of school. But she didn't have time to care. She took out her defunct warrant badge and flashed it at the girl.

'It's all right, love. I'm not here for you. It's the boy who sold you the gear I'm after.'

The girl looked like she was about to implode with fear. 'I'm sorry but I don't know what you're talk—'

Raine reached forward and snatched the wrap out of her hand. 'Just his name, and maybe his address, and you're free to go. Alternatively, we can finish this conversation down the nick with your parents. Completely your choice.'

'But . . . won't you have to arrest me for possession or something?'

Raine held up the wrap. 'Not unless you've got more than this on you. All you need to do is tell me his name and I'm gone. No trip to the cells. No phone call to your parents. No suspension from school.'

'Jamie Callow,' the girl said promptly. 'He lives on Lake Avenue.'

Maybe there was hope for her yet. 'Great. That wasn't so hard, was it? Do you know the house number?'

The girl shook her head, releasing little diamond-shaped tears from her eyes. 'No, but it's the one with the roses growing up the wall. Near the shop-arcade end.'

Raine stood up and started walking away.

'That's it?' said the girl in a small voice. Raine turned back to face her. The girl's face was full of hope, but no belief.

'Almost. But if you touch drugs again, I'll come back and arrest you in front of your cuddly toys. Understand?'

Before the girl could say anything else Raine walked quickly on.

* * *

'Here.' Echo jabbed his finger at the tablet. 'There's a whole article about students turning to prostitution to supplement their loans.'

Hume looked over Echo's shoulder at his screen. The phone against her ear continued with its attempt to connect her to Leicester Police.

'Good work. See if you can get hold of the computing department at the uni. Find out if any of the lecturers working there were employed at the time of the attack.'

'Hello, can I help you?' said a voice in Hume's ear as her call was answered.

Hume turned away from Echo and straightened.

'Hi. This is DI Hume of the Met. Who am I speaking to?'

'The desk sergeant, ma'am. DS Gulati.'

'DS Gulati, pleased to make your acquaintance. I wonder if you can put me in touch with anyone at the station who would remember a case from 1990? It was a violent assault on a student in Clarendon Park.'

There was a pause as the DS processed the request.

'That's quite a way back, ma'am. Before my time. Would you mind holding on while I check with my colleagues?'

'Not at all, Sergeant. And please don't call me "ma'am". It makes me feel ancient. "Sir" will be fine.'

'Right. One moment, please . . . sir.'

The line went silent. Hume wondered if the officer would first check Hume was who she said she was, and not some reporter digging up an old story. Echo was chatting to someone on his own phone, while typing furiously. Hume looked up at the smartboard while she waited. They had added the name of the last victim next to the three others. Mr Porter from HFEA had said there was one other child conceived with the donor's sperm, but the information on this child had been erased.

Why? wondered Hume. *Why had he hidden himself and one child, but left the others on the agency database? He must have known that once he started his killing spree the police would eventually find the connection.*

'Inspector Hume?' A different voice in her ear. Older.

'Yes,' she said into the phone, dragging her attention away from the board.

'This is DI Tom Hall. I understand from our sergeant that you're interested in a cold case from thirty years ago.'

'Not as such, Inspector. I'm working on a multiple murder case down here in London, and there's a possibility that my suspect started his journey on your patch. Were you around in 1990?'

'Patrolling the streets, and much happier for it.'

Hume smiled. She understood exactly where he was coming from. Walking the beat was a lost art. Changing police methods and cutbacks had all but destroyed the concept of community policing. Boots on the ground gave you a visceral contact with the community you served. The further you got from the street, the harder it was to feel that connection.

'Understood. Do you happen to remember the case of a student who was attacked in the summer of that year? They say she was selling sex to pay her way through uni and it ended badly . . .'

'Rape victim?'

'No, I don't think so. She was dragged into the park and beaten up, but not raped. She had her top ripped off and some words written on her chest with lipstick.'

'Game over,' said DI Hall promptly. Hume felt the hairs on the back of her neck stiffen.

'You remember,' she said softly.

'Difficult to forget. The girl was one of my first twisters, you know what I mean?'

Hume nodded. She understood about twisters — those cases that completely changed your perspective on everything. Took you out of the comfort of thinking the world was basically decent and forced you to see the truth: that underneath the skin of society was something much darker than you could imagine. Something rotten. A twister was a case that tore the house up, spun it round and dumped it in a whole new world. Leaving you feeling like Dorothy in *The Wizard of Oz*.

'Damn, this is something to do with those code murders, isn't it?' The detective's voice broke through her thoughts. 'I knew there was something bugging me.'

'What makes you say that?'

'Because of the leet. The words were written with numbers as well as letters. And there was some sort of code.'

Hume's stomach tightened, and she walked to the window, hitting the record button on her phone. Outside the air was grainy with heat. Even the builders on the scaffolding opposite looked smudged somehow.

'F-0-0,' she said.

'That's it. Means you're a poor player or something. I can't quite remember.'

'It would be a big help if you could tell me everything you *do* remember, Tom. We're getting closer, but the dots still aren't connecting.'

There was a pause while the detective marshalled his thoughts.

'No problem. Let me see, I was not long on the force. I'd been given the baby-beat.'

'The baby-beat? Like playgroups and the school run?'

'Are you kidding me? Those mothers are sodding animals! The school run is a nightmare. Road rage and child envy. The school run requires combat experience.'

Hume smiled again. She liked DI Tom Hall.

'So what's the baby-beat?'

'University patrol.'

Hume felt a cog engage in her brain.

'Breaking up house parties when the music got too loud. Making sure the disco biscuits were under control. It was a way of giving new police officers a taste of the world in a little microcosm of society.'

'Except something went wrong, yes?'

'All the way,' said the detective. 'That summer there was a big prostitution problem at the university. Students getting rent discounts for sexual favours from private landlords was the beginning, but the whole thing escalated.'

'How, exactly?'

'I'm not sure. It was the time before the internet and dating apps. Everything was done either via classifieds or left on message boards in the halls of residence. No one even had mobile phones. All those kinds of transactions were facilitated by text-pagers. Do you remember them? Little gadgets that you could only write limited texts on.'

Another cog. Hume noticed that Echo was off his phone and working his tablet.

'But what do you mean, it all escalated?'

'I guess it was just a mad summer. There was a lot of ecstasy around. A lot of cocaine, too. The idea of rent boys and girls was almost acceptable. Everything seemed kind of normalised. Odd to think of it now, but the kids didn't view it as abuse.'

'That's because they were kids. They didn't have the perspective.'

'Right. Anyway, a few of the students got into drug dealing, and a few got sucked into prostitution. You know, fuck a student and all that. Feeds straight into the fantasies of the type who would request such a service.'

'And this girl was one of those? The one who got beaten up?'

'Yes, but she wasn't cut out for the stress or the horror of it. Some of the kids just took it as a laugh, or at least seemed to. But she was deep in a hole. After the attack, she dropped out of university. Dropped out of life, really, as much as I remember.'

'Game over.'

'Game over,' he agreed.

'Did you ever get anywhere with the case? I've searched through the records but there was no follow-up from the original attack, as far as I can see.'

'Dead end. The girl couldn't give a description of her attacker; she was pretty high at the time. We investigated, of course, and that put an end to most of the prostitution. Then it was the summer holidays. By the time the new term started, the kids had moved on. You know what they're like.'

'Not sure I do.'

'The summer of love was over, and the students had moved up a year. And the new students had a different income stream.'

'Like what?'

'Clinical trials, I think. Private clinics started springing up, and students could make a packet by offering themselves as pincushions, so to speak.'

'Right. You mean by testing new drugs for pharmaceutical companies?'

'Exactly. And the games industry was just kicking off. Kids were being paid to road-test the latest titles. RPG — role-playing games — were quite big at the time, as far as I remember.'

Hume felt the two cogs begin to grind together. She heard DI Hall clear his throat, the sound metallic in the small speaker of her phone.

'Some of them even donated sperm. There was good money in that, back in the day.'

Hume looked across at the builders. One of them seemed to be staring straight back at her. She turned away from the window to see Echo waving frantically, trying to get her attention.

'I wonder if you can put all this down in an email and send it to me at the station? Your desk sergeant will have the details. You've been really helpful, and I appreciate it, but my colleague needs me urgently.'

'No problem. Do you think it's the same person? The one who attacked the girl? Doing these murders? There was something . . . obscene about the way she was treated. With the code on her. Like she was merely a cypher or something. All these years and I can still remember her face.'

Hume glanced at the smartboard, covered with images of the killers' four dead offspring. The code cut into their bodies as if they were part of some game.

'Oh, yes. I think it's the same person.'

* * *

I feel everything now.

It's like back in the day. Like when you're young. You feel every bit of air on your skin. Every touch on your body. So long ago.

A different person. That's not who I am anymore. Not the mask I made myself.

If the young man hadn't knocked on my door that day, and brought the past crashing in, then maybe things might have stayed as they were. Maybe I could have stayed living in my shell. Who knows? But now I don't have to. I should thank him, really. Make him a cake and put on a party hat.

Because it's been a party, this past couple of weeks. Taking care of the things I'd tried to bury. Taking care of the past.

Although it was never really the past, was it? There isn't really a past, no matter how we try to convince ourselves otherwise. I, more than anybody, should know that. Everything is just the present, getting more and more cluttered. Nothing deleted. Nothing erased. Everything always existing somewhere.

But I have had a bit of a spring clean. First then, in the pretend past. And now here, in the pretend present.

CHAPTER 51

Raine stood opposite the house in Lake Avenue with the roses growing up the side. The house next to the small gaggle of shops that looked like they were all run by middle-aged matrons who believed that cake and flowers and wine were all a person could need if they had to nip out for extra supplies.

Maybe they were right, she thought. It sounded pretty good to her.

Raine pulled out her phone and tried Hume again, but got an engaged signal. She closed the call and tapped the device against her front teeth, debating what to do.

She looked across at the house. She couldn't loiter here much longer; it was a nice middle-class neighbourhood and her face, still covered in faded bruises, really didn't fit in. She put the dead phone to her ear again.

'Tarquin? I'm trying to find your house, but all these boxes look the same. Did you say yours was the one with the swimming pool?'

She crossed the road.

Raine opened the gate to the property and walked up the little garden path.

'It's OK, Tarquin. I'm just going to pop in and see Jamie on my way. I'll be round in a jiffy.'

Pocketing the phone, Raine raised her fist and knocked briskly on the door.

* * *

'Leon Steward,' said Echo, his eyes shining.

'Who's Leon Steward?'

Hume leaned against the desk and raised her eyebrows. Echo was practically vibrating with excitement.

'He is, or was, according to the head of the computer-science faculty, one of the brightest computing stars who ever passed through the university.'

'OK, and why is he of interest to us?'

Echo pulled up his tablet and started scrolling through. 'Leon Steward. Straight "A" student, but not popular with his peers. Seemed a little disconnected.'

'Echo, I was a little disconnected as a youth. That's sort of the point.'

'But Leon was showing enough warning signs for his head of year to red-flag him. He thought there might be money troubles or possible mental-health difficulties. Suspected eating disorder, too.'

'OK, but what puts him on our board?' asked Hume. The hairs on her neck were still tingling, and her stomach still felt tight.

'There was an altercation, just before the summer holidays. Leon beat someone up. A girl from the year above. Or more correctly, they beat each other up. Neither party would say what it was about, and the term ended shortly after. The person I spoke to thought that maybe they were in some sort of relationship.'

'I'm still not getting it. Why did the lecturer you spoke to—'

'Head of department.'

'Thank you, Mr Pedantic. Why did the head of department think this Leon might be of interest to us?'

'It was the same girl,' said Echo. 'The girl from the park. Laura.'

Hume remained perfectly still for a couple of seconds.

'And why wasn't it reported to the police?'

'Laura didn't press charges. The only reason the professor even remembers it is because of something that happened later. Something weird.'

The tingling increased. It was like little electric shocks tracing up and down the back of Hume's neck.

'What sort of weird?'

'Laura died, apparently. Never returned for her third year. Suicide.'

'Awful, but not weird.'

'She'd removed all her teeth with pliers.'

'Jesus . . . The head of department told you this?'

Echo shook his head, causing his hair to flop over his brow. He pushed it aside. 'No, but he remembered where she came from. Near Canterbury. There was a story about it in the local press. The pop psychology at the time was that she'd removed them because she'd run out of ways to express her inner turmoil.'

Echo pointed at the smartboard, where he had already added the piece next to the article from the *Leicester Chronicle*.

'I called the newspaper, except it's all gone digital now. It's just a two-person operation with syndicated stories, but it's the same reporter.'

'Local newspaper hell. Once you're in, you never get out,' murmured Hume. 'Which I'm guessing is to our advantage?'

'Very much so. He told me all the gory details. How she'd laid them all out in a line on her desk.'

For a moment, Hume thought he was talking about the reporter. Then realised with a lurch he was talking about the girl, Laura. About her teeth. Hume wondered if anyone had even checked to see if one was missing.

'The fingerprints on the pliers were hers?'

'Yes. And there was a note.'

Echo should have looked triumphant, pleased with his detective skills, but he didn't. His skin was pale and there was a light sheen of sweat on his face.

'You need to cut down on the coffee, DC Echo. What did the note say?'

'"I can't take it anymore. Game over."'

Echo pointed to the smartboard. On it he'd written:

g4m3 0v3r

'Jesus,' whispered Hume again. 'It's him.'

'For sure. The reporter sent me through a picture of the teeth on-scene. it wasn't released publicly because . . . well, for the same reason I've just used the term "teeth on-scene".'

Echo swiped and an image of a dressing table appeared on the smartboard. It was the sort you would find in a teen-age girl's bedroom. There was a mirror and make-up and a trinket box. There was also a row of bloody stumped teeth and a set of pliers.

'Christ!' murmured Hume.

'Do you see it?' said Echo.

'I'll see this in my nightmares,' said Hume. 'It's . . . completely fucked up.'

'No— I mean yes, it is, but that's not what I'm talking about.'

He expanded the image until it was just the teeth in the frame. Hume really wished he hadn't. With the magnification, every ripped bit of tissue looked stark and somehow naked.

'There,' he said. 'Do you see the gap?'

Hume saw it. On the right-hand side there was a space between the teeth. Unless you knew what to look for, there wouldn't be any significance to it, but Hume understood. She knew exactly what it meant.

'Our missing tooth,' she said. 'The one we found in David's mouth.'

'More than that. You see where it is? It's the molar.'

'So?'

'So the gap is at the back. It's another little in-joke he's playing.'

'I don't get it.'

'He created a space in her teeth. At the back.'

Echo looked at her expectantly.

'Spell it out for me, Echo.'

'Control plus backspace. The two keys you hit on a computer keyboard if you want to delete something.'

She stared at him. 'That's a bit far-fetched.'

'Maybe. But if we're right, and the physical body — the DNA — is viewed by him only in computing terms, it makes a kind of sense. Like he's just playing.'

'So everything really is just a game. Nothing is real to this man.'

'Including himself, it seems.'

'What do you mean?'

'I mean I can't find him. There are no records of him anywhere since 1993. Nothing on the electoral roll. No driving licence. Nothing. It's like he disappeared off the face of the earth.'

Echo swiped again and a picture appeared on the board. A young man in his late teens, stick-thin with long blond hair tied back in a ponytail. His face was a battleground of acne scars. He was smiling at the camera and had his arm around a girl. Hume guessed it was from some university event. End of year party, perhaps. She gazed into his eyes and felt the synapses fire into life at the back of her brain, new connections forming just out of reach.

'Parents?'

'Both dead.'

'Maybe he's just so hot at computers he's made himself disappear — at least from the internet,' she mused.

'Computers weren't like that then,' said Echo. 'There was no internet, remember? Everything was held on separate systems. You couldn't just wipe your identity.'

As Hume studied the picture of Leon, her phone buzzed: a reminder that she had voicemail. She realised she hadn't finished listening to Raine's messages and swiped her screen, calling up her inbox, then turned to Echo with a big smile.

'This is great work, Echo. See if you can get Professor Flynn on the line. Maybe he's thought of something to help us profile.' Then she swiped the phone to listen to Raine's message.

'*Hi. Don't worry — I'm not about to do anything stupid, but I'm following your drugs. If you don't hear from me in two hours get Echo to ping my phone and come and rescue me.*'

Hume checked the time: the message had been sent an hour ago. She recalled what DI Conner had said about intelligence given on a London drug depot, and that the killing of Raine's misper, Heather, had possibly been a mistaken gang hit. Knowing Raine, she had probably gone off to some postcode hell in an attempt to get information.

She fired off a quick reply: *Let me know you're OK, or I'll send in the troops. Now.*

'Professor Flynn is on the line,' said Echo.

'Great, put him on speaker.'

There was an amplified 'click' as Echo dropped his phone into the speaker pod on his desk.

'Hello?' Flynn's voice filled the small office. 'Am I still here?'

Hume blinked at the question. 'Hello, Professor? It's Detective Inspector Hume. Thank you for taking our call.'

'No problem. I was actually going to call you. I've been giving some thought to our friend.'

Echo raised his eyebrows, but Hume shook her head. 'Excellent! Has anything new occurred to you?'

'It's the circular nature, you see.' The intellectual excitement was clear in the professor's voice. 'At first, I assumed that it was as I described, a closed circuit. He had made the code, so to speak, but the life choices of his programs — his biological children, that is — had corrupted it. The code was now damaged, and the programs needed to be shut down. The teeth were possibly a way of doing that. Similar to what you suggested.'

'A biological USB,' said Echo.

'But the more I thought about it, the more it didn't fit. There would be no need for the mask, for a start. Why wear a mask if the person you are killing — the program you are shutting down — will never be able to identify you to the authorities?'

'Because they'll be dead. Good point,' said Hume. 'And do you have an answer?'

'You know, I think I do. I think the mask is not meant to disguise how he sees himself now but to amplify what he was then.'

Hume looked at Echo, whose expression told her he didn't know what Flynn meant either.

'Sorry, Professor. I'm not getting you,' she said.

'Have you ever heard of body dysmorphia?'

'Is that when you think there's something wrong with your body? Like you think you're overweight or whatever?'

'In simplistic terms, yes. Body dysmorphia is the belief that an aspect of one's physical appearance is defective in some way. I think what we're dealing with here is someone who despises their body and wishes to alter it. In fact, even deeper than that, I think they saw their very DNA, or code, as somehow wrong.'

'Like Blackpool rock,' said Hume quietly. 'Wrong all the way through.'

'I beg your pardon?'

'Professor, we've recently come upon a suspect. He was a student at Leicester University, as you suggested he might be—'

'In the computing department?' Flynn interrupted eagerly.

'Yes.'

'You see! It all fits the pattern. Dysmorphia on a fundamental level. If your man had been studying computer code, looking at the building blocks of logic, then he could easily have transposed his psychological dissymmetry; combined the two realities.'

Echo seemed lost, but Hume was listening intently.

'I sort of understand what you're saying.' She paused for a moment. 'It's possible he was also working as a prostitute to bolster his income. Do you think this would feed into the psychosis?'

'Most definitely!' said the professor cheerily. 'Only, he wouldn't have done it for the money. It would be a way of disassociating himself from a physicality he found repugnant. Not just on the outside, but all the way down to a cellular level. There have been several studies on sex workers feeling alienated from their own bodies. But his separation would have been more fundamental.'

'Bad code,' Echo chipped in.

'Exactly,' said Flynn. 'The act of prostitution itself would feed into his body-hate, unless he started treating his flesh as a separate entity. Something he could control.'

'Like he was the driver,' said Hume.

'Or the games master,' added Echo. 'We think he was into the burgeoning game culture.'

'That would explain the . . . leetspeak, I think you called it?'

'Which feeds back to the disassociation, coupled with a sense of elitism,' ventured Hume.

'A feedback of mental superiority, while hating one's physicality. Yes,' added the professor, 'the perfect storm. The entire physical structure becomes unreal. Only the code is pure.'

'Hang on a moment, Professor, while I process. It's a lot to take in.'

'Of course.'

Hume thought through the implication of Flynn's words for several hard seconds. Meanwhile, Echo began reorganising the smartboard, swiping his tablet and transferring all the files to the screen. Placing the new information alongside the old. The board was becoming cluttered. Difficult to read.

'So, if I've understood what you're saying, Professor,' Hume said at last, 'Leon—'

'Is that his name? The suspect?'

'A person of interest,' corrected Hume, mentally kicking herself. 'He has this condition . . .'

'Body dysmorphia,' prompted Flynn.

'Right, but some extreme variant of it, that makes him despise his entire physicality.'

'Down to his genetic make-up, yes.'

'And the sperm donation?'

'Would be an attempt to expunge that code, rather than propagate it.'

'OK, I get that. But why now? And why the large gap between kills? Did he become well — stay well for thirty years? Is that even possible?'

As Echo shuffled the display, Hume gazed at the board, as if mere concentration could solve the problem.

'No,' said Flynn firmly. 'He must have done something that satisfied his psychosis. Or at least masked it enough for him to live a normal life. Like a functioning sociopath. Hidden in plain view.'

Hume nodded.

'And the catalyst? The thing that made him seek out his biological children and—' Hume couldn't help but grimace — 'shut them down?'

'That I don't know. But it must be something that bridged the gap between who he is now and what he was then.'

Hume looked at the board. At the picture of the teen-age Leon, with his ravaged face. She thought that he'd have wanted to do something about that skin if he'd worked as a prostitute. Foundation or concealer. Or a mask. Then she thought about David searching for his biological father. Idly, she let the strands of the case web her consciousness, as if memory alone could catch a fly.

And something tugged.

She refocused and concentrated on the board again. Her eyes widened as realisation hit her.

CHAPTER 52

The door opened and, for a nanosecond, Raine was frozen. The person in front of her was the same man she had photographed with Cale a few nights ago, drinking vodka in the cafe in Soho.

'Hello, can I help you?' The man smiled at Raine, with a slight crease of puzzlement between his brows. Up close she realised why his face had seemed so smooth. His skin seemed too tight for his skull, stretched and taut, as if it had been tensioned.

Raine blinked, then smiled back. 'Hi, I wonder if I might have a word with Jamie? Is he in?'

The man's smile slipped a little. 'Jamie? My son? I'm sorry, but what is this about?'

Raine held out her old warrant card, keeping her smile open and friendly, obscuring the date stamp with her fingers.

'DC Raine. Mr . . . ?'

'Callow.'

Raine could see the tension in the man's shoulders as he crossed his arms.

'Mr Callow, yes. Well, it's nothing to worry about. There's just been a little trouble at school. I wonder if I might step inside for a moment?'

The man glanced over Raine's shoulder into the street, as if to check whether any of the neighbours were watching — curtain-twitching while a police officer, albeit plain-clothes, was standing on his doorstep. He peered down at Raine, the smile on his face now laced with worry.

'I'm not sure. My wife normally deals with these things. Perhaps you could come back later—'

He began closing the door, so Raine placed a hand against it, halting its path.

'It won't take long, Mr Callow, and it is quite important.'

The man looked at her hand, then back at her face. His puzzlement changed to fear.

'Something's happened, hasn't it? Has Jamie been involved in something bad?'

'It's really best if we talk inside, Mr Callow. Is Jamie in?'

The man stepped aside. 'He's upstairs in his room. Please come in. I'll go and get him. I wish my wife was here. I'm not good with people. She's the one who liaises with the school. I'm expecting her back any minute now, actually.'

Raine's mind was racing furiously as she entered the house. Upstairs she could hear the bass of an EDM track. What the fuck was going on? Why was the father of a teenage drug dealer meeting up with the boyfriend of a murder victim?

Because it was a family affair? Was his son supplying drugs for him to sell on? Raine mused.

Then she shook her head. It just didn't fit. A father–son drug operation, like some middle-class version of an old East End family gang? Not very likely.

Mr Callow closed the front door and stepped past her.

'Come through to the sitting room. He'll never hear me calling over that racket. I'll get you seated and then fetch him. Can I get you something to drink — tea or coffee?'

'No thank you, Mr Callow, and I'm sure we can sort this out. It's not really your son who's in trouble. There are some kids at school who have been bullying a younger girl. I'm checking all the children in Jamie's form to see what they know, or may have witnessed.'

Jamie's dad looked over his shoulder, obvious relief on his face. Raine followed him down the narrow hall past the stairs. There was an old-fashioned telephone table with a brass lamp on her left, and a framed photograph of Jamie and his father on the wall to the right. Mr Callow stopped at the bottom of the stairs.

'Please, go through. I'll just pop up and get him. He's a popular boy at school, so I'm sure he'd be able to help if he saw anything.'

Raine squeezed past. She figured she'd just about have time to message Hume before the man came back down with his son.

'Thank you, Mr Callow. I'll try not to take too much of your time—'

Raine paused, wondering why there was no wife in the photo. The man had clearly stated she was due back at any moment. She began to turn even as the base of the lamp crashed into her skull, sending her spinning to the floor.

* * *

Hume's gaze fixed on the two photos, the gears in her brain shifting up.

'Professor,' she said, her voice tight, 'hang on a moment, please.' She turned to Echo. 'The photo you've just uploaded of Leon. Put it on a separate screen.' She spoke into the phone again, addressing the professor. 'What if he did something with his face to disguise it? Could that tie in with the DNA psychosis or whatever?'

'Like plastic surgery? Unlikely. This isn't some James Bond baddie we're talking about—'

'Thing is, I'm looking at a picture from a surveillance asset here that closely resembles our suspect. Only, there's something about the face . . .'

'What about it?'

'I'm not sure . . .'

Hume glanced at Echo. 'Could you put the photo Raine took in Soho next to the one of Leon? The one of Cale and his mysterious drinking buddy.'

Echo immediately began swiping at his tablet, reordering the board.

Meanwhile, the professor was in full flight again. 'Leon, if I'm right, doesn't even see his body as real. He wouldn't do anything as mundane as plastic surgery to escape capture. That would be investing too much belief in his own flesh. In fact, I'd say his psychosis is a form of body dysmorphia within a technological matrix that probably requires an entirely new category. Existential dysmorphia, perhaps.'

'Great,' muttered Hume. 'I hope you enjoy your book deal.'

'However . . .' Professor Flynn sounded thoughtful. Even through the phone's small screen, he was able to pin Hume with his piercing gaze. 'Did you know, Detective Inspector, that the term "computer bug" actually has a biological origin?'

'In what sense?'

'I'll crop out Cale and leave the two next to each other,' said Echo.

'Just the faces, and make them bigger,' said Hume.

'In 1947, at Harvard University, a moth found its way into a computer mainframe, causing it to malfunction. That's why we use the term "bug". It was an actual bug. A sliver of biological matter that shorted a relay, triggering corruption in the programming.'

'That's . . . amazing.'

The professor smiled graciously in agreement. 'Since the killer views the body merely as wrongly encoded material, he would not have any compunction about rewriting it.'

'Sorry, Professor. I'm not getting the connection.'

'The moth permanently altered the program. Its body fused with the machine, becoming part of it. Even after the insect's remains had been removed the program didn't default back. The fact of its physical presence, its biological footprint, could not be reversed. The whole system had to be wiped and reprogrammed.'

Hume felt the puzzle shift again. 'And that's what the killer has been doing with his children? Wiping the program?'

'Perhaps. Trying to get back to a time before the moth, if you will. Before the DNA dysmorphia was triggered. In fact, it would even fit with the mask theory, given the information you have supplied.'

'Go on.'

'It's possible that our man believes the mask to be his true form: an external representation of what he feels internally. So, for him, the mask wouldn't be a mask at all.' The professor leaned forward, his face now filling the screen. 'Rather, he would see his real face as the mask. A biological disrupter, if you will.'

Immediately Hume recalled what the traumatised sex worker had said about seeing a devil at the scene of Alice Watkins' murder. *What did the mask look like to cause such terror? Exactly how did Leon see himself?*

'Boss?'

Echo had placed the two photos side by side on the board. *Even with the poor quality . . . Even with the age difference . . . Even with the*— she baulked inwardly at the jargon — *existential dysmorphia, it was the same person.*

Echo tapped his tablet once more. On the smartboard, the photograph Raine had taken and sent in with her report expanded to fill the space. Up close, it was clear there was something strange about his face. An unnatural smoothness, like it had been ironed. She looked across at the other picture: Leon with his acne scars and discolouration.

'Professor. The image I'm looking at . . . The suspect has done something to his face. Maybe Botox or some sort of skin graft. How would that fit in with your thesis?'

'Interesting. Apart from the smoothness, is the shape basically the same?'

'What do you mean?'

'Nose. Chin. Structure identifiers.'

'Right, got you.' Hume studied the pictures a moment. 'No, it's just the skin. Everything else seems to be—'

'If it is the same man, he must have had some cosmetic work done. No way would the skin stay that tight round the eyes and neck,' said Echo, expanding the image further.

'Then it could certainly fit in.' Professor Flynn was warming to his theme. 'Leon could be attempting to bookmark his face. Stop it changing at a particular moment in time. Erase any possible future and freeze it at the moment that he felt most himself. I'm sure such a procedure would have been possible. Plastic surgery was like the Wild West back in the '90s. There were private clinics that would do just about anything, given the right financial incentive.'

'Thank you, Professor. You've been really helpful,' said Hume.

She thought about the money Leon might have made from prostitution. About the dissociation that the professor had discussed. Then she turned to Echo. 'We need to get hold of Raine. See if she noticed anything that could help us find our man.'

'Do you think we'd better check on Cale Brindley first?'

Hume looked up at the picture of the two of them outside the Soho cafe. The man's finger, Leon Steward's finger, touching the young man's wrist.

'Shit.'

* * *

Oh dear. And it was going so well.

Still, that's the trouble with the physical; it always fucking lies to you. Corrupted data.

That's why the code is all that matters. The code that I've become.

One more on my list. He should have been at the top, really, but I thought I might be able to rewrite him. Make him pure.

And in a way I suppose he was *at the top of my list. After all, he was the first one I found, once I'd looped the program. Overwritten my face.*

Finding his mother was a doddle. The HFEA database could have been set up by Wombles, for all the security protocols they fucked up; especially back then.

Killing her had been a doddle, too.

The boy was only a baby, and one parent is as good as another after a while. After a little more time had passed, he didn't even remember her.

We had to move, of course, but that was fine. People only see what they want to see. A father and son. My son. My new son.

Oh, well. Easy come, easy go.

CHAPTER 53

Raine felt roughness against her cheek, itchy and somehow hostile. She couldn't remember where she was and she seemed to be having trouble opening her eyes. Every time she tried, a bolt of pain exploded at the back of her head.

She concentrated on breathing and not throwing up. Slowly, the pain subsided to a manageable level. She tentatively explored the area with her fingertips. It was warm and wet and spongy. And she smelled the coppery scent of blood, almost like a taste.

Then it all came flooding back. Following the boy home. The man opening the door. The same man who had been drinking in the Soho cafe with Cale. Smiling and touching his hand.

Raine opened her eyes.

Not Cale's dealer, then. Not supplying him with drugs so he could murder his boyfriend. Something else.

She was lying on her side on the floor of the living room. The roughness she felt on her cheek was carpet. She could see the door to the hallway, the heavy brass lamp on the wooden floor next to the stairs. Mingled with the thump of pain in her head, which pulsed with her blood, she could hear the bass of the EDM track vibrating through the house.

Which meant the son might still be listening to his music.

Beyond the lamp, she could see the front door. It was maybe fifteen metres away.

Raine centred herself.

She could make fifteen metres. She could hold the pain and the nausea and the fear inside long enough to make fifteen metres and get the fuck out of here. Phone Hume. Call in the cavalry like she should have done earlier.

'I'm surprised that whack didn't kill you. I really put everything I had into it.'

Or maybe not.

Raine closed her eyes, letting go of the idea of immediate escape. The voice was behind her, unflustered and amused. As if its owner hadn't just tried to bash her brains out.

'But I suppose you'll be used to being hit, in your line of business.'

There was something else in the voice, as well as amusement. A kind of detachment, as if only half the thought process required was being directed to the conversation. Also, there was a slightly muffled aspect to the tone, as if the man were holding a newspaper in front of his face.

'It must be filthy down there. Why don't you let me help you up? I've been quite busy this week. I haven't really had much time to concentrate on housework.'

Raine felt herself being grabbed under the arms. She wanted to cry out, but the pain was too great. All she managed was a low moan as the pain fireworked, flaring inside her skull, and she slipped back into unconsciousness.

CHAPTER 54

'Cale's dead. The uniforms we sent say he's been dead for some time. Maybe a day or more.'

Hume felt heavy with the weight of Echo's words. She stared out of the window across at the building opposite. The scaffolding was down now and the outer stone wall was newly washed and pristine. Hume gave it a year before the acid in the rain began to make inroads.

'How?'

Echo read from his tablet. 'Both of his eyes have been removed, along with his right hand. We'll have to wait for the lab report but, according to the crime report, it was definitely done while he was alive.'

Hume focused now on her own reflection in the window. Lots of blood meant the heart was still pumping. She turned around.

'And on his chest? What was written on his chest?'

Echo gestured towards the smartboard. He had posted the photograph of Cale's pale chest onto the screen.

9h0578411

'Ghostball,' Hume read. 'Right?'

She glanced at Echo who confirmed: 'Ghostball was an early computer virus.'

'A virus,' repeated Hume, inspecting the cuts on the body. She remembered the young man's face. So beautifully kept.

'Yes. And we've had the CCTV back from HFEA. It was Cale who visited the institution, posing as David.'

She examined the other photographs that appeared on the board. The severed wrist. The empty eyes. She felt her brain spinning everything around, pulling it all together.

'So Cale is the catalyst, not David. Cale is the virus. The start of it all. He saw something on David's computer. Or maybe they saw it together. Then went to HFEA. Reached out to Leon.'

'Except Leon doesn't exist anymore,' said Echo, standing. 'Because Leon's code was wrong. After the killing back in Leicester, Leon wipes himself off the grid. Becomes someone else.'

'No luck in tracing him?'

'No. And we're still trying to track down the last donor child, but it seems Leon scrapped all the data referring to them.'

Hume clenched her fists in frustration.

'So he ghosts himself. And because he's good with computers he can do it. Then he changes himself. But he doesn't just grow his hair or whatever. He needs something more fundamental than that. His body . . .' Hume glanced at Echo.

'Dysmorphia,' he supplied.

'. . . is existential. He needs to become a "biological disrupter", as the professor put it, a moth within the machine. What's the one thing the body does without fail?' Hume looked at Echo expectantly.

'Age.'

'Exactly — age. So Leon stops the process. At least on his face. Gets some surgery done on the black market, as a means of separating himself from the DNA inside.'

Hume started pacing, slotting the pieces into place in her head.

'But Leon still keeps tabs on his old life. His old code. When Cale reaches out to him, he replies. Maybe he doesn't know his little student money-earner had any takers. Or maybe he did, but he had shut that part of his life away.

'He still keeps a line open to his old identity. Because he understands that information is never destroyed, only changed into different forms. When he gets an alert to say that somebody is looking for him — the old him — he finds out who it is and engineers a meet. Then Cale turns up with the ultimate up-fuck proposal. Give him some money or he'll drag Leon into the open. Or — who knows? — if Cale believes Leon is sufficiently affluent, with a nice comfortable life, then this man might pay to keep David a secret.'

'But Cale doesn't know that Leon is a fruit-loop,' said Echo.

Hume stopped pacing and raised an eyebrow. 'Fruit-loop? Is that an approved psychological term?'

Echo's expression was solemn. 'One hundred per cent. Professor Flynn told me.'

Just for a moment Hume's mouth twitched.

'Anyhow, Cale brings it all back. Triggers the old code.'

'And thereby sets in motion the killer-command program,' finished Echo.

They look at each other in silence for a couple of seconds.

'You know I think that's it. I think that's what happened,' said Hume.

'But what about the drugs? How did Leon get the drugs?' Hume looked at Echo, then at the board.

'The Donkey Kong,' Echo realised.

Hume's smile slipped. 'Raine,' she said, opening up her phone. 'She was checking out the drugs.' She listened as the phone went to voicemail.

'*Hi, this is Raine. Do it.*'

Hume barked at Echo: 'The phone thing — can you do it now?'

'What phone thing?' said Echo, confused.

'Track it or whatever. Find out where she is! She gave you all her passwords and stuff, didn't she?'

'Oh right. Hang on.'

Hume watched on tenterhooks as Echo did his thing.

'The last time it was used was a couple of hours ago,' said Echo after a minute.

That would tally with when she'd left the message: *If you don't hear from me call in the troops*.

'Nothing since then?' asked Hume, the desperation plain in her voice. Echo shook his head, still tapping. 'No. I can only track it to its last used location. Any further and you'd need the network supplier, or a court order to Google.'

Hume thought furiously, trying to think if Raine had told her anything that might give a clue as to where she had gone.

Echo showed her the screen of his tablet. Displayed was a map of south-east London with a red pin lit up. 'Her last location was outside a school.'

Suddenly, Hume remembered the schoolboy. The last Raine image had sent through to her before going off grid.

Hume grabbed her coat.

'Get me a patrol car. Now.'

CHAPTER 55

When Raine came to again she was tied to a chair with duct tape. The man had gone, but the EDM track was still pumping.

Now she was upright the pain in her head had receded a little. She guessed it might have something to do with blood flow. Or adrenalin. Or the anger she felt at herself. What the fuck had she been thinking? Of course the schoolboy wasn't supplying drugs to a crazed killer. When would he find the time for that? Between homework and Pokémon?

It was the father who was supplying drugs to the crazed killer.

Raine tested the duct-tape bonds. They felt secure, immobilising her hands behind her back and fastening her to the spine of the chair. She stared wildly around the room, desperately searching for something to cut the tape, but nothing sprang immediately to view.

That was all right. She was a former police officer with years of training in hand-to-hand combat and working under pressure in stressful environments. She'd be able to get out of this situation in no time at all.

She felt blood slugging down the back of her neck and closed her eyes. When she opened them again, an apparition from a horror film was standing in the doorway. In his hand was Raine's old warrant card.

'Hello, Detective Raine. Shouldn't you have handed this in when you were fired?'

It was the man who had hit her. The drug dealer. The man whom she had photographed with Cale outside the cafe. The man who had let her in to his house — Callow. She could tell by his voice. But she couldn't tell by the face, because he was wearing a mask.

The man — or *monster*, as Raine had decided to think of him — walked across the room and sat at the table. The mask was made out of some form of rubber or latex. An off-pink colour, like childhood medicine. The only holes in it were for the eyes and mouth. There was something vaguely sexual about it, perhaps the shininess. It looked like it would be slick to the touch. Not that you'd ever want to touch it. Raine thought about the woman in the disused warehouse, the sex worker who had glimpsed a scene from hell.

It was a devil. That was what she'd said. She was right.

The entire mask was covered with letters. They varied in size and colour, and seemed to be arranged in patterns, crammed together in tight groups. In between the letters were what appeared to be pictures of ladders that had been twisted in the middle.

Raine told herself not to be stupid, not to be scared of some ridiculous mask. 'Actually, I wasn't fired. We came to a mutual decision. Did you kill my cat?'

Callow tilted his head. Raine couldn't read the expression in his eyes, but his posture spoke of his confusion.

'Your cat? Why would I kill your cat?'

'Don't worry. I get a little confused when I'm scared. How about, "Did you kill David Webb?"'

The man's eyes sparkled. 'What do you think?'

'I think you've got a really freaky mask on. What are all the numbers and symbols?'

As she talked, Raine tried to use her peripheral vision to scope the room. Tried to find some way out of her situation.

She saw her phone on the table. Callow must have removed it while she was unconscious. The thought of this monster touching her made Raine sick with dread. There was something . . . very seriously off about him.

He raised a hand to the mask and gently stroked it. 'These? These are part of my code. Do you know there are over three billion letters that make up the human genome, each one representing a chemical symbol?'

Raine stared at the mask, not understanding. She now saw that some of the letters had tiny numbers above them.

'This is only a representation, obviously. Written out in full it would stretch for five and a half thousand miles. I've isolated the core, so to speak. The bit of code that is uniquely me, and not replicated anywhere else.'

'I thought it was all unique,' said Raine. Apart from the phone, there was a vicious-looking knife on the table. More of a scalpel, really, Raine thought. The sort of thing that could slice through flesh with absolutely no bother at all.

'Oversimplification. Lots of it is replicated in all organic matter. In fact, all of it is repeated in each body trillions of times, as it is copied into every cell.'

Raine wondered if she was going to die here. A part of her wouldn't mind. She'd been so tired for so long. If she died she'd be able to rest.

But another part of her, the tinfoil part, continued to scan the room. Continued to work the maths. Continued to find the cracks in the situation that would give her leverage.

'Why did you kill David and the others?'

'Why?' The man laughed. It was a bright tinkling sound, like a musical box with its insides broken — all the notes out of tune and in the wrong order. Above them, the bass of the EDM track continued. Raine prayed that the boy wouldn't come down, because she was fairly certain the madman in front of her had snapped and would kill him, son or not.

'I didn't kill them. I merely turned them off.'

CHAPTER 56

'This isn't a child protection issue, sir. I've already sent you a photo of the boy. I just need you to give me his name, please.'

Despite the evenness of her tone, Hume was fuming. She kept her phone clamped to her ear with a grip so tight her knuckles were close to poking out of her skin as the car hurtled towards St Edmond's Academy, the last known location of Raine's mobile.

'I understand that, Detective Inspector,' said the voice on the end of the line, 'but the children's welfare—'

'The boy's a drug dealer! Where is your concern for children's welfare on that issue?' Her voice dropped menacingly as the patrol car bombed across a busy junction, sirens blazing.

'And I'm pretty sure your school will have CCTV surveillance. How would it be if I sent a Digital Forensic team down there? To go through absolutely every datapoint you have? Do you think we might turn up the odd teacher who is one of his clients? Someone suspiciously looking the other way?'

'I don't think there's any need for that—'

Hume pressed mute on her phone.

'Fuck!' She shot a look at Echo. 'Send a picture of Leon through to him.'

She unmuted.

'Of course there is. Drug dealing is a very serious offence. If you won't tell me who the boy is, then at least you can tell me if the man whose image I just sent you has been hanging around the school. Maybe the boy sold him some drugs, or got in his car or something.'

Hume thought that if that was the case they'd have a good chance of picking up the licence plate from the CCTV.

'I don't understand,' said the headmaster, his voice full of confusion. 'I thought you said you didn't know who Jamie was?'

'Jamie? Is that the boy's name?'

Hume felt a tightening around her chest. 'And why do you suddenly think I know who he is?'

'Why, because of the photo you sent through.'

'Do you recognise the man in the photo, then?' But she'd already guessed the answer.

'He's Jamie's father. Marcus Callow.'

Hume muted the phone again. 'Marcus Callow. That's the name Leon is using.'

She unmuted.

'Headmaster,' Hume's voice was ominously quiet. 'You need to give me Marcus Callow's address right now. There's a good chance Jamie's life might be in danger.'

* * *

Raine couldn't think straight. Between the blow on the head and the mask, her cognitive processes were completely scrambled.

'Turned them off? What are you talking about? I think you're very fetching. Kind of fucknut-chic.'

She had a vague sense that if she could get the man annoyed, then maybe he'd come close enough for her to head-butt him.

The man chuckled and picked up the scalpel.

'I'm getting bored with you, ex-detective. I think I might cut your tongue out and stuff it down your throat because

287

the only one you're talking to here is yourself. The language I talk is on a much more . . . fundamental level.'

Raine eyed the knife. Even though she was certain there was only one blade, she could see two. She shook her head. 'Your son will hear.'

'Are you kidding me? An atom bomb could go off and he wouldn't hear a thing! What with the PlayStation, the ketamine and the house music, he's completely cocooned.'

'You know, you really don't have to do this. I could just walk away . . .'

'Plus I strangled him.'

The laugh that dribbled out from behind the mask told the whole story. It was flecked with madness and laced with a large dose of 'couldn't give a fuck'.

'Or maybe not,' said Raine. 'Why would you strangle your own son?'

The man paused and seemed to consider the question.

'It wasn't my first choice. If I'd had time, I would have drowned him in acid. Degraded his corrupted DNA completely.'

Raine stared at him in horror.

'Because I'd grown fond of him. Still, never mind. It's you we're concerned about now, isn't it? It's what we're going to do about you.'

'I think letting me go should be the first choice,' said Raine.

The man chuckled again. 'I think we need to find a way for you to tell me everything you know, then I'll be able to work out if I can just . . . turn you off like the others and dump you somewhere or . . .'

'Or what?' said Raine.

He did the strange questioning movement again. Half a shrug, one shoulder lifting while his hands twitched. 'Or whether I need to break you down into parts.'

That Raine was going to die here she had no doubt, but she was not going without a fight.

'Why don't you untie me and we can discuss this?' she said. She twisted her wrists, testing the strength of the duct tape. It was not going to tear apart. She shifted in her chair, hearing it creak slightly.

'Not today, I'm afraid,' said the man, picking up the scalpel and moving behind her.

Raine felt the blade as it softly stroked its way down her face. She didn't feel the cut because the blade was so sharp, but she did feel the warmth of the blood as it leaked its way out onto her cheek. She held her breath as the cold steel reached her throat, then let it out slowly as it passed on down to her chest, pressing hard.

'Please . . .' she began, a wet catch in her voice.

'Oh, don't beg. It means nothing to me. All it will do is delay the inevitable—'

Raine thrust her feet hard against the floor and forced her body upward, bringing the chair with her. As the scalpel split open her chest, the top rail of the chair behind her head smashed into the man's chin, slid over the mask and continued up to his nose. He cried out, the noise distorted by the blow, and collapsed on the floor. Raine then accelerated backwards, legs pumping, sledgehammering into the table. The body of the chair shattered, along with her right arm just above the wrist. She screamed with pain and fell to the ground among the wreckage of the chair.

In front of her, the man was on his knees. Despite the mask, Raine could see his nose was clearly broken, along with many of his teeth. As Raine struggled to get to her feet she saw him spit blood. In the struggle, the mask had slipped a little, obscuring his vision. Raine ran forward and kicked him in the face. The force of the blow reverberated through her body. She slipped and fell to the floor, her head connecting with the hard surface. She greyed out.

She regained consciousness when she felt the first fist connect with her face.

The man straddling her looked horrific. His mask was slick with blood, the genome code glistening beneath the red. His mouth was a gaping hole of ripped gums and shattered teeth, and his eyes were spinning stars of pure hatred.

'You fucking bitch!' he screeched. 'Look what you've done to me!'

Raine wasn't sure if he was referring to his body or the mask. As she gazed up at him she felt a great calm enter her. The pain in her arm receded and she felt almost happy. She was going to die now.

'Don't call me a bitch,' she said, although the words came out slurred from the beating. 'It is just so bloody boring.'

The man hit her — again and again.

As the blows pummelled her body, Raine closed her eyes and tried to picture Clara. Tried to tell her that she was coming. She barely heard the door smash open as Hume and Echo burst into the room, batons extended.

The man they knew as Leon made a keening sound from the ruin of his mouth, but kept punching down on Raine's face.

At the sight of Raine's prone body, Hume froze in shock, then ran forward and kicked Leon in the head, sending him sprawling. Echo pulled his arm up and back, pinning him to the ground.

Hume knelt beside Raine. 'Raine! Raine, it's Mary. Are you all right? Raine!'

Ignoring the rip in her friend's skin that stretched from her breast to her stomach, Hume put her ear close to Raine's chest. She listened.

'Is she alive?' asked Echo, his eyes wide, his weight on Leon.

'She's breathing.'

'Jesus, look at all the blood!'

Hume pulled out her radio and called for an ambulance, shouting for them to hurry. Then she gently stroked Raine's cheek, sticky with blood, telling her that she would be all right. That there was no need to worry. She was still stroking Raine's cheek when the paramedics arrived seven minutes later.

CHAPTER 57

'Hello, Robert. Mary. Thank you for coming.' Raine let her smile widen further when she turned to Echo. 'And I see you've brought a plus one!'

Robert kissed Raine on the cheek and walked past her, navigating the boarding plank with exaggerated care. 'Hello, Raine. You look absolutely terrible. When did they let you out of the hospital?'

Hume gazed at the detective's battered face, her arm rigid in a sling, and at the place beneath her grandfather shirt where her wound must be itching. Raine noted her gaze and grinned defiantly.

'Once it heals I'm going to get it enhanced with a tattoo. And they didn't let me out; I ran away in the middle of the night.' She smiled at Robert. 'I hate hospitals. They're full of ill people.'

'Love a tattoo,' said Echo, sticking out his hand. Raine glanced at it, then leaned forward and kissed him on the lips.

'I don't kiss men, but for you I'll make an exception,' she said. 'Thank you for finding me.'

Before Echo's entire quota of blood darkened his face, Raine turned and joined Robert on her boat. No trace of the break-in remained. On the deck, she had set up a small table, laden with nuts and crisps, plus a bottle of sparkling wine.

'I see you've gone all out,' said Hume, eyeing the spread.

'Difficult to cook with your arm in a cast,' said Raine, pouring everyone a glass. 'Plus I don't cook.' Once she'd handed them round, she raised her own in salute.

'Just to get it out of the way, I'd like to say thank you for saving my life. If you'd arrived any later that fuckbucket would have killed me. He was, without doubt, one of the creepiest people I have ever met. When I came to and he was wearing that mask . . .' Raine shuddered and took a gulp of wine.

'Technically, according to Professor Flynn, the real mask was the persona Leon had decided to inhabit in his daily life. The biological date stamp signifying when he stopped being human. The thing he put on when he tried to kill you was, to Leon, his true self. His unmasked mask.'

'Like he was an avatar from a computer game,' Echo chipped in.

'Which is completely fucked up. Why make life so complicated? Work, yoga and the unconditional worship of your wife,' said Robert. 'That's all you need.'

Hume looked at him. He shrugged. 'Well, it works for me.'

'That's because you're not a fuckbucket, dear,' said Hume, fondly.

Raine glanced out across the canal as she listened to Hume and the others chat. Talking about work and London and Aotearoa New Zealand. She felt it wash over her. The itch on her chest was intense; like ants were trying to eat her. She watched as a cruise ship motored by, ignored by a neighbouring swan.

Raine turned and picked up the small cardboard box that had been delivered to her boat yesterday. 'If I might just say a few words?'

The chatter stopped and Raine began. 'As you know, two weeks ago someone broke into my boat, my home, and stole my laptop. It now seems that it is in some way connected to the misper, Heather, who was murdered. They also killed my cat, Melania. I had her body cremated and now I'm going to throw her ashes in this canal.'

Raine opened up the box and tipped the contents into the water. She half expected the water to turn red, as if the ashes were bath salts of pain.

After a few moments Hume said: 'Well. That was . . . quite brief.'

'I'd also like to add that when I catch the person who did this, I will break their fucking arms and force-feed them dead squirrels,' finished Raine, turning away from the water and smiling at them. It was not a pleasant smile. 'Uncooked.'

'O-kay,' said Echo, filling the awkward silence. 'And are you any nearer with that?'

Raine shrugged, as if putting away thoughts of revenge, and turned to him.

'Nothing else from the alert you set up for me,' she said, placing the box that had contained the ashes of her cat down on the table next to the crisps. 'No one's used it since Watford Gap services on the M1. I've asked Inspector Conner to revisit the digital autopsy, now that we know Heather was cremated — in case there was something they were trying to hide.'

'And by "they" we mean . . . ?' asked Robert, eyebrows raised.

'She means the parents,' said Echo.

'Because nine times out of ten the murder is committed by someone known to the victim,' said Hume, her voice tinged with melancholy.

'The email they used to contact me has been shut down, and the address in Nottingham was fake.' Raine's voice was hard. 'They completely played me.'

'What about the apartments in Lewisham?' said Echo. 'Where your laptop connected to the web?'

'Accommodation for refugees from West Asia. Pakistan. Iraq. Afghanistan. Syria. Inspector Conner thinks they are being recruited as scavengers, hoovering up the grab-bag crime for phones and laptops; easy-sell hardware that can be moved around the country.'

'Right,' said Robert. 'Makes sense.'

'Apparently, due to government policy of distributing refugees and asylum seekers countrywide, Conner thinks there is a burgeoning network affiliating itself with local crime syndicates.'

'Brilliant,' commented Echo, his voice laced with sarcasm.

'What about the serial killer you all caught?' said Robert. 'Leon?'

'Assessment.' Hume's voice was refrigerator-cold. 'Then a high-security psychiatric hospital. The courts have accepted the professor's diagnosis of existential body dysmorphia. I believe our good academic is even getting a book deal out of it.'

'And the son?' said Raine softly. 'The schoolkid?'

'In a coma,' said Hume. 'It's a miracle he's not dead.'

'I still find it amazing,' said Robert, 'that someone would treat their physical self, their face, so casually that they'll change it as if it were a suit.'

'Except Leon didn't consider it a face,' said Hume. 'Or at least not as we understand it. It was more of a—' she glanced over at her colleague — 'what did you call it, Echo?'

'An avatar. Or ident. An image you wear in the virtual world.'

'That's it. As far as he was concerned, that's where he lived. That's why he had to destroy the children produced from his sperm. They were part of his false biological code.'

A cloud moved in front of the sun and Echo shivered. Raine finished the rest of her wine.

'Well, thank you for coming. You've made Melania's send-off a special occasion. Really. Now I'd like to be alone with my memories. Please mind your heads on the way out.'

Hume looked at her, then at the wide-open sky.

'You know what, Raine — you're really quite odd.'

'That's why you love me,' said Raine.

Raine guided Echo, Robert and Hume off the boat. Just before Hume stepped ashore she turned and spoke in an undertone. 'Will you be OK? I mean, really?'

Raine grinned back.

'I'm always OK; you know that.' She pointed out at the canal, where the swan was still ignoring everyone and everything. 'Do you know swans are amazing? They are one of the few species that mate for life.'

Then she gave Hume an awkward one-handed hug. And whispered in her ear. 'How's Clara?'

Hume stiffened, but only slightly. Her daughter had been gone for five years and the wounds had healed. But never the loss. The loss just got deeper. More textured.

'Still dead, Raine,' she said. 'Still dead.'

Raine kissed her on the cheek, butterfly-light. 'Not to me.'

Raine pulled away and walked back down the boarding plank onto the deck of her boat. Hume didn't move until she had disappeared below deck without looking back. Not even once.

Hume breathed in slowly, rearranging the features on her face to cover the pain, and turned to face her husband. 'Come on, love. Let's go home.'

She turned to Echo. 'Can we drop you anywhere?'

'No, I'm good. I'm going to hook up with Bitz at Kooks.'

Kooks was a super-trendy retro-gaming bar the coder had introduced him to.

Hume smiled with genuine affection. 'Of course you are.'

* * *

Raine lay on her bed, the picture of Clara on her chest. Her tears had long dried, but their tracks were still visible on her skin. She stared up at the roof, feeling the water's gentle movement through the hull. She thought it might be a little like being in the womb. She let her mind unfetter itself. Just let her senses take in her surroundings. Anchor her to them.

Her phone rang. She looked at the ident: it was DI Conner.

'Inspector! It's like we're dating! What can I do for you?'

'Raine.' Conner's voice was full of velvet, warm and soft like a comfort blanket. 'I've had a report back from Doctor Sing. I thought you'd want to know.'

Raine sat up. 'The pathologist guy — sorry, radiologist — who did the digital autopsy on Heather? Definitely. Anything interesting?'

'Actually, yes. He was very embarrassed about it. Said that he was only briefed to confirm the cause of death, not to look any closer.'

'So spill. What did he find?'

'Well, as you know, Heather was shot and then run over, creating multiple bruising and contusions all over her body. She was a total mess. But when Dr Sing re-examined everything, he found that underneath all that damage there was more bruising, and marks consistent with being restrained. Not recent, but historical. Scarring on the wrists and ankles.'

Raine closed her eyes. Thought about the fear in the young woman's eyes when she was being attacked in the alley. Thought about their conversation in the cafe.

You really believe that? That most people are good?

That's what Heather had asked her, and Raine hadn't picked up on the signs.

Heather had learned that most people aren't good. Not even the ones who were meant to protect you.

'Right. Thank you, Detective Inspector. I wonder if you could get me a copy of the latest autopsy report? Just so I can close down my records?'

'After the drug bust you handed me? I can probably get you just about anything.'

Raine thanked him and ended the call. She lay back on the bed and looked at the ceiling, wondering if it was possible for her to feel any more guilty.

Another buzz on her phone. She guessed it would be Hume. Mentioning Clara had not been wise. Their relationship was built on such a fragile bridge, but Raine couldn't help herself. Hume was her only connection to Clara, and she needed to reach out. Find a way of healing. She just didn't know how.

She looked at the phone, checking the ident. It wasn't Hume. It was the number Heather had given her. The number which had ghosted.

I'm so sorry. Please help me.

Raine stared at the message for several long moments. Then she thought back to the image of Heather lying on the pavement, her face obliterated by a shotgun blast.

Unrecognisable.

The body only identified by her parents, then sent straight off for cremation.

Her eyes unfocused for a moment as she considered the implications.

'Oh, my,' she said eventually. Then pressed the dial button.

THE END

ACKNOWLEDGEMENTS

Christine, Dominique, Gabriel, Joseph, Josephine, Lula and Michelle: thank you for reading the novel in its *proto-stage* and giving such needed feedback.

Wren. One down and four to go!

Philip for being adorable.

Kate and the team at Joffe for welcoming me with open arms.

Anne-Marie for the horrible task of making my work presentable and for always being in my corner.

And finally to all of you who have read *The Skin Code*.

Hope you enjoyed it!

S.

Thank you for reading this book.

If you enjoyed it please leave feedback on Amazon or Goodreads, and if there is anything we missed or you have a question about, then please get in touch. We appreciate you choosing our book.

Founded in 2014 in Shoreditch, London, we at Joffe Books pride ourselves on our history of innovative publishing. We were thrilled to be shortlisted for Independent Publisher of the Year at the British Book Awards.

www.joffebooks.com

We're very grateful to eagle-eyed readers who take the time to contact us. Please send any errors you find to corrections@joffebooks.com. We'll get them fixed ASAP.

Made in the USA
Middletown, DE
14 June 2022

67136501R00182